ALSO BY KATEE ROBERT

Court of the Vampire Queen

Dark Olympus
Stone Heart (prequel novella)
Neon Gods
Electric Idol
Wicked Beauty
Radiant Sin
Cruel Seduction
Midnight Ruin
Dark Restraint

Wicked Villains
Desperate Measures

Black Rose Auction
Wicked Pursuit

SWEET OBSESSION

SWEET OBSESSION

KATEE ROBERT

sourcebooks
casablanca

To those who continue to fly too close to the sun,
no matter how often it burns us.

Published by Sourcebooks Casablanca, an imprint of Sourcebooks
P.O. Box 4410, Naperville, Illinois 60567-4410
(630) 961-3900
sourcebooks.com

Cataloging-in-Publication Data is on file with the Library of Congress.

Printed and bound in the United States of America.
PAH 10 9 8 7 6 5 4 3 2 1

Sweet Obsession is an occasionally dark and very spicy book that contains parental abuse (historical, non-graphic), torture (briefly on page, not overly graphic), attempted spousal murder (historical, non-graphic), violence, murder, explicit sex, elements of dubious consent (because of captor/captive power dynamics), and panic attacks (on page, brief).

THE RULING FAMILIES OF *Olympus*

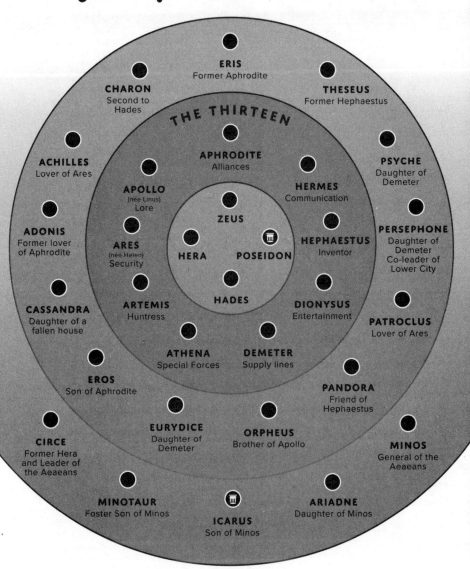

THE THIRTEEN

ERIS
Former Aphrodite

CHARON
Second to Hades

THESEUS
Former Hephaestus

ACHILLES
Lover of Ares

APHRODITE
Alliances

PSYCHE
Daughter of Demeter

APOLLO
(née Linus)
Lore

HERMES
Communication

ADONIS
Former lover of Aphrodite

ZEUS

HEPHAESTUS
Inventor

PERSEPHONE
Daughter of Demeter
Co-leader of Lower City

ARES
(née Helen)
Security

HERA   POSEIDON

CASSANDRA
Daughter of a fallen house

ARTEMIS
Huntress

HADES

DIONYSUS
Entertainment

PATROCLUS
Lover of Ares

ATHENA
Special Forces

DEMETER
Supply lines

EROS
Son of Aphrodite

PANDORA
Friend of Hephaestus

EURYDICE
Daughter of Demeter

ORPHEUS
Brother of Apollo

CIRCE
Former Hera and Leader of the Aeaeans

MINOS
General of the Aeaeans

MINOTAUR
Foster Son of Minos

ICARUS
Son of Minos

ARIADNE
Daughter of Minos

MUSEWATCH

Previously in Olympus...

OLYMPUS'S SWEETHEART GONE WILD!

Persephone Dimitriou shocks everyone by fleeing
an engagement with Zeus to end up in Hades's bed!

ZEUS FALLS TO HIS DEATH!

Perseus Kasios will now take up the title of Zeus.
Can he possibly fill his father's shoes?

APHRODITE ON THE OUTS

After a livestream in which she threatened Psyche
Dimitriou for marrying her son Eros, Aphrodite is
exiled by the Thirteen. She chooses Eris Kasios to
be successor to her title.

ARES IS DEAD!

A tournament will be held to choose the next Ares… and Helen Kasios is the prize.

…LONG LIVE ARES

In a stunning turn of events, Helen Kasios has chosen to compete for her own hand…and she won! We now have three Kasios siblings among the Thirteen.

NEW BLOOD IN TOWN!

After losing out on the Ares title, Minos Vitalis and his household have gained Olympus citizenship… and are celebrating with a house party for the ages. We have the guest list, and you'll never guess who's invited!

APOLLO FINDS LOVE AT LAST?

After being ostracized by Olympus for most of her adult life, Cassandra Gataki has snagged one of the Thirteen as her very own! She and Apollo were looking very cozy together at the Dryad.

MURDER FAVORS THE BOLD

Tragedy strikes! Hephaestus was killed by Theseus Vitalis, triggering a little-known law that places Theseus as the new Hephaestus. The possibilities are…intriguing.

HEPHAESTUS AND APHRODITE ARE OUT!

Our new Hephaestus and Aphrodite have stepped down unexpectedly! But can a leopard really change its spots? We don't expect Eris Kasios and Theseus Vitalis to fully turn their backs on Olympus politics… even for the love of Pandora and Adonis.

THE WAY TO THE LOWER CITY IS BLOCKED

After a series of attacks in the lower city, Hades has strengthened the barrier along the River Styx! There's official word on the reasons why, but an inside source says that he won't lower the barrier until the Thirteen present a unified front. We hope he's prepared to wait…

THE BARRIER HAS FALLEN!

The unthinkable has happened: for the first time in Olympus's history, the protective barrier keeping us safe from the outside world has fallen. Newly vulnerable, all Olympus can do is wait and hope…

OLYMPUS UNDER ATTACK!

A squadron of enemy ships has been spotted forming a blockade in Olympian waters. Rumors say they are led by Circe, who was once our very own Hera, long presumed dead. Has this ghost returned to burn Olympus to the ground in revenge?

MINOS KILLED IN DARING ESCAPE

Minos and his children may have managed to tear down Olympus's barrier for their ally Circe, but not all went according to plan: while Ariadne and the Minotaur escaped, Minos was killed and Icarus captured. We can only hope our own Poseidon means to bring the full fury of Olympus down on this enemy of the state...

ICARUS

IT FEELS LIKE I'VE BEEN KNEELING ON THE DOCK FOR DAYS, weeks, months, years. Maybe I've always been here, watching the people I care about walk away—or sail away, in this case. The ship Ariadne and the Minotaur stole disappeared in the storm that rose when the barrier fell, the sea surging violently enough to make *me* sick even safe on land.

Every time her ship was swept into a gully between waves, my heart lodged itself behind my teeth. And every time it appeared again, a white smear against the whitecaps, farther and farther from us each time, I exhaled shakily.

And through it all, Poseidon stands at my back, a threat I cannot escape. So be it. I don't have to escape. My sister will be okay. The monster who loves her will ensure it.

It was supposed to be me. I was supposed to be the one who defied all expectations and saved the day—for once. The son and brother who was no longer the disappointment but the hero. At least to Ariadne.

Maybe it's better this way. I would have fucked that escape up—I *did* fuck that escape up. Better to be left behind to occupy the Olympians. It will keep them from searching too hard for my sister.

That and the squadron currently taking up residence across the mouth of the bay. First three giant warships and then five. They're too far away yet to see their names, but they'll be familiar. The most powerful in Aeaea have come to conquer Olympus. The wall coming down now wasn't part of Circe's plan and yet somehow she managed to stay one step ahead, creating a net that only Ariadne and the Minotaur managed to slip through before it closed.

"Up. We're done here."

I follow the rough voice to my captor. Poseidon. A large white man with a broad chest, a thick gut, and thighs as big as my waist. He's handsome in a salt-of-the-earth way—or whatever the sailing version of that is. He's also the one Olympian my father didn't have much information on.

Poseidon, one of the three legacy members of the ruling body—the Thirteen—whose title moves from parent to child like the monarchs of old. This particular Poseidon isn't from the direct line, though. He was brought into the role something like fifteen years ago when a sickness wiped out his cousins, clearing the way to the title for him. But since then, he's kept his head down, and the most illicit thing my father could find about him was an alleged affair with Demeter, which ended ages ago and without a whisper of drama.

In short, he's a stick-in-the-mud.

Said stick-in-the-mud grabs my upper arm and hauls me to my feet with no apparent effort. We're nearly the same height, but all that does is give me another glimpse of his freckles. Fucking *freckles*.

I should say something as he muscles me down the dock and through the marina to the parking lot. I mean to. Truly, I do. But exhaustion hits me like a freight train, bowing my shoulders and making my feet drag. It's been a long and terrifying day in a string of long and terrifying days, and I don't have any fight left in me.

His people watch us closely as he steers me to a large SUV and yanks open the door. "Inside."

"I'm going to get the seats wet." It's such a silly thing to say. He's the enemy. I should be gleeful at the idea of ruining his fancy Olympian car with salt water.

"I don't care." Poseidon pushes me roughly into the back seat and slams the door before I can dredge up some response.

I stare through the tinted windows as he speaks with two of his people—a short, petite Black person with box braids and a giant of a white person with an eye patch. It should make them appear ridiculous, but their fists look big enough to beat my skull to pieces, so I'll keep my mouth shut for now.

I slump back against the seat. My wet clothes are really closer to damp by now, and they're starting to stiffen up from the salt water. Pure misery. I shift restlessly, but that only makes it worse. I'm in the middle of contemplating the intelligence of stripping naked when the driver's door opens up and Poseidon himself slides behind the wheel. He's just as damp as I am, courtesy of my ill-advised attempt to take him hostage. How the tables have turned.

"What are you doing?"

He doesn't look back at me. "Driving."

I blink. From anyone else, that word would have been coated in sarcasm, but from him it's merely a statement of fact. I shake my head. "No shit, you're driving. Why are *you* driving? And where are your people? I could choke you to death with your seat belt."

His gaze lifts to meet mine in the rearview. He has whiskey-colored eyes, a deep amber that someone more foolish than me could lose themselves in. Someone who isn't the fucking *captive* of a man who stares at me with something like pity.

Poseidon puts the car into drive. "Trying that is a bad idea. You won't be successful; you'll just end up getting hurt." He says the words with a tense confidence that makes me believe him.

"You mean *you'll* hurt me."

"I would prefer not to."

I huff out a choked laugh. "Yeah, that's what they all say." If there's one thing I've learned about living in Olympus these past few months, it's that the ruling class here is just as corrupt and fucked up as the one in Aeaea. They murder, cheat, and steal and people applaud them because it's *entertaining*. Poseidon might not appear to enjoy it, but he's obviously just as willing to get his hands dirty as the rest. At least back home, the general public has the good sense to fear their leaders. Here, they're a strange form of celebrity.

My father loves it.

Loved it.

Just like that, the events of the night come rushing back. He's gone. The man who cast a long shadow over my entire life, moving goalposts I could never reach, constantly reinforcing the fact that I'm a disappointment of a son... Gone, felled by a single bullet.

To save *my* life.

I shudder and wrap my arms around myself. "Whatever. Take

me wherever you want. A dungeon? Maybe Olympus has stocks you can lock me in and let the public toss tomatoes at my head."

"Stocks are for your feet. You're thinking of a pillory." Poseidon huffs out a breath, but he doesn't continue. He just drives. Later, I'll worry about looking for an angle to leverage this shitty situation into one I can use to my advantage. Later, I'll start crafting an escape route. Later...

It feels like between one blink and the next, the car is rolling through an impressive-looking wrought-iron fence and up to a startlingly massive Victorian-looking home...and then we drive past it, looping around the curved driveway to a much smaller building tucked into the trees behind the main house. It looks like an in-law setup, or maybe somewhere for the staff to live if the family didn't want them in the house proper.

So this is where I'll be held.

But when Poseidon hauls me inside, it's hardly the cold, dank cell that I expect. The glimpse I get of the space as he drags me down the hall is startlingly cozy—low light, deep colors, sturdy furniture. This looks like a place that's *lived* in. Cared for. Loved.

The hall ends in a staircase so narrow, Poseidon's shoulders nearly brush the walls. I'm so bloody tired, more tired than I've ever been. My head feels like it's floating a foot above my body. Everything hurts.

So when Poseidon opens a door and shoves me inside, I barely manage to turn to face him before he slams it shut. The click of a lock snapping into place feels very loud in my ears. "Locked in," I murmur. "Of course."

I turn and dredge up the energy to survey my new prison. It's nice, as prisons go. The bed is large and looks comfortable enough that I have to fight against the urge to drop onto it and let unconsciousness take me. There are a sturdy-looking dresser and nightstand, both probably too heavy for me to move on my own. A TV mounted on the wall. Two gaming consoles situated on the shelf below it. Past that is a door into a decent-sized bathroom with a shower and tub, fully stocked with high-end products.

Stranger and stranger.

My immediate priority is to get these clothes off and scrub the salt from my skin. The bed looks inviting, but I know better. I haven't slept properly in weeks, haven't slept at all in days. I'm destined to lie there and watch the minutes tick by until dawn comes and it's time to go through the motions all over again.

But thirty minutes later, when I'm clean, wearing someone else's lounge pants I found in the bathroom, and between the sheets...I'm out like a light.

Apparently all I needed for a good night's sleep is to be captive to an enemy who wants me dead.

POSEIDON

GOING HOME TO SHOWER IS A WASTE OF TIME, BUT I CAN'T fucking *think* with my damp clothes pressed to my skin, pulling with every movement, the salt starting to make everything crusty. It's more than an irritant. It's agony. My people—Olympus—need me at my best, and my best requires a shower and a clean set of clothes.

I move as fast as possible, but there are still half a dozen missed calls when I step out of the shower. Five of them are Zeus, who is very much alive despite the plans, weeks in the making, to change that. The sixth is from Hera.

It's Hera that I call back even before I get dressed. She's not a patient woman, and I highly doubt failing to make herself a widow has sweetened her temperament.

Sure enough, she answers almost before the phone actually rings. "Where are you?"

I prop the phone between my shoulder and ear and reach for a pair of pants. "Securing my prisoner. I take it Zeus is alive, judging from all the times he's called me."

"Yes." Her voice is so cold, I'm surprised the phone doesn't ice in my hand. "A small setback, but not a permanent one."

Previously, I found her confidence inspiring. She plays the same games the rest of the Thirteen do, but she at least has the aim of protecting the people of Olympus. Well, she intends to protect her family, but it benefits the general population, which is the only reason I agreed to support her attempted coup. The enemy is literally at our gates; we can't afford to have the Thirteen divided, and they will never be unified under this Zeus. He's not charismatic enough, and the others see his attempts to bring the group together as weakness. He should have taken a note from his father's playbook and ruled by fear, but it's too late for that now.

"I assume there's a reason you called. Unless you're actually ready to discuss the navy currently laying siege to our bay." Unlikely. Hera moves fast, but this is too much, even for her. We all feared the barrier would come down, but I hardly believed it was possible. It's held for my entire life, my parents' lives, my grandparents', back more generations than I can count. The barrier was just a fact of life, and now it's gone and Olympus is not prepared to deal with an outside threat.

"He's called a meeting. I'm sure you'll get a notification of it shortly. Afterward, I would prefer you linger here so we can discuss our next steps."

Our next steps. She means to continue with her plans to murder her husband, and obviously she needs my help. Not that she ultimately asked me for much help when it came to putting together the plan to annihilate Dodona Tower. The only reason I agreed with *that* recklessness was because she promised to clear the tower of everyone except Zeus before bringing it down. The amount of destruction is hard to quantify, but the tower has served as an image for Zeus's power for generations, ever since it was built so long ago. Bringing it down serves to undermine that title.

It all seems rather petty now. I thought we had more time. I was certain of it. But here we are; the barrier has come down. *The barrier has come down.* I can barely comprehend what that means. For so long my entire role in Olympus was to ensure our imports and exports came through the barrier smoothly. To ensure the people of Olympus wanted for nothing. To ensure we were safe.

Safety is going to be a foreign concept moving forward, I suspect.

I have no interest in making Hera my enemy. She's much more useful as an ally, and we'll need all the alliances we can get in order to protect the people who need it the most. So I swallow down my distaste and say, "I'll be there." I hang up before she can. It takes mere moments to finish dressing, but I still feel uneasy.

Everything is changing. And I can't say it's changing for the better.

It's tempting to check on Icarus, but nothing I've learned about this man has given me any indication that he's actually dangerous. Yes, he's Minos's son. Yes, he attacked Pan at the country party. Yes, he even took me captive and tackled me into the icy waves of the marina. But once we hit the water, the fight seemed to go out of him. *I'm* the one who had to drag *him* to safety. He hardly attempted to drown me.

No. There's no reason to check on him. There is, however, every reason to ensure that the meeting of the Thirteen doesn't progress without me present. There are people among that number who I trust to put the city's safety first, but unfortunately they're in the minority. I need to be there to act as a balancing force.

I run into Polyphemus near the front door. He looks just worried as I feel. "You're off to the tower?"

"Yes. I need you and Orion to gather all the people we have and set up a network of sentries along the coastline to ensure that none of those ships land without our knowing about it. Use phones but have radios as backup in case something happens to the cell towers." I don't want to believe Circe would be able to dismantle our communication so quickly, but better to plan for the worst outcome. "I'll be back as quickly as possible."

"Everything with the Thirteen takes longer than it should. But yeah, I'll see it done." He shakes his head, his strong brows drawing together. "And the captive?"

Despite myself, I can't help my gaze tracking to the door of the room Icarus is currently locked in. There isn't a sound coming from behind the thick wood, which is just as well. He can't escape. "He may have information we need. I'll deal with him when I return."

I don't bother to call for a driver as I leave the house. My truck will serve my purposes fine, and I prefer to drive myself unless having a driver is absolutely necessary. I recognize that employing one is the normal way of doing things among the legacy families in Olympus, but it's silly to employ someone just to drive me around on the rare occasions I need it. My people have better things to do with their time. Most of the rich and powerful in this city already think I'm odd, and this is just one additional piece of proof to support that belief. Having realized they couldn't use me to further their goals, they mostly leave me alone.

At least until Hera recruited me for her coup.

It takes far too long and yet no time at all to drive into the center city. I hate to spend time in this part of the upper city. No one says what they mean, and everything is a lie. Even the buildings themselves participate in the illusion, each of them nearly identical despite their disparate purposes. A bar looks the same as a pharmacy, which looks the same as an office building. It's a low-level irritation, but an irritation nonetheless. It's also a perfect representation of what Olympus is. Of what the Thirteen are.

I'm one of the last to arrive. It makes sense, since I had the farthest to come, except for Hades…but Hades isn't here. Neither is Hermes, now that I start counting heads. The latter makes sense; she's been missing more often than she's been present in the last few months. But Hades? He shows up for every meeting like clockwork. He's the one other member of the Thirteen that I can depend on to have a cool head and to have his priorities in order.

At least until the attacks in the lower city had him raising the barrier that runs along the River Styx. I assumed it had fallen with the exterior wall and that he would be present, but maybe my assumptions are false.

I take my customary seat midway down the large rectangular table, between Demeter and Artemis. Artemis is about ten years younger than me with light-brown skin, dark curly hair, and a selfish streak a mile long. That trait hasn't gotten better with the death of her cousin, the former Hephaestus. Demeter…is more complicated. She's a soft-looking white woman who's on her way out of middle age, not that you can tell by looking at her. She has deep laugh lines around her full mouth and crow's-feet branching from her hazel eyes, but there's something about her that continues to be ageless.

It's what drew me to her initially, at least long enough to have a short, ill-fated affair. Ill-fated because I had no interest in becoming one of her ex-husbands and she had no interest in sharing power, even if it was only the perception of shared power. I wouldn't say we're friends now, but we have an uneasy truce.

Across the heavy wooden table, Athena watches me with unreadable dark eyes. She's a beautiful Black woman about my age with her hair cut fading up the sides of her head and leaving her curls longer on top. She's not happy I chose to spare Icarus, and while I can understand that, I'm not one to let my emotions get the best of me. Most of the time. Icarus is a tool to be used; I didn't spare him out of the goodness of my heart. But Athena doesn't like to leave loose ends, especially when that loose end sent her on a wild-goose chase through Olympus before the confrontation in the marina.

Zeus clears his throat, drawing everyone's attention to the head of the table. He's only a few years younger than me, but there's something untried about his energy. I can appreciate his having no interest in playing the games the others do, but that lack of interest is a weakness all the same. The last Zeus may have been a monster, but we relied on his charm to keep the people happy and the streets relatively safe.

Not that I think he would have been better suited to handle the crisis before us now. Knowing him, he would've tried to make a deal with the enemy so he could come out on top, even if that meant sacrificing large numbers of people. That wouldn't work now anyway, not when *she* is the head of the enemy forces. The monster threatening Olympus is of the former Zeus's making. A reckoning that has been a long time coming.

"Circe is here." I don't mean to say it, but I hate this pregnant silence. We don't have time for this. We need to move, to plan, to orchestrate some kind of defense. We squandered what little time we had to prepare for her with infighting. Now she's here and all that's left to do is scramble for our lives and those of every person in the city.

Or surrender.

Zeus plants his hands on the table and half rises. He's an athletic white man with dark-blond hair and piercing blue eyes. He's handsome in the way of all Kasios family members, but where Ares and Eris—and even Hercules—are the beauty of warmth, Zeus is all ice. His cold doesn't thaw now. If anything, the sensation of a freezing barrier closing around him only seems to grow. "The time for personal vendettas and bullshit is past. The enemy is at our gates, and if you think Circe will spare a single one of us, you're a fool. She has more reason than most to hate the Thirteen and Olympus. She'll show no mercy. She won't be satisfied until the city is reduced to rubble and every person in this room is dead." He takes a deep breath. "And that's why I'm calling for the vote of war. We need to attack the ships before more arrive, to cut Circe down before she has a chance to do more damage."

I accidentally catch Hera's eye. I look away almost the moment I make contact, but even in that brief glimpse, I see satisfaction. The idea of the Thirteen ceasing to exist doesn't seem to bother her. It's strange. Her family has more connections to the various members of the Thirteen than most—her sister married to Hades, her mother occupying the title of Demeter.

Those connections should make her fight all the harder to protect the Thirteen. They don't. Maybe she craves a simpler time, before her mother became Demeter and brought her and her sisters into the city proper. It's those connections that resulted in her becoming Hera, a bargain to protect her family—not to seek power herself.

It's a similar enough story to several of the past few Heras. Our current Zeus's mother was a social climber, but Circe was just a beautiful woman with no connections. The Thirteen sure as fuck didn't protect her when the last Zeus picked her up off the street and married her in a whirlwind ceremony. No one stepped in as he swept her off to a honeymoon that only one of them returned from. A swimming accident, he said. His fresh bride drowned in the ocean. Her body was never recovered.

Now we know why.

She's back for revenge, and if her plan didn't involve a navy laying siege to the city itself, I would step back and allow her to do it. Except the man who hurt her has been dead for nearly a year. Our current Zeus was a teenager when all of that happened, and while I was freshly named Poseidon at the time, I wasn't much older. Perseus couldn't be expected to do anything. Not when his father saved the worst of his torments for his eldest son. Or that's what the rumors say.

But I should have done something. The guilt for the past Zeus's actions have been a weight for the entirety of my tenure as Poseidon. I'm one of the three legacy positions. I should be able to use my power to protect people. Except nothing works like it should in Olympus.

The only people I can protect are *my* people, so I've spent the last decade focused on doing exactly that. Maybe it was a mistake not to fight for more power, not to try to expand my circle of protection past my territory... I don't know. Even if I had tried to push back against Zeus's abuse of power and people, I'm experienced enough to acknowledge that nothing would have changed.

Except there would be someone else of my bloodline occupying this seat right now, observing the same bitter rivalries play out, again and again.

While I've been musing, a heated discussion has started. Not that I need to be present to know the familiar routes this conversation takes. Zeus makes a declaration. Immediately, Artemis and the new Hephaestus begin listing all the reasons he's wrong. It doesn't matter what statement he begins with; it always progresses the same. Now Demeter will step in, making a big show of striving for peace while really riling up both sides. Hermes and Dionysus will whisper back and forth, lobbing a well-aimed insult from time to time to increase the chaos. All while Hades and Hera watch with unreadable expressions on their faces.

Except Hades and Hermes aren't here.

I clear my throat. "We're missing two key members."

"A vote of war only needs a majority. They aren't necessary." Zeus meets each person's gaze in turn. "As long as those of us here tonight are united."

He might as well wish on a star for all *that* is going to happen. I shift, drawing his attention back to me. "That's true, but I don't know how we can formulate a defense for Olympus without taking the lower city into account."

Ares is Zeus's younger sister, her skin reflecting a rosier tint than his, which is mirrored in her auburn hair. I had my reservations when she won the tournament and took her title, but in the time she's held it, she's showed every evidence of being a fair leader. She certainly elevated what fighting troops we have. But is it enough?

"You're right, but it's one and the same. Hades said he will deal with the Thirteen once we are a whole and unified front. He's not interested in wasting time bickering." Ares makes a face. "Neither am I, honestly. Zeus called a vote and it's time to actually vote. I'm in support of war against Circe."

Artemis snorts. "You might as well lick his boots while you're at it, Ares. Circe hasn't attacked yet, so there's no reason to think she will. I vote against."

"On the contrary," Apollo cuts in. "We have *every* reason to believe she'll sack the entire city. She's done a good job of it even before she actually arrived. I vote in support of war."

Two in support. One against. We need seven in support to have the majority—and without a majority, we cannot act. I study the table, trying to anticipate which way the rest will go. Athena votes for war, which is expected. Obviously Zeus does. Hephaestus and Aphrodite, both being new and cautious, vote against it.

Four and four.

Dionysus looks sick to his stomach when he speaks. "I don't think war serves anyone, but I've seen firsthand the damage done to this city and I'm not interested in letting Circe run rampant. I vote for war."

Five and four.

"I vote for war," I say softly. I don't want it, but it's the only option. That leaves us with six in favor of war, four against...and only two left. We just need Demeter or Hera to vote in favor and it will be done.

Demeter keeps her chin high, her hazel eyes steely. A pit forms in my stomach. I know this look. Sure enough, when she speaks, it's firm and frank. "While I applaud your initiative, we don't have troops in the traditional sense. We don't have a navy. We are not prepared for a war, and throwing our people into combat will only end in them dead and Circe still victorious. There is another way. We just have to find it." She takes a deep breath. "I vote no."

"No," I whisper.

All eyes in the room turn to Hera. I already know what she's going to say. It's there in the barely hidden satisfaction on her face and the way her lips curve ever so slightly. She shuts it down immediately, presenting a perfectly composed mask as she meets her husband's eyes. "I agree with my mother. There must be another way. I vote no."

And with that, Zeus's plans die a terrible death. He doesn't flinch, doesn't show even the slightest bit of disappointment. "So be it." He rises. "This meeting is over."

I watch the rest of the Thirteen file out of the room, my heart sinking at the implications. While Demeter isn't wrong—we have no navy to speak of, and Ares's troops are hardly trained in active combat—her vote spoke volumes. It undermined Zeus to a point where I don't see how he recovers from this.

I heft myself to my feet and sigh. No matter how fractured the

Thirteen, the fact remains that Circe *is* a threat. Our only chance to get ahead of her is to have the people in charge unified. Hades knows that; it's why he's refusing to waste his time until we can actually agree on something. Whether that happens at all, let alone before Circe attacks…it doesn't seem likely at this point.

And *my* people will be the first harmed if she stages an attack with those ships.

ICARUS

I DON'T KNOW HOW LONG I SLEEP FOR. NOT LONG, JUDG-ing from my headache and the drowsiness clinging to me, urging me back to blessed unconsciousness.

Unfortunately, the one-eyed man from earlier is currently standing over me, so close to the edge of the bed that I could reach out and touch him. He doesn't look particularly happy with me. *Shit.*

Without meaning to, my gaze skates toward the door. Looking for Poseidon? But that doesn't make any sense. He hates me just as much as the rest of the Olympians do. And why not? My father was instrumental in the events that brought down the barrier protecting Olympus from the rest of the world. Or at least that was always the plan. That, and destabilizing their power structure so that when Circe finally sailed up with her squadron of ships, the city was ripe for the plucking.

By all accounts, there's no reason to keep me alive. I might have a wealth of knowledge about the key players in Circe's inner circle, but it's not like anyone in this city would believe me. The only person who gave me the benefit of the doubt sailed off with her monster of a boyfriend. The Minotaur will protect Ariadne. That, at least, I don't have to worry about.

I don't have to worry about...anything. Not even my unwelcome guest. I'm not going to survive this. My chance of obtaining freedom is gone forever, and maybe if I live long enough I'll mourn that loss, but right now all I feel is relief. There's no one left to disappoint.

None of that explains why this man is in my room, though.

I stretch out carefully and prop my arms behind my head. "Go ahead. Look your fill."

He looks at me like I'm dog shit on the bottom of his shoe. "I don't expect you to know this, but when your people killed Triton, there were others caught in the crossfire."

My bravado threatens to buckle. I had nothing to do with any of that. Responsibility would require my father to trust me enough to tell me anything. It would require me to be something other than the son he never wanted. The son he claimed he never needed. Apparently, my failure as a son was so spectacular he had to foster two sons to fill the void created by my disastrous performance.

"Sorry?" I don't quite manage to sound as irreverent as I'm aiming. The word crumples around the edges. "That wasn't my op."

"But it *was* your father's. He bribed Triton to bring people into Olympus. And once he did, they murdered him and his guards. Including my sister."

Growing up as Minos's only biological son, I may not have had a front-row seat to all of the sins he committed, but I was privy to enough of them to develop a thick skin. It was the only way to survive. He wasn't going to change his actions just because I find murder stomach-turning. If he knew how much I hated everything he did, he would have taken away the sliver of freedom that made my life worth living. I could say I didn't have any other choice, but somehow I don't think this stranger wants to hear it. "I'm sorry," I say again, managing to make it sound more sincere this time.

"Maybe." He lifts his hands, and I go cold at the sight of his leather gloves. "You *will* be sorry. I'll make sure of that."

I don't stop to think. I burst into motion, rolling across the bed away from him. Some part of me already knows what I'll find when my hand lands on the knob: it doesn't turn beneath my grasp. Locked. Of course. This person, intent on revenge, wouldn't leave anything up to chance. Of course he locked the door behind him when he came to murder me.

He grabs my arm before I have a chance to decide on a different course of action, spinning me around and slamming me back against the door. He pins me there with a hand across my throat. "What is Circe planning?"

I might laugh if I had the breath for it. So, not a murder. An interrogation. Of course. It was my mistake for thinking Poseidon's honesty would prevent him from getting his hands dirty—or allowing his people to get their hands dirty. Naive of me.

"Answer the question."

I let my head fall back to rest against the door. "The answer to that is above my pay grade. But even so…it doesn't take a genius to look around and draw the obvious conclusions. Her squadron is in the bay, so she intends to take the city."

He tightens his grip around my throat and slams me back against the door. "No shit. Give me the details."

"I don't have details." If I did, I would've bargained for my freedom and my sister's freedom long before now. Gods, *that* is what I should have been focusing on. If I'd managed to get those details, I could have saved us both.

It was only in the last couple of weeks, when our father turned on my sister, that I realized there was no coming back from this. There was no gaining his approval. We had disappointed him one time too many, and he'd rather see us dead than see us turn against him.

If I live long enough, eventually I'm going to have to deal with the truth that he turned a gun on me, with every intention to pull the trigger and end my life. That my sweet, precious sister killed him first. That she bloodied her hands to keep me among the living. That she will bear scars on her soul because of my failures.

Fortunately, I'm likely to die before I ever have to face that reckoning properly. Maybe it'll even happen today.

The stranger glares. I think he might question me again, but instead he moves too fast for me to brace, punching me in the stomach. The breath rushes from my lungs, and every muscle in my body seizes up as I bend in half with an instinctive need to protect myself from the blow that already happened. One would think I'd have learned to take a punch by now. Apparently not.

He uses the opportunity of my agony to haul me back to the bed and throw me down on my back. I'm still trying to force air into my seizing lungs when he straddles me and shoves my hands over my head. A click of handcuffs registers before the feeling of cold metal against my wrists. The man sits back on his heels, his disgust written all over his face. "It's pathetic that someone so weak helped orchestrate so much pain. So many deaths of people better than you."

My first full breath comes out in a rough laugh. It's painful that everyone from my own father to this stranger have such an accurate read on me, but it's nothing new. "Tell me something I don't know."

"Okay." He reaches into his pocket and withdraws a switchblade. "I'm going to cut you, again and again, until you tell me exactly what I need to know. Poseidon might be pissed that you bled out all over his fresh sheets, but the information you give me will make it all worthwhile."

"Torture." I make a face. "I would think a big, strong man like you would know that torture doesn't work. That's practically Bad Guy 101. Except I suppose you think you're the good guy? Color me not convinced."

He presses the tip of the knife to the center of my chest, right at the bottom of my sternum. "Yeah, that's the thing. *Poseidon* is the good guy. Not me. I figure if you blubber like a baby, at least *something* that comes out of your pathetic little mouth will be true. That's enough for me."

He might say he's a bad guy, but it's not the truth. He's convinced himself he can make this work. He can make himself strip me apart piece by piece and come out okay on the other end. It's sad. Somehow, I don't think he will thank me for saying as much, though.

I take a ragged breath. "I'll be honest. All it will take is you cutting me once, and I'll tell you anything you want to know. I'm more a fan of giving pain than taking it. That doesn't mean my information will be accurate. I don't have what you're looking for."

"We'll see." There's no further warning. He drags the knife down my stomach in a shallow slash. I thought that getting punched was agony. It's nothing compared to this. It's no mere scratch that he's dealt me. It fucking hurts.

"I don't know anything," I gasp. I can't breathe, not even to cry out. Somehow, a part of me didn't really believe he'd do it.

"I think you do." He drags the knife in a parallel line to the first. Another searing stroke that has me clamping my jaw shut to contain a scream. "What is Circe planning?"

"Death and destruction to all Olympians, probably. Definitely the Thirteen. She doesn't seem to like them much." I hardly sound like myself. Surely that's not my voice, so rough and thready?

He cuts me a third time.

This time I can't stop myself from crying out. "I told you what you wanted to know! I answered you. You're supposed to stop hurting me."

He grins, but not like anything is funny. His eyes look almost sad. "When did I ever say that I would stop hurting you if you answered me?" He cuts me again before I can find an answer.

And so it goes. My world narrows to each cut, to each new pain that blossoms in the wake of the last. I answer his questions…I think. But I don't know what I say. There's no space for intention when all I can experience is agony. At one point, I start screaming and I can't make myself stop.

That's when the door slams open and *he* appears.

Poseidon, looking like an avenging angel, but maybe that's the haze of pain talking. His fury is written all over his roughly hand-some face. It only becomes more pronounced as he takes in the scene: his man straddling me, the mattress soaked with my blood. I half expect him to step back and close the door and let the torture continue.

Instead, he crosses the space in two large steps and hauls my torturer off me, picking him up by the back of his shirt and flinging him away. "What the fuck are you doing?"

The man hits the wall, but manages to keep his feet. "Getting answers."

"Absolutely not." Poseidon *roars* the words. "This is not what we do. This is not who we are, Polyphemus. This *cannot* be who we are."

The man—Polyphemus—stammers, his face gone waxy. "Poseidon, I—"

"*Get out.*"

In the back of my mind, I expect my tormentor to keep arguing. To bluster. Maybe to get a little stabby with Poseidon himself. Grief makes people do strange things, and Triton was only killed a couple weeks ago. Not nearly long enough for this man to process the death of his sister.

But he doesn't. He wilts as if Poseidon has ripped out his spine with his words. The knife drops to the floor and his voice turns almost pleading. "I thought this was what you needed. I thought you just didn't want to command me to do it. I didn't know—"

"You know nothing!" Poseidon is still roaring, the walls practically shaking with his fury. "If I want you to do something, I will give you an explicit order. You've worked for me long enough to know that. Now get out of my sight."

My torturer flees. Everything hurts—every breath, every minute movement of my muscles. I stare at my unexpected savior, watching the fury sweep out of him, draining away as quickly as it arrived. I swallow painfully. "I think I'm going to pass out now."

Poseidon gingerly places his knee on the mattress next to my hip. "I'm sorry."

I must be suffering from blood loss, because there's no way that one of the Thirteen just apologized to me. Impossible. Absurd. "I'm your enemy."

"You are." He produces a key from somewhere and unlocks the cuffs binding my wrists to the top of the bed. "This is going to hurt. I truly am sorry." I don't have a chance to ask him what he means when he wedges his arms under my body and lifts me, cradling me to his chest. I don't think I've been held like this since I was a child, and maybe not even then. But there's no space to enjoy the strange moment of care. My entire body screams in protest. Maybe I scream in protest. I can't be sure.

Poseidon shifts off the mattress…and everything goes black.

POSEIDON

THE LAST THING I EXPECTED UPON ARRIVING HOME TO check on the prisoner was to find Polyphemus straddling him, a knife in his hand and covered in blood. Later, I'll berate myself for misjudging one of my people so thoroughly, for not noticing how grief had turned his moral compass flexible in a way that I don't fully understand. Later, I'll worry about how angry I was and how close to fully losing control. Right now, I have an unconscious Icarus in my arms, and my hands are covered in blood.

The sensation is sticky and makes me want to scour my skin with sandpaper, but I muscle past the response as I shoulder my way into the bathroom and carefully lay Icarus in the tub.

He's too pale, his light-brown skin gone waxy and his beautiful face standing out in stark lines. Like this, I can clearly see the dark circles beneath his eyes that suggest he's had more than a few sleepless nights in his past.

That matters less than the cuts streaming blood. Panic threatens to derail my logical thought process, but again I muscle it down.

One does not work in a shipyard without knowing how to deal with wounds in a crisis. Granted, I'm not particularly familiar with knife wounds, but the premise remains the same.

I hurry to the cupboards under the sink that house a first aid kit. But, even in the midst of all this, I can't help pausing to scrub the blood from my hands. I know it's a lost cause, but the compulsion is too overwhelming. I *have* to give in once in order to release the pressure enough for me to be able to think. To help him.

If I were going to let him die, I would have done it on the docks. He's under my protection, which means it's my responsibility to get him back into fighting shape. Or at least back into consciousness.

It takes longer than I would like to clean his wounds. Long enough that they have mostly stopped bleeding by the time I'm done. There are a dozen long cuts, but none of them are deep enough to require stitches. It means Polyphemus intended pain and not death; I don't know if that's better or worse.

I'm going to have to deal with *him*.

Except...it feels wrong to leave Icarus in the tub like this. He needs rest to recover, and he's not going to get that here, sticky and shivering. I can't very well take him out when his lounge pants are soaked in blood—and there're the sheets and mattress to attend to. There's so much fucking blood.

I grip the edge of the tub and force myself to take several steady breaths. Inhale, one, two, three. Exhale, one, two, three. On the third round of this, I feel slightly more in control. Slightly.

The pants have to come off. I can wrap him in a clean blanket to keep him warm while I deal with the bed. That is the sequence of events that makes the most sense.

It sounds great in theory until I have my fingers on the band of his pants and the reality of sliding them down his body hits me. He's not wearing anything underneath them. Even if he were, I'd have to take those off, too. There is something inherently wrong with seeing him naked while he's not conscious and aware. I recognize that nurses do it all the time, but I'm hardly a medical professional. And he's so damn pretty.

Frustrated with myself for wasting time, I still grab a towel and drape it over his hips. It's awkward business working his drying pants down his body and keeping the towel in place, but I manage to do it. Barely. I try very hard not to notice how smooth his skin is. I'm mostly successful.

Next is the blanket. I find a spare, unblemished one in the closet and take the time to tuck it around him, angling his body so it's between him and the cool porcelain of the tub. Through it all, he doesn't make a sound.

Am I wrong about the severity of the wounds? They've bled a lot, but they're not bleeding anymore. Surely he just passed out from shock. Surely he isn't...dead.

Panic threatens to override everything. I place my hand to the side of his throat, measuring the slow beat of his heart. Possibly too slow, but it's there nonetheless. I'm not a doctor. I know slightly more than basic first aid but... "Damn it." I know better than to panic in a crisis, and yet here I am, forgetting the important and vital step to getting him on the mend.

The motions of stripping the mattress of its sheets and muscling it out the door are comforting in their simplicity. I don't have to worry about accidentally exposing a mattress to my eyes. As I shove it through the door and out into the hallway, I nearly smother Orion.

They jump out of the way and hold up their hands. "What's going on? Did you kill the captive?"

"No. Polyphemus was overzealous in his questioning. His *unsanctioned* questioning."

Orion flinches. "I'd wondered where he'd gotten off to, but I didn't realize what was happening. I'm sorry. I should have paid closer attention."

We all knew the death of Polyphemus's sister hit him hard, but not even I understood the risk of having Icarus under this roof. "It's my fault."

"Is he...alive?"

"Yes. But I need you to get me another mattress from a different room. And dispose of this one. And also new sheets." I'm not normally this scattered. My household is run in a methodical, streamlined manner that never changes. There's comfort in always knowing what each day will bring. I operate the shipyard the same way, though there's a little more flexibility required there. We don't get the same shipments in every day, or even every week. But the process of shipping in and shipping out is the same, regardless of the cargo.

Nowhere in that regularity is there space for a captive. A captive that is currently unconscious in the bathtub. I don't know what the fuck I'm doing. I can feel myself spiraling, but that's unacceptable with the stakes as high as they are. I can*not* afford to lose control.

Orion, thankfully, doesn't comment on the erraticism of my orders. They simply nod. "Consider it done. Where will you be?"

It occurs to me that I could leave this situation in their capable hands, but I immediately reject the notion. It feels wrong. I've failed Icarus, and I should be there when he wakes up. Apologizing again won't accomplish anything, but I can't shake the urge. I don't know what the rules are for captor and captive. I've never had one before.

I fucking hate this.

I drag in a deep breath. "The bathroom. Let me know when the new bed's set up."

"Will do." They pull out their phone and start dialing. That's where I leave them, bloody mattress and all. Orion will take care of it. I can trust them. They aren't going to go rogue. But then, I didn't think Polyphemus would go rogue, either.

Too much is happening. Too much change. Too much stimulation. I need a moment.

I step into the bathroom and close the door softly behind me. Icarus's eyes are still closed, but his chest rises and falls in a comfortingly steady rhythm. I grab the stool from the corner and set it next to the tub. It's ridiculously small for my body, but it's sturdy enough to hold. I perch on it and tap my middle finger against my thigh, mirroring the rhythm of Icarus's breathing. Each tap calms my breathing and my heart rate further. Within a few minutes, the world stops feeling like it's spinning out of control and I can think again.

This situation with Polyphemus was an unfortunate series of events, but ultimately it changes nothing. I need whatever information Icarus has. Circe is invading. I don't know what hope Olympus has of prevailing when we can't even manage a simple majority vote to go to war to protect the city. Even if we had, we have limited armed forces with no actual experience, no equipped navy, no barrier to protect us. But if Circe wants the whole of Olympus ground to dust, then surrendering is not an option. The risks are too high. She might very well decide to murder everyone, right down to the last civilian.

More, surrender would require a united ruling body the same way going to war would. We don't have that. Not even with the threat of invasion breathing down our necks. The only thing we managed to come to an agreement on during that meeting was that we would start evacuating civilians to the country, under Demeter's oversight. There's space out there, but I highly doubt there's enough to house an entire city's worth of people. At least not for any extended period of time.

Despite myself, my attention shifts to Icarus's face. He truly is beautiful. High cheekbones, a sensual mouth, a delicate bone structure that makes me feel ham-handed just sitting in his presence. I had thought him young, probably in his early twenties, but in sleep, the weight of his years sits on his features. He has to be approaching thirty.

He groans faintly and his eyes flicker open. They're just as dark as his sister's, just as wide. Just as haunted. He shifts and groans again. "So. Still alive."

"My personal doctor is on the way, but I don't think you were in any danger of dying." I ignore the fact that it was something I was actively worried about for a few moments. "Don't move too much, though. I don't want you to reopen your wounds."

"Why not? Like I told your little torture buddy, I don't have the information you need to stop Circe. No one does. She's going to win. There's not a damn thing you, I, or anyone else can do to stop her." He shifts again and frowns. "Am I naked?"

Embarrassment heats my skin until it feels like an inferno just beneath the surface. "I didn't see anything. I kept you covered the whole time. But you couldn't stay in those bloody clothes. Are you warm enough?"

He blinks those big eyes at me. "I've just been cut a dozen times, and you're asking me if I'm warm enough?"

When he puts it like that, it does sound ridiculous. I clear my throat. "Yes."

"Oh." He shifts a little and winces. "Well, in that case, I'm happy to report that everything hurts and I kind of wish I were dead, but I'm a perfect temperature."

This is one of our first actual conversations, and it strikes me that he communicates very similarly to so many of the Thirteen— charming, oily lies. I've had fifteen years of learning to read the things he's not saying, though. I suspect that when he's in full health, he's better able to lie with his face and body, but right now his discomfort and fear are clear.

I have the strangest urge to find the words to make him feel more at ease. What a ludicrous idea. He shouldn't be at ease. He's not safe. I may not have ordered Polyphemus to harm him, but that doesn't mean I'm not capable of doing it. I wouldn't feel any joy, but ultimately the life of one person comes nowhere near outweighing the lives of everyone in this city. Most of the Thirteen don't take that responsibility to heart, but I do. I've felt the burden of those people's safety for my entire adult life. I'm not about to fail them now, not when they need me the most.

Still, words spring from my lips despite my intention of staying silent. "This won't happen again, but I need you to tell me what you know, even if you say it won't help. We won't know what will or won't be an asset until we have all the information available. For that I need you alive. You're safe with me. At least until this ends."

Icarus laughs bitterly. "And here I heard you were the honest one. Silly man. I'm not safe, and neither are you. Circe. Is. Coming."

ICARUS

I WAKE TO WAVES OF AGONIZING PAIN. MY ENTIRE CHEST is a blazing firestorm. Even before I open my eyes, the events of the last however long come rushing back. My father's death. Ariadne sailing off into the horizon. The one-eyed man torturing me.

And…Poseidon himself attempting to patch me up.

It's that last that has me opening my eyes to take in my new situation. I'm back on the bed, but it feels different. The mattress has changed; I'm nearly certain of it. It doesn't make any sense. I could have sworn I was somewhere with a hard surface, cool against my naked skin, but maybe I imagined it.

Poseidon is nowhere to be seen, but the room isn't empty. There's a small, wizened white woman with a cloud of colorless hair standing next to the bed. Her face is a map of a life well lived, showing the years in every line and wrinkle. It's the kind of aging I've been trained to avoid at all costs. All I have is my beauty. The moment time whisks that away, I'll truly be as worthless as my father always said.

I guess he'll never say that to me again, being as how he's dead.

The dark thought makes me laugh, but I immediately regret it when the motion sends fresh pain surging through me. "Ow."

"Stop that. You're going to undo all my hard work." The doctor—because who else could she be?—taps my shoulder in a no-nonsense way. "You'll live, if that's what you're wondering. I've stitched you up. Your bandages will need to be changed regularly, but I'll discuss all that with Poseidon. Your job is to lie there and rest your pretty head. It's the best way to heal."

I want nothing more than to touch the bandages I can now feel wrapped around my torso, but I have a feeling she won't let me do it while she's in the room. I paste my best angelic expression on my face and smile at her. "I'll be a model patient."

She purses her lips. "You're going to be as big a pain in the ass as the rest of them. I can already tell. Oh well. You're Poseidon's pain in the ass now. See that I'm not called back here because of your ridiculousness." Without another word, she whisks from the room. I like her. Her brusqueness is refreshing. It's *truth*. Rare enough in both Olympus and Aeaea to be worth more than gold.

But no matter what I told the doctor, I have no intention of lying here on my back and waiting for my body to heal. I have plenty of experience in negotiating my way through ongoing pain. Of ensuring no one will notice the hitch in my step or the way I tense when I pull bruised muscles in the wrong way.

I'm in the process of trying to sit up when Poseidon steps back into the room and closes the door softly behind him. "What are you doing?" His deep voice stops me short. He really is too good-looking. It's the kind of attractiveness that grows on you the more time you spend in his presence. He was handsome enough in a generic sort of way when I'd seen him previously, but now there's something that draws me to him even though he's the worst possible choice of a bed partner.

Maybe that's why I'm attracted to him—because he *is* the worst choice I could possibly make. My captor. One of the Thirteen. A leader of this doomed city and, by all accounts, one of the few honorable ones. I'm sure that means his skeletons are buried deeper than most. No one in Olympus has hands free of blood.

He wasn't even supposed to be Poseidon. His uncle held the position and had three children who should have inherited it after his retirement or death. And yet this man now stands before me, possessing one of the legendary legacy titles. I wonder if he's responsible for their deaths?

"I asked you a question."

He did, didn't he? "I'm sitting up. I would think that's obvious."

"I heard your orders. Be still, heal."

"Ironic that you're telling me I should heal when it's *your* man responsible for this." I finally manage to struggle my way up into a sitting position, propped against the headboard with pillows under my elbows. It's not entirely comfortable, but admitting as much feels like conceding defeat. "Or do you just want me in tip-top shape so that you can torture me yourself next time?"

"No one is going to torture you," he snaps. His face flushes with color until the redness blends in with his freckles. "Not again."

I shouldn't find his blush charming. We're talking about torture, after all. But it *is* charming and I'm only human. "So you killed your man?"

He blinks slowly. "What are you talking about?"

"Eye patch. The one with the big knife. He blames me for his sister's death. Once you're that wrapped up in grief, logic holds no sway. If he's still alive, he'll come for me again."

"His name is Polyphemus. And yes, he's grieving currently. A lot of my people are. We're a tight-knit group and so the loss of even a single person, let alone several, hits deep. Not that you would understand. Your own father's dead and you're making jokes."

Minos is dead, isn't he? Every time that thought rolls through my brain, I wait for the emotional backlash sure to follow in its wake. My father is the specter that overshadows everything in my life. The one person I couldn't convince to love me. There was no manipulation that worked on him. There was no living up to his impossible standards. Even suffering silently through his abuse wasn't enough for him. I was never good enough. Never strong enough. Never smart enough. Never *enough*.

And yet I loved him. Pathetic. I should be rejoicing now that he's gone, now that I can finally be my own person. But I don't feel anything at all. Not joy, not relief, not even grief. Just a yawning emptiness that feels like it might swallow the entire world whole.

"You wanted him dead, and yet you're not celebrating," I finally say. "Let's not throw stones from glass houses."

He frowns, his amber eyes flicking over my face as if he's trying to read my thoughts. He's welcome to them. At least right now. Finally, he crosses his arms over his broad chest. "Only a couple of the cuts on your chest actually needed stitches. You should be healed in a relatively short time as long as you don't aggravate the wounds.

So you'll stay in this room and avoid doing anything to aggravate the wounds while I deal with the mess your family made."

Right. The mess. Circe. I seem to remember saying something incredibly dramatic before I passed out a second time in the tub, but I had almost forgotten that particular sword hanging over all of our necks. Circe deals with failure as well as my late father did. She's hardly going to spare me out of the goodness of her heart. Which means I have to get out of this city before she invades properly.

I don't know how I'm going to do that, but hopefully I have at least a couple days to figure it out.

My best bet is the man who stands before me. He's *Poseidon*; he's bound to have access to a wide variety of water vessels that could potentially slip through Circe's net in the dark of night. But first I have to escape him…or turn him to my way of thinking.

"You stripped me," I say. I don't particularly care that he took off my pants and underwear, but this kind of accusation is a surefire way to get a bead on the kind of person he is.

Did I think he was blushing before? This new flush to his pale skin puts that one to shame. He practically turns as crimson as his hair, and he shifts from foot to foot like a small child caught with his hand in the cookie jar. Interesting.

He clears his throat a few times. "I put a towel over your hips. I didn't see anything. You were covered in blood, and so the pants had to come off. It was all very respectable."

How infuriatingly charming. "Respectable. What's respectable about someone unconscious and bleeding as you ogle their naked body? And not just anyone—the man you're holding captive." Every word is designed to worm its way into the crack he's exposed to me. Because he is supposedly a man of honor, and people of honor are inherently more manipulatable than others. They expect you to hold the same moral center that they do, and so they never see you coming.

"That's not... I didn't..." He clears his throat. "You're trying to provoke a reaction out of me."

"If I was, it'd be working. You feel guilty. And you should."

He glares. "I am sorry for the harm you came to while under my care, but you aren't going to be able to manipulate me. You tried to harm my city and everyone in it, which makes you the enemy. I need to leave now, but when I return, I fully expect you to give me the information I need to protect my people and the rest of the city. Do you understand me?"

Do you understand me?

He says it softly, evenly. He's not yelling at me. He's not even really threatening me. And yet my body locks up all the same. I'm thankful for the blanket covering my lower half because it hides my clenched fists from his gaze. It takes more effort than it usually does to paste my charming smile on my face, to force my shoulders to relax as if his words have found no purchase. It's vitally important not to show your weak underbelly to those who want to hurt you. It doesn't mean they *can't* hurt you, but at least they won't be able to find your soft center. "It's cute how you're so committed to the bit. Even Demeter breaks character sometimes. I'm your enemy. Why are you pretending you care about the people of Olympus to *me?*"

Poseidon's brows draw together. "What are you talking about?"

If he keeps this up, it's going to jump straight past charming into irritating. I wave my hand. "It was a smart move taking the strong, silent stance and gaining a reputation as a man who's for the people or whatever. I can see why you'd go that route instead of the others when you came into the title so unexpectedly...unless it wasn't unexpected."

I'm watching him closely, looking for that character break. Usually, I can talk quickly enough for a time to get anyone angry at me—certainly angry enough to stop this ridiculous act.

But he just looks more confused. "Did Polyphemus hit your head, too? What are you talking about?"

"Stop pretending!" I flinch as soon as the yell leaves my lips. This isn't strategic. I'm being stubborn for no damn reason at all. "Never mind. It doesn't matter."

"Icarus."

"I understand that you want information from me." And I do. He's given me the path to cracking him wide open. Because he's an *honorable* man, and people pretending to be honorable are even easier to manipulate than those who are actually honorable. They're predictable.

"What I *want* is to protect the city from Circe. More importantly, the people in the city."

Not himself. Not the Thirteen. The helpless people who rely on those stronger for safety. Surely he's not *actually* an honorable man. That would be too good to be true...

I shake my head roughly. "It doesn't matter what you want. It's all the same to me."

I'll give him everything he asks for. I can't stop Circe—I don't think anyone can at this point—but part of Circe's power is her support base, and I've slept with more than a few of them over the years. I'm good at pillow talk, good at delving into the little nooks and crannies that hide their secrets. They love to brag, love to tell me things no one else knows. Things I can exploit. And what they don't brag about, I find on my own. I'm not as good with computers as Ariadne, but I'm no slouch, either.

I already intended to use the information I've painstakingly compiled to blackmail them into giving me enough money to live a lavish lifestyle until I die of old age. That money would've gone a long way toward protecting Ariadne and me, into getting us far away from Olympus and Aeaea. An entire world away, even.

I'll still need money if I survive this, but if I'm still in Olympus when Circe takes the city, I'm going to need every bit of blackmail to ensure I don't end up dead along with the rest of her enemies. Unfortunately, I don't have blackmail on *Circe*—her preferences lean more in the sapphic direction—but depending on who she brought as generals, I should have a decent chance of living through this.

I just need to string Poseidon along until that happens. If he's going to insist on pretending to be an honorable man, then I'm going to use it against him to ensure I stay alive.

I settle back down into the comfort of the bed. Now, when I'm finally properly alone, I allow myself to picture my sister, to witness the desperation on her face as she forced a promise from me: Carnaval next year. We're supposed to meet there. I don't know if I believe that it's even possible…but Poseidon has given me an avenue forward. And I mean to take it.

POSEIDON

ICARUS'S WORDS RING IN MY EARS AS I LEAVE HIS ROOM and head downstairs. Most of my people have homes in the area surrounding the docks, but I keep the rooms in the guesthouse stocked with all the necessities for those who need it. No questions asked. Polyphemus has been using one of those rooms ever since his sister, who he lived with, died in the attack on Triton.

I check there first, but it's empty. It only takes a few minutes to find him sitting on a chair in the small sitting room tucked just off the entrance, head bowed. Even as I tell myself to be calm, the words burst from me in a furious rush. "What the fuck do you think you were doing?"

Polyphemus digs his hands into his pockets and hunches his shoulders. "I'm sorry."

"Do you understand how dire our situation currently is? I sympathize with your loss. We are all mourning those who died that day. But if we don't do something—and *quickly*—more people will die. Do you understand, Polyphemus? I have to be able to trust you, and if I can't, then I have to send you away."

He jerks as if I've reached out and struck him. "Don't send me away, Poseidon. Please. I'm sorry I fucked up, but I won't do it again."

I want to believe that. I need to be able to trust my people, and before I came home to find Polyphemus torturing a bound Icarus, I would've said I *could* trust them beyond a shadow of a doubt. But war changes people. And there's no more denying that we're in the midst of a war, a majority vote for the Thirteen or no. "Did it make you feel better to hurt him?"

He opens his mouth, pauses, and wilts. "No. It didn't bring her back. I thought punishing someone who was at least partially responsible would help, but all it did was highlight the fact that I'll never see her again."

I know the steps of this dance, even if it makes me deeply uncomfortable. I never wanted to be a leader. I never wanted people depending on me, relying on my reading of events and enemies being accurate. But I *have* learned, oftentimes despite myself. If he'd wanted Icarus dead, he had plenty of time to make it happen. I can't excuse the pain Polyphemus caused, but I can understand it. I can offer empathy in return.

I pull him into a rough hug. It's the right call because he instantly clings to me, sobs racking his large body. Even though the contact feels strange and awkward, there's comfort in knowing I made the right choice. My slight discomfort is making him feel better—or at least allowing him to release some of the grief he has bottled up.

When he starts to loosen his hold, I step back. "Go talk to

Orion. They'll get you sorted. But, Polyphemus." I wait for him to look at me. "If this happens again, I *will* send you to the country. You understand?"

"I understand." He takes a deep breath and as he exhales, his spine straightens and his shoulders go back. When he walks out of the room, he moves much more like the man I've relied on for so many years. It's not a guarantee that Icarus is safe around him, but Orion will ensure Polyphemus has plenty to occupy himself—and keep him far away from our prisoner. There's no reason to tempt a second disaster.

Speaking of disasters…

My own personal one walks through the door like a gale-force wind, her long dress sweeping out behind her. Hera. Like so many of the Thirteen, she's beautiful, but her beauty is a warning rather than an invitation. It's as sharp as a blade and twice as deadly. I have no idea what motivated our new Zeus to marry her and put her in a position of power, but that choice will ultimately be his downfall. She has the same coloring as her mother, pale skin and deep-brown hair, the same hazel eyes that all the women in her family seem to share, but if I learned to be wary of Demeter, my wariness is a thousand times stronger with her eldest daughter.

None of that explains why she's here. Our communication is usually in the form of phone calls. We rarely have cause to interact in person outside of the mandatory meetings with the rest of the Thirteen. It's better that way. It would be unfortunate if others started to realize there's an alliance between us. It would be even more unfortunate if they realized the goal of that alliance—the death of Zeus.

Her eyes alight on me and she pivots in my direction with the grace of a ballet dancer. "You didn't wait for me after the meeting."

Damn it. I completely forgot. "I'm sorry. I was a bit flustered by your voting *against* us going to war."

"It's no matter. This is preferable."

I should let it go. She's not the only one to vote against war, and Demeter is perhaps more of a shock than Hera, but... "Why did you do it? Circe is *right there*. No matter what the others said, we don't need a navy to remove her threat. Athena's people have been doing violent tasks like this since the beginning of Olympus."

Hera meets my gaze, no guilt evident on her face. "She'll be expecting that. It's what Olympus would have done under the old Zeus."

I flinch. I can't help it. She's right. "It would minimize the violence against civilians."

"It won't work." She looks around pointedly. "You have one of them here."

If I'm hesitant to allow my people near Icarus, there's no way I'll put Hera in the same room as him. Not until I know what her plans are—and what knowledge Icarus possesses that might be useful. "You should be focusing on Circe."

"I *am* focusing on Circe. But she's only one part of this cluster-fuck we find ourselves in." Her hand falls to her stomach. It's still appears flat to my eye, but if she was telling the truth several weeks ago, it now holds the next Zeus. That little cluster of cells ensures that, should our current Zeus die, Hera will become regent until her child is born and comes of age. Without her husband in the mix, there's a solid chance we can get the entirety of the Thirteen to finally agree on something. To become a complete body, unified and able to meet the threat at our gates.

Or at least that's the theory. I'm not so sure it will work anymore. "Your plan is in ruins. Zeus is still alive, Circe is here, Hades is unwilling to come to the upper city, and the Thirteen refuse to align in a vote for war—which is *your* doing. The lower city is completely inaccessible, but there's no telling if that barrier will hold up against a proper assault by our enemies."

She waves that away with crimson-tipped nails. "Hades set his condition when he put up the secondary barrier. When the Thirteen are unified, he'll come back to the table. Our goals are still in alignment. Nothing has changed except the timeline. There's no space to fuck around any longer."

She has a strange definition of fucking around. I know for a fact she worked with Minos, at least indirectly, to bring down Dodona Tower. Even evacuated, its destruction would have caused untold devastation. I never agreed to that plan, but I was outvoted. And, to be honest, better that we knew when Minos would strike. I understand the logic, even if I find the whole thing distasteful.

I cross my arms over my chest. "I'm assuming this desire to cease fucking around is the reason why you're in my home right now."

"Precisely. If all the information about Circe is correct, then her vendetta is against Zeus. Not Olympus. That doesn't require a war to rectify."

I'm already shaking my head before she finishes speaking. "If that logic held true, she would've sent an assassin instead of an army—and she would have done it years ago, before the last Zeus died. She's coming for *the city*. I know you're not naive, so there's no way you're entertaining the idea of handing over Zeus and hoping she'll be happy enough with that to walk away."

Hera lifts a single eyebrow. "Doing so would certainly solve one of our problems." She shakes her head. "But no, that wasn't my plan. It's one thing for Zeus to die, but if we hand him over to our enemies, the rest of the Thirteen will turn against us. His death can't be linked back to us. It's unfortunate that the best patsy to blame for that outbreak in violence is now dead."

She doesn't out-and-out accuse me of being incompetent, but the meaning is clear beneath her words. Minos died in the fight at the marina—or, more accurately, *before* the fight at the marina. I was there, so the blame lands with me.

For all that Hera is someone whose purposes align with mine for now, she's no different than the rest of the Thirteen. She lies as easily as she breathes, shielding her true meaning under different words and tones. She's better at it than most of the others, but we've interacted enough that I have a relatively good bead on the truth of her.

Most of the time.

I wait. She obviously has a reason for being here, but she'll get around to it in her own time. People like to talk. I've found that staying silent often provokes them to speak even if they have no intention of divulging information.

Sure enough, it only takes a few sparse seconds before she continues. "You have a member of Minos's family in your custody. If would be a shame if he escaped and went on a murderous rampage. Or at least the beginning of a murderous rampage, starting with my dear husband. We would accost him directly after, of course."

I think about Icarus, mostly naked and covered in cuts. He's as much a liar as the Thirteen, but a murderous rampage? "That surpasses the realm of belief."

"Does it? He attacked Pan at that cursed party, after all."

Yes, Icarus smashed Pan over the head, but it wasn't a fatal wound and when his foster brothers were out attempting to murder the other members of the Thirteen at that party, he took no part in it. By all accounts, he hasn't done anything remotely violent since. Still, Hera has a point. He's an enemy. Even if he's not quite a believable perpetrator of violence, what does that matter when the fiction is so compelling? It's as good a plan as any, and yet I find myself hesitating. "I still think the time for this particular plan has passed. Circe isn't going to sit out there in her ships for long. She's going to attack, and we need to call another vote before then so we can present a unified front when she does. We need to get defenses in place..."

Hera looks around. I have to wonder what she sees. I inherited the property when I inherited my title, but in the years since, I've preferred to spend my time here in the guesthouse. Even that's still rife with elegance and luxury that makes me feel ill at ease, like if I move too fast, I might knock a painting off the wall or do some damage to the dainty furniture.

The main house is worse. Every time I turn around, I expect my uncle to appear, red-faced and furious. I'm tempted to raze the whole building to the ground, but that feels like letting him win, even though he's dead and I'm still among the living.

I much prefer my little apartment in the shipyard. I tend to sleep there more nights than not. It's simple there; no conflicting emotions. That space has only ever been mine.

Finally, she gets tired of whatever she sees on my face and says,

"What defenses, Poseidon? We have none. We've relied for so long on that damned barrier that we have no naval forces. What will Athena's assassins do against an army? And while my sister-in-law has done quite a bit of work to whip her forces into shape, they're untried. There's every chance they'll fold at the first confrontation and leave this city entirely defenseless."

I want to argue with her, to offer a perspective with more hope. But facts are facts, and she's not wrong. Without the barrier, Olympus is incredibly vulnerable. We have no defenses, no *barrier* to hide behind. The closest thing are the mountains that border the countryside, but even they could be surpassed with enough resources and knowledge.

If it comes to a proper confrontation, I don't see a path to victory. I don't see a path to *survival*. "The only way to save our people is to avoid a confrontation entirely."

She smiles, the expression sharp and dangerous. There's no surprise on her face. She came to the same conclusion before she sought me out. "Precisely."

The pit of my stomach drops out. So we finally get to the truth of what she has planned. "Tell me why you really voted against going to war. Tell me what you're planning."

Hera drifts to a gilded painting in the corner. It's of some ancestor of mine, though I can't begin to guess what sin she committed to have her portrait here instead of the main house. A thick woman with a riot of red curls and the same blue eyes that have passed down through the core family of Poseidons back to the beginning of Olympus. My own eyes are a different hue. But then, I was never supposed to rule.

She turns back to me, her long, dark skirt swirling around her legs. "I intend to have a conversation with Circe." Her smile widens, but there's no amusement in her hazel eyes. "One Hera to another."

ICARUS

I KNOW POSEIDON EXPECTED ME TO BE A GOOD LITTLE captive and stay put like he commanded, but I'm not the kind of person to let an opportunity pass me by. Survival is the only thing that matters. Maybe if I think that enough times, it'll actually feel true. I know it's what my sister would want. I promised her I'd meet her in Brazil, and the only way I can do *that* is if I'm alive and free when Carnaval comes around next year. The thought of everything standing between me and a reunion with her is almost enough to drive me from the new bed that was made up while I was in the bathroom, as pristine as if violence never happened here. I am so godsdamned tired. Tired of fighting. Tired of failing.

But Ariadne committed the most unforgivable act in existence to keep me alive—she killed our father. Apparently I *do* have some honor within me because I can't let my baby sister bathe her hands in blood on my behalf, only for me to die a few days later.

Shame, more than anything else, finally gets me to test the door. It was locked previously, but I was certain I hadn't heard Poseidon lock it when he left earlier. Sure enough, the knob twists easily against my palm. Every move is an understated agony, but that's life, isn't it? I'm used to it by now. Granted, my father's "punishments" never reached the level Poseidon's man committed against me, but I've learned to move smoothly even while in pain.

I slip out into the hall and look around carefully. I only got a glimpse of the rest of the house as Poseidon hauled me in here… yesterday? It's hardly a maze, though. Best I can tell, it's laid out in a perfect square. The hallway is a straight line that turns at a right angle on either end. I pick a direction on instinct, retracing my steps toward the entrance. I know better than to try to escape. I won't last long on my own. There are too many people in this city who blame my father—rightly so—and my family for all the horrible changes in the last few months. Since my father's dead, one of my foster brothers is now protected by the Kasios family, and Ariadne and the Minotaur have escaped the city entirely. That only leaves me.

If I'm going to keep my promise to my sister, I can't play scapegoat for an entire terrified city.

My best option is to stay here and convince Poseidon I'm an asset worthy of being protected. At least until I can find a way to make contact with whoever Circe has brought with her to threaten the city.

Voices slow my pace. I recognize Poseidon's deep timbre, but it's his light, lyrical conversation partner that has my heart beating faster. I know that voice. I've heard it in interviews my father played during his research on the Thirteen. She's no longer the newest member, but she is the one who interested him mightily. Hera. The woman holding the same position Circe did, albeit *this* Hera has now held it longer.

What's she doing here?

I pad to the top of the stairs and stop just before stepping into view. Truly, if they wanted to have a private conversation, doing it in the foyer is just ill-advised. Anyone could listen—and *I* fully intend to. Every piece of information is a weapon I must mold to my own use, because becoming invaluable is the only way to survive.

And, dammit, I *will* survive. If not for myself, then for my sister. That'll have to be motivation enough to put one foot in front of the other against these seemingly insurmountable odds. I've faced impossible odds before, and even though I've faltered before accomplishing true victory, I'm still here and so many of my tormentors aren't. What is that if not success?

I carefully lean my shoulder against the wall and concentrate on keeping my breathing even so there's nothing to give my presence away. Only once I have myself under control do I slide forward a little until I can see them both at the bottom of the stairs.

Poseidon is visibly agitated, his hands shifting at his sides and his entire body tense. "Hera, you can't."

She looks so tiny next to him, for all that she's not a particularly short woman. I've only met one of the Dimitriou women during my time in Olympus—the youngest, Eurydice—and while I can see some similarities in their beauty, Eurydice practically radiates kindness and Hera is cold enough to freeze the unwary.

Her voice demonstrates none of the emotion brimming in Poseidon's. "On the contrary, I must. We have no naval forces. We have no defense. The only way forward is compromise with a healthy dose of trickery."

He actually takes a step back, as if her words are a physical force battering against his big body. "You sound like Hermes—and we both know she's a traitor."

"*Do* we know that? Because the more we find out about Circe and her reasons for hating this city, the more I wonder." Hera looks particularly elegant this afternoon. In her interviews, she tends to favor menswear or sharply designed dresses that fit her lean form. What she's wearing now is almost a gown. A dress fit for a dark queen, the black fabric hugging her chest while leaving her shoulders bare and then billowing out around her stomach and hips to fall in smooth lines to the ground. All she needs is a crown to complete the picture.

I wonder about Hermes too, but she's not my problem and neither are her motivations. Most importantly, she's not here to be an asset to help me accomplish my aims.

"Are you listening to yourself?" Poseidon rumbles. "The only reason I agreed to work with you is for the betterment of Olympus. I thought that's what you wanted."

"It *is* what I want." Her voice is so cold, I can't tell if she's speaking truthfully or crafting an artful lie. "We have an opportunity to stop this entire invasion before it gets properly started. To save lives. That is what *you* wanted, isn't it?"

She's boxed him in rather neatly, if I do say so myself. It's increasingly clear that Poseidon's greatest weakness is the perception of his honor. If it's *not* an act...

I have no idea how he's survived as long as he has when he wears his emotions on his face and in his hands. Or, more accurately, in his fingers tapping nervously against his thigh. It's obviously an expression of discomfort; he might as well have posted a neon sign above his head saying as much. If he wasn't in a legacy position, he never would've become one of the Thirteen.

He probably would've been happier that way.

"Fine," he says flatly. "What do you have in mind?"

Her gaze flicks over his shoulder, catching mine. *Caught.* Fuck. Her smile widens, a pleased cat inviting a mouse to come play between its paws. "We have an eavesdropper—and just who I wanted to see. Come down, Icarus. You may as well have a voice in this conversation since I intend to utilize your resources."

Poseidon whips around, and I'm not expecting the betrayal that flickers over his face...or the strange guilt that flickers in my chest in response. I have nothing to feel guilty for. He's my enemy, just like everyone else in this godsforsaken city. My goal of surviving Olympus means the only rule I hold to is doing whatever it takes to come out on top and escape with my life. I don't have another choice.

I wish I could say that I float gracefully down the staircase, but the truth is that I white-knuckle the banister and take each step slowly to avoid my knees buckling. Every breath is agony, and my body is *not* on board with all this moving around. When I finally come to a stop on the ground floor, it's everything I can do not to pant for breath and shake. Only a lifetime of training keeps my body steady and my haggard exhales trapped in my lungs. I even manage a smile. "Hera herself. I'm honored."

"I want a meeting with Circe. How do I contact her?"

"Hera!" Poseidon roars.

I ignore him, keeping my attention on her. "So abrupt." The more I speak, the smoother my tone becomes. I know how to do this. How to flirt and charm and take everything while giving the bare minimum. I have at least some of the knowledge she needs, and while I'm obviously not immune to torture, blunt doesn't seem to be *this* Hera's style. "You're not even going to buy me breakfast first?"

She flicks her long dark hair over one shoulder. On anyone else, the move might seem flirtatious. With this woman, it's a threat. "As I'm sure you're aware, I don't have time to waste with this song and dance. If I have to drag you out of here by your hair, then I will. Your father had a way to contact Circe. How did he do it?"

This, at least I have the answer to. I shrug. "It's this deliriously clever device called the telephone. You should try it sometime."

"You do have a quick mouth, don't you?" She moves closer to me, and even with the new clothing now covering my body, I somehow get the sensation that she sees my wounds. I barely have a moment to tense before she grabs the back of my neck and presses her hand to my chest. Hard.

It happens so quickly, there is no bracing for it. Agony sends me to my knees, and Hera follows me down, bending to keep the pressure on my wound. "Let's try this again, shall we?" Her voice is perfectly even while I'm fighting not to scream. "How do I contact Circe?"

"That's enough." Just like that, it ends. Hera's still in front of me, still gripping the back of my neck, but the hand causing me so much pain has been removed. Poseidon has his fingers wrapped around her wrist, and he holds her touch several precious inches away from me. "Let him go."

"I knew you were soft, but I didn't think you were suicidal." He releases her so she can rise to her feet and take two cautious steps backward. Somehow, it doesn't look like a retreat when she does it, but more like a recalculation. Hera examines her wrist. "I should kill you for that."

I don't miss the way Poseidon half steps in front of me, shielding me with his large body. "I didn't hurt you, and you know it. I simply stopped you from hurting him." For all his firm words, his finger has started that tapping on his thigh again. "Icarus."

I jolt. Has he ever said my name before? Surely he has. And yet it feels different this time. It feels, somehow, like he's reached out and touched me. Dangerous. Ill-advised. I know better than to fall for the good-cop, bad-cop act. I'm not entirely certain Poseidon has the duplicity to pull off that sort of ruse, but I can't entirely rule it out. It's possible they're manipulating me. I have to keep that in the back of my mind.

Poseidon glances over his shoulder at me. "Do you have her number?"

"It's hardly something my father would just give out."

He narrows his amber eyes. "So you *do* have it."

Dammit, I thought that non-answer might distract him. But then again, pain is making me slow, swirling my thoughts as if they were molasses. If I give them Circe's number, what use do they have for me?

No, I can't afford to think like that. Circe is hardly going to entertain a compromise at this stage of the game. I don't know her overly well, but I know enough of the moves she's made to be sure of that. Giving them the phone number ensures they continue to believe I have information they need. They'll call her and be shut down immediately, and then they'll come back to me for more. This is the right move. I'm sure of it.

I stagger to my feet, ignoring the way Poseidon starts to reach out to help me. "Fine. You can have it." I rattle it off, watching as Hera wastes no time pulling a phone out and typing in the number. I half expect her to make the call right then and there, but she slips her phone back into the pocket of her dress and nods.

"Lovely. I'll be in contact." She turns and sweeps from the room, and a few seconds later the front door slams to signify her exit. It's the only outward sign of her anger. Surprising that she'd allow even that much on display. Interesting.

But I'll consider that more when I've rested. Right now, I'm swaying on my feet. I start to take a step but my body won't cooperate. Poseidon catching my elbow is the only thing that keeps me off the floor. His expression is downright forbidding as he studies me. "You're supposed to be in bed."

"Aren't you glad I'm not? Look at what an asset I am. Look at how cooperative I am. Just like a good little captive."

His dark-red brows draw together. "What game are you playing, Icarus?"

Now is the time to ensure he'll continue to protect me. To go on my best behavior and play by the rules he's set out. I don't. Instead, that perverse little impulse inside me, the one that always gets me into trouble, takes the reins. I lean against him, pressing my hand to his chest right over his steadily beating heart. "I'll play any game you want me to, lover."

"What are you talking about?"

I blink up at him, searching his expression. Normally, when I drop some innuendo, the target of my desires picks up on it quickly enough. Most people are simply looking for an excuse to do the "bad" thing, the opportunity to take my hand and be led into the lust-filled night. And all the while, they tell themselves that it's not their fault, that they have no choice but to go to bed with me.

But there's none of that with Poseidon. He genuinely looks confused. Either he's a better actor than I could have dreamed or... I push forward, testing him. "I'm talking about *sex*, Poseidon. Down and dirty fucking. Whatever flavor you're into, I guarantee I've done it. I'd like to do it with *you*."

"You're talking about..." Poseidon's face flares a delicious crimson. His mouth moves, but no words come out. I actually made him speechless. I don't know if I've ever done that to a potential lover before. Not that I had plans to make Poseidon my lover five minutes ago, but now it seems like a great idea.

"You're probably asking yourself why I want to fuck you." I keep talking on pure instinct, but my mind is moving a mile a minute. This...isn't an act. I had my doubts before, but now I'm sure of it. He genuinely isn't playing hard to get. It literally never crossed his mind that I might set out to seduce him.

Aw, wee lamb.

"We're not... We can't... Absolutely not." He's sputtering. I shouldn't find it so charming, but I do. Especially when he shifts back as if putting more distance between us will change the possibility I've put to voice. "It would be a horrible abuse of power," he finally manages, voice strangled.

"You're one of the Thirteen," I say slowly, still determined to test him. "Experience says that power is meant to be abused."

"It's wrong."

"That just makes it even hotter." Oh yeah, I'm going to seduce the fuck out of Poseidon. Because he's handsome, yes, and power-ful, of course, but most importantly, because he truly *is* honorable. If he feels like he's taking advantage of his captive, guilt will take residence in that impressive chest of his. It will ensure he continues to protect me until I no longer need him.

And I'll get to have a bit of fun in the process.

POSEIDON

"YOU NEED TO EAT." I DON'T MEAN TO SPEAK THE WORDS.
"I...uh, you should have a meal. I should feed you." Putting a little
distance between myself and Icarus seems like the smart thing to do,
but here I am offering him a meal. It's too late to take back.

Especially when he smiles suspiciously widely. "I could eat."

Did I really think he was going to turn me down? He's already
shown himself to be resourceful and that he will end up in places he
shouldn't be. I have him trapped in my house. Of course he's going
to be looking for a way to create some leverage for himself. Every
person wants to survive, after all. He's no different just because he's
an enemy to Olympus.

But he's already experienced unacceptable amounts of harm
while he's supposed to be under my care. Depriving him of a meal
simply because his presence—his *offer*—makes me feel strange isn't
acceptable. So I motion for him to follow me.

Whichever one of my ancestors built the guesthouse apparently
didn't think their guests deserved a kitchen, so we have to make the

short trek to the main house. It looms in the fading light, a monster intent on devouring.

Except, no, it isn't. It's not a monster. It's just a house. Four exterior walls and an absurd number of rooms. Too much money spent on decorations for how hideous it is. There are no ghosts haunting the place, for all that my uncle and cousins died there.

For once, Icarus has nothing to say, but when I glance at him, I wish he were prattling on because, instead of talking, he's watching *me*. I can't even pick up my pace because he's barely staying on his feet, and if I leave him behind, he's likely to pass out in the rosebushes.

Instead, I push open the door and hold it so he can precede me into my uncle's kitchen.

It's weird to still consider it my uncle's kitchen. I know that. He's been dead for well over a decade at this point and I've been Poseidon for nearly half my life. But this house doesn't feel like home. It never has. It's impossible to walk through these halls and not have the small hairs on the back of my neck rise just like they did when I was a child. *Trespasser. Freak.* He called me that and more when he was still alive. I truly don't believe in ghosts, but sometimes when I have reason to be in this house late at night, I can almost convince myself that they're real.

The kitchen is nice, though. And while it *is* part of the house that still feels like it belongs to my uncle, I highly doubt he spent any amount of time in this particular room. I still maintain the staff—what's left of them—from when he was Poseidon, but that's mostly because it feels wrong to let them go.

It also feels wrong to sit down while someone else cooks me a meal, as if my hands aren't capable of labor. Thankfully, the cook has long since gone home. He usually only comes by in the morning these days to prep a day's worth of food for me and my people, on the off chance that we come through these doors.

That's where I go now, to the large industrial-sized fridge tucked into the corner. Sure enough, there are neatly labeled containers with the makings for a ridiculously extravagant meal. It makes Louis happy to cook them, so I don't ever complain. And they *are* delicious. Almost enough to draw me here just for a taste when I don't technically have business within these walls.

Icarus watches with narrowed eyes as I pull the containers out and line them up on the counter. "Leftovers?"

I pause and give him a long look. "These leftovers are probably the best thing you'll have eaten in recent memory. Don't be a snob."

His brows wing up. "If we're back to throwing stones about being a snob, you're the one who is a member of the most powerful group in this city. If anyone's a snob, it's you."

I don't bother responding to that. He's obviously looking to provoke a reaction, and I know for a fact it's not true. If anything, the criticisms lobbed my way are that I'm too different to fit in with everyone else. Ironic, that.

My entire life, I've been a square peg trying to fit in the round hole of societal expectations. I can fake it, I can shave down my corners, but it fits like a too-tight coat, like I can't catch my breath.

Since I became Poseidon, I stopped having to try as hard. Because of that power. People criticize me for not being charming or witty or a number of bullshit things related to playing nice with the press, but I fulfill my duties better than the last three Poseidons combined. I don't cause problems, and I stay out of the petty power plays the rest of the Thirteen indulge in. The rest of the Thirteen mostly leave me alone, just like I prefer.

At least until Hera's coup. Or attempted coup, as it were. She hasn't quite pulled it off yet, and it worries me that she's continuing with her plan despite the enemy literally at our gates.

A few minutes later, I set a warmed plate full of food in front of Icarus. "Eat."

He makes no move to pick up the fork that I slide across the counter. "What about you?"

"What about me?"

"You can't honestly expect me to eat a meal while you stand there staring. Besides, have you even had dinner?"

"I haven't, in fact." Stress has a way of annihilating my appetite, and it isn't particularly intense during the day anyway. It's late at night when my body usually decides to inform me that I haven't given it nourishment in far too long. We're hours away from that point, though.

Maybe he thinks it's poisoned? I would hardly waste good food on that sort of thing, but it's not like he knows me. I grab a second fork and take a careful bite of everything on the plate. "Satisfied?"

His smile is slow and a little wicked and makes my stomach flip. "Hardly. But it's a start." The words are smooth except for the barest edge. It takes me a few seconds to place the tone. Flirtation. But that doesn't make any sense, even if he was talking about sex earlier to fluster me. He's my captive. He rightfully hates me, and people may be all sorts of twisted up and do things against their better interest, but surely he draws the line at *actually* trying to seduce his captor...right?

"Share a meal with me, Poseidon." His grin is still there, morphing into something playful. Does he realize it doesn't meet his eyes?

Disappointment quells that small flip in my stomach. Icarus is a liar just like all the rest. I expected nothing less, but it still feels bad. All the same, he has a point about me needing to eat. It's only when I'm standing across the island from him with my own full plate that he picks up his fork and begins to eat as well.

I expect the silence to be jagged and filled with peril, but it's strangely comfortable. Icarus is moving stiffly, but he will be for quite some time with his injuries. I still can't believe I misjudged Polyphemus so intensely. If I had known he was a danger to Icarus, I never would have left him in charge of our captive. That failure was paid for in Icarus's blood.

Icarus takes another bite and shivers. "You know, this is amazing, even reheated. Your chef is something special."

"Yes, Louis is." This, at least, is a conversation easy to navigate. "He's old enough to be a grandfather several times over, and I'm pretty sure his eyesight went out a decade ago, but his taste buds remain as youthful as ever."

"Sounds charming."

"I don't know if I'd say that." Charm and Louis hardly go hand in hand. He's a cantankerous old bastard who treats me just like the two assistants I hired for him a while back. He's bossy and snarls as often as he talks, and I enjoy spending time in his presence immensely—or I would if he wasn't *here*, in this damned house. Louis says exactly what he thinks, and he never couches his words in hidden meanings. I know where I stand with him at all times. It's a relief.

"You know, Hera's plan won't work. Circe won't be satisfied with anything less than fully sacking the city."

There's no reason to feel disappointed that he's turned our conversation back to the pending attack. It's why I kept him here, after all. I need the information held in his beautiful head. "Do you know Circe well?"

"No one knows Circe well. I know her less well than most. My father wasn't exactly proud of me, and he took great pains to ensure I wasn't exposed to more of the council on Aeaea than absolutely necessary. That went doubly true for Circe. He was certain I would embarrass him and endanger his upward mobility. I'm the ultimate disappointment as a son, you know." The words ooze charm, but his smile still doesn't reach his dark eyes. A truth within a truth. His father's disappointment cuts him like a knife. His father who has been dead less than forty-eight hours.

Guilt stabs me. Somehow, in all this, I'd almost forgotten. Athena's people took Minos's body, and it wasn't an Olympian who killed him, but all the same, I should have remembered. I push my plate away. "I'm sorry for your loss."

"No, you're not."

I shrug. "No, I'm not. But it's the thing people say in situations like this. So I said it."

Icarus surprises me by laughing. It's not the calculated sound I've heard him make a few times when he attended the same parties I suffered my way through. It's too loud, and he snorts. It's cute.

He sits back in his chair. "I suppose it *is* what people say in situations like this. But to elaborate on what I said earlier, I may not know much of Circe *personally*, but I've had plenty of personal experience with people who interact with her daily. People talk. As a result, I know as much about her as anyone. She's bent on revenge; I can't imagine what you could possibly offer her that she wants more than Olympus burning."

I understand it, at least in theory. I even met Circe once, long ago, at her wedding to Zeus. She was a beautiful bride, but that's no surprise. Nothing but the best for that monster. Rumor had it that he saw her walking down the street and had to have her as his own. I don't know why that translated into marriage for this particular victim, but even I could tell that she was filled with barely contained fury as she walked down the aisle to him. Throughout the reception, he kept her close, as if afraid she would try to escape. A few days later, they whisked away to their honeymoon.

A honeymoon he returned from as a widower.

"She was mistreated greatly by Olympus," I say, my mind still in the past. "Not just by Zeus."

"You sound almost like you agree with her."

"Do I?" Damn it. I've let myself be too honest again—and with someone who I can ill afford to be open with. I clear my throat. "You may think dealing with Circe is a fool's errand, but Hera tends to get what she wants. She might surprise you." I dearly hope she does. There are so many innocents in this city, and even more are spread through the countryside. So many lives under the protection of the Thirteen, and we're failing them. We have been for a long time, but it's never been clearer than in the moment when the barrier came down and instead of taking decisive steps to protect the city, we're still engaged in political manipulations and power plays.

"Maybe." Icarus shrugs and sets his fork carefully on his plate. "Maybe not. I suppose it won't matter to me overmuch anyway, since I'm going to be dead."

I blink. "What do you mean?"

He gives me a long look. The fake charm pulling at the edges of his mouth fades away and he becomes uncharacteristically serious. Did I think he was beautiful before? He's so much more so now, when he's not pasting a mask on his noble features.

"You have to kill me." He says it almost gently, as if breaking bad news. "As long as I'm alive, I'm a threat to the security of the city. What remains of it, at least. I'm not a fan of being tortured, but Polyphemus had the right idea. You need whatever information I have, and then you need to dispose of me. It's the smartest move."

No matter how many times I replay his words, they don't change. "Are you seriously suggesting that I torture and then murder you?" That can't be right. It *can't* be.

"Like I said, I'm not exactly advocating for that kind of violence. But I'm not a fool. This only ends one way, and it's not with me riding off happily into the sunset, whole and alive." He looks away. "Which, frankly, is a damn shame. It will break Ariadne's heart when I don't meet her next year. She's strong, though. She'll get over it. It might take a while, but I'm sure the Minotaur will be there to comfort her through her grief...and I'll be too dead to worry about it either way."

ICARUS

I NEEDED THE FOOD, BUT WHAT I DIDN'T NEED WAS THE confusion this meal brought. Poseidon isn't playing a game like I originally thought. Some of the other Thirteen I've met have been almost smarmy. Power does weird things to people, particularly the Olympians. But apparently not Poseidon.

At least he's talking to me. It's very hard to seduce someone who flees the room the moment you enter.

"No one's going to murder you, Icarus." He says it intensely, forcefully. As if he can will it into being true. "You're under my protection now."

"So that means I can leave?" I say, testing exactly how far his so-called protection extends. From the way his expression shuts down, that's a no. It's nothing more than I expected. I just wanted to see if he'd admit as much. I shrug, the very picture of nonchalance. "Like I said, it's fine. I knew what would happen when I decided to stay behind so Ariadne could get away. I accepted it."

Poseidon plants his large hands on the countertop and glares at his plate of food as if it's insulted his mother. "It was a very brave thing you did."

I stare. Did he just *compliment* me? Surely I'm hearing things. "I took you captive, threatened to murder you, and then when that didn't go to plan, almost drowned us both." It wasn't brave. It was reckless and desperate and more than a little fatalistic.

I honestly didn't think they'd let me leave the docks alive once they pulled me out of the water. My sister has spent her life enduring the same gilded captivity that I have, but it hasn't broken her. She still has hope, and joy, and plans for the future. She deserves to be happy. My life is a small price to pay to ensure she has a real chance to make it happen.

But going on and on about how I'm sure to die obviously won't garner the sympathy I was aiming for. Time to try a different tack. I stand, doing my best to cover up my wince as the movement sends a jolt of agony through my chest. Poseidon is watching me closely, but he doesn't leap forward to stop me from moving, so I must do a good job of masking my pain. Perfect. It's hellishly hard to seduce someone who thinks you're about to fall unconscious at any moment. That sort of thing puts a damper on the mood.

"I'll tell you anything you want to know...on one condition."

Poseidon doesn't move as I circle the island and come to stop in front of him. I've been close to him before now, but it feels different in this moment. Charged. That adorable flush is back in his cheeks, drawing my attention to the smattering of freckles over the bridge of his nose. I've never been one to enjoy beards, but his close-cropped beard looks good on him. It smells good, too; obviously he takes care of it.

And then there are his shoulders, stretching the fabric of his shirt damn near to bursting. Some people wear too-small clothes to show off their bodies, but on him it feels almost like...neglect. Like maybe he yanked on the first shirt he found and it just happened to be a tiny bit too small. It pulls tight across his muscular chest and even tighter across his round stomach.

It...makes my mouth water.

"Icarus?"

Right. I'm staring. From the tension in his thick muscles, I can tell he's considering putting some distance between us. I make the big guy nervous, and it delights me to no end.

He takes what I can only assume is an attempt at a fortifying breath. "What's your condition?"

"I'm very scared, you see. I went to bed alone and woke up being carved to pieces." It takes effort to put a quiver into my voice...but not as much of an effort as I would like. The truth is that Polyphemus scared the shit out of me. I have no tolerance for torture, it seems. Not for enacting it and not for receiving it.

Another way my father was right about me.

I shove the thought away and focus on the man before me. "If you mean to give me your protection, I want it twenty-four seven. I want to be by your side every hour of every day."

"Out of the question."

I didn't honestly expect him to agree, but when bargaining, it's important to start with the most outlandish ask and then negotiate your way to what you really want. "I understand that I can't attend confidential meetings, but aside from that."

"The shipyard is no place for tourists. You're going to get

yourself killed, and I just got done promising to keep you safe. No."
He shakes his head sharply. "I'll put Orion on your security detail,
but you're not leaving the house."

We're getting closer, but we're not quite there yet. "Poseidon."
The way his body clenches when I say his name brings to mind
all sorts of interesting possibilities. I'd love to say that my focus is
solely on manipulation, but the truth is I've been depressingly cel-
ibate since arriving in Olympus. It's too dangerous to take people
to bed not knowing where their alliances stand. Ironic, considering
the very outcome my father was afraid of is the one I'm living right
now. Captivity. Being used against Circe. A traitor to my people.

Poseidon licks his lips. They're very nice lips. Sensual and full
and completely at odds with his perfectly groomed beard. He's
such an interesting combination of rough and gentle. It intrigues
me despite myself. Finally, he says, "What?"

"You're the only person in this city who seems to give a damn
if I live or die." The words are intentional, but it doesn't make them
less true. Fuck, that's depressing. I push through, not willing to
spiral right now. There will be plenty of time for that later. "I only
feel safe with you."

I'm close enough to him that he has nowhere to back up to, but
he crosses his arms over his chest, almost as if they can be a barrier
between us. "There are places I'm going on a day-to-day basis where
you can't come with me, Icarus. You want safety, and not being at
my side is what's required to give you that safety."

Almost there. I have him just where I want him. I allow my
shoulders to dip, my spine to wilt. It hurts, but it's worth it to see
the way his eyes go soft. "But what about at night? I don't know if

I'll be able to sleep, considering the last time I did, I woke up with a knife embedded in my skin." Not strictly the truth, but it serves for dramatic purposes.

He shifts from foot to foot. It's a slight movement but it's there all the same. I really do make him nervous. How fucking delightful. He swallows. "What do you suggest?"

"I want to sleep with you." I sink enough insinuation into the words to make his flush deepen quite prettily. I laugh and press a hand to my cheek. "Wow. That sounded like I was coming on to you, didn't it? But you understand what I mean, don't you? I feel safe with you, which means I'll actually be able to sleep. That's what you want, isn't it?"

He stares at me for a long time. Long enough that I have to fight the urge to fidget. There's a wealth of knowledge in his amber eyes, and I have the sudden sneaking suspicion that he sees right through me. I've done this song and dance before; I've used seduction to ensure safety or gather information or any number of things I've needed in the moment. It's *seduction* that paved the way for my archive of blackmail material. I'm good at it. Fucking spectacular, even. And yet this big man doesn't seem to be falling for it.

I guess I need to up my game. Or that's what I tell myself as I take the small step forward that brings us almost chest to chest. He drops his arms in surprise and I take advantage of that new space to press my hands to his pecs. Fuck, he's huge. He's easily six inches taller than me and his shoulders are twice as wide. He could destroy me.

But he stands there, perfectly still, as I shift up onto my toes. "Unless you want me to seduce you?"

His mouth moves and he stammers. Actually fucking stammers. "I…uh…what?" It's the most adorable thing I've ever seen. Poseidon clears his throat. "No. That isn't necessary. I said I would protect you, and you don't need to be in my bed to ensure it happens."

Maybe not, but it's a good way to tip the scale in my favor. Sex creates intense emotions in most people. Maybe not at first, but give it enough time and that shared intimacy starts to mean something. I've never let that get in the way of my end goals, but my partners start to feel special, valued, like they can trust me with their deepest secrets. And *that's* where the real value is. Having sex with Poseidon is no great sacrifice. He's handsome and shows every evidence of being kind and considerate. I'd still do it even if he wasn't, but it certainly makes for a more pleasurable experience.

I press even closer until our breath mingles in the bare space between our lips. "I don't *need* to be in your bed…but maybe I *want* to be."

"Icarus." On his lips, my name is a plea for mercy.

Too bad I have none. "Poseidon." I shift one of my hands to the back of his neck and dig my fingers into his thick red hair. I pull, mostly to angle his head to where I want it, but the moment I do, his knees buckle.

His. Knees. Buckle.

He catches himself on the edge of the counter and stares down at me with something like wonder. Maybe that's the sensation in my chest right now, warm and strange and confusing. Surely Poseidon isn't submissive. He's one of the Thirteen, for gods' sake. I've read my father's reports. He runs his teams of people with an iron fist and a mutual respect. I anticipated him being tough and strong and maybe a little kind, but not enough to outweigh his dominance.

And yet that same man is staring down at me with his eyes too wide and his lips parted. As if I've shocked him. As if I've introduced him to something he didn't even know he needed.

This development should be enough to cause me to retreat, to come at this from a different angle, but I can't escape the look in his eyes. I can't stop myself from tugging on his hair again, harder this time. He *whimpers*.

Holy fuck.

I don't make the decision to kiss him. My body does it for me. I guide him closer, and he moves with my touch, putty in my hands. And then his mouth is on mine, and all my plans dissolve in the rush of sheer need. He tastes like the spices of the meal we just ate, and he has to be approaching forty, but his lips are almost tentative against mine. As if he's waiting for me to guide this connection.

Later, I'll have to figure out what the fuck I feel about this, but right now I'm riding on instinct. I bite his bottom lip, wanting to hear that whimper again. Wanting to taste it. He gives me exactly what I desire. I suspect he's gripping the counters right now because he very carefully doesn't touch me. He lets *me* touch *him*.

But only a hand in his hair and one pressed against his chest so I can feel his racing heart—and it *is* racing. For me. Because I'm kissing him. Power surges through me, heightening my desire, turning it into something even stronger than I could have anticipated. I kiss him harder, deeper. This was meant to be a soft, careful seduction. But there's no room for either of those things now. Not when his hands finally touch me, his palms pressing to my hips, his fingers digging into the curve of my ass. He moans against my tongue and pulls me hard against him, obviously craving more contact with as much fervor as I do.

The press of his chest to mine sends a wave of agony through me. My wounds. I'd completely forgotten. My sound of pain is barely a whisper, but somehow he hears it. Poseidon rips his mouth from mine and uses his hold on my hips to set me away from him. "That's enough."

I stare at him, my breath coming hard in my lungs. There's no space for argument, but as my heart slows and my lungs settle in my chest once more, knowledge takes root inside me. It's not enough.

It won't be enough until I possess him fully.

POSEIDON

I END THE EVENING QUICKLY AFTER THAT. IT'S EASY enough to usher Icarus back to his room. As much as I want to flee to my room, as much as I'm certain his words were meant to incite a particular reaction in me, I can't deny the truth of them. I intended for him to be safe here, and he wasn't. I may not have been the one that drew a blade across his skin, but that doesn't change the fact that I'm responsible; it was one of my people who did it.

Leaving him unprotected is unacceptable, and as much as I want to trust my people implicitly, there's been too much pain to go around. It changes people, and often not for the better. The only person I can fully trust with his safety is *me*.

I slide down the wall next to his door and stretch out my legs. I'm tall enough that they nearly touch the wall on the other side of the hallway. It's going to be an incredibly uncomfortable night, but it's a small price to pay for failing him.

I can't allow him into my bed. I...shouldn't. I really, really shouldn't. Not only because of the complicated power dynamics—he's obviously bargaining in an attempt to save himself—or because I can't afford to have my loyalty to Olympus muddled at a time when I'm needed the most. No, the fear fluttering in my throat is solely because of my reaction when he pulled my hair during that kiss.

I've had lovers—a few, at least—but they were such careful encounters. There was never anything remotely like pain involved. Icarus didn't *hurt* me when he pulled my hair, but it was the promise of hurt that buckled my knees. Something I wasn't even aware I might want, and should I decide to explore that, it most absolutely can*not* be with one of the enemies to my people.

No matter how handsome he is. Or how good he tastes. Or how skillfully he kisses. Or how my stomach flutters when he says my name just so…

I shake my head, force thoughts of him from my mind, and settle myself down for a long night.

Orion finds me in the early hours of the morning. They raise their brows but make no comment on my choice of sleeping location. Instead, they simply hand me my phone. "You've been summoned."

I blink blearily up at them, trying to focus. "Has the invasion started?"

They shake their head. "As best we can tell, none of the ships have moved. They haven't sent out people, either. We have a watch set along the coastline like you wanted, so even if there were divers, we would find them. There's been nothing."

Maybe that should reassure me—I hardly want Olympus invaded—but all I can do is wonder why Circe is hesitating. There's a reason for it. There's been a reason for every move she's made, skillfully and with great intent. There's a reason for this too, and I have a feeling that by the time I find out, it will be worse than if she raided us on the first day.

I accept Orion's outstretched hand and allow them to pull me to my feet. Only then do I check my phone. Sure enough, there's a single text message from Zeus himself.

Zeus: We meet at eight. Be punctual.

He hasn't commented on the fact that I didn't return his phone calls the other day, and it's just as well. I don't have a good excuse. It's not as if I can tell him I've been in league with his wife to see him dead. That I still am, technically. Zeus and I have never been friends and never will be friends, but planning for his death is nothing personal. It's for the good of the city, just like everything else I do.

Within an hour, I've showered, changed, and grabbed a quick breakfast. I walk into Dodona Tower with minutes to spare. Even so, I'm not the last to arrive. That falls to Hera herself, sweeping in the room right before the doors close. She's back in her customary menswear, the black suit tailored perfectly to her body and some kind of lacy top in a deep purple color peeking out from underneath the suit jacket. She meets my gaze for a beat and then moves to her husband and sits at his right hand.

Zeus doesn't look at her. "Report."

Hephaestus shifts in xyr seat. "This is a waste of time and a pathetic little power play. You didn't need to summon us all here for a damned report. *We* are busy being actually useful."

Zeus doesn't flinch at the venom in xyr tone. "Be that as it may, we're here now. *Report*."

Demeter leans forward, breaking the tension a little. "Evacuations are well in progress. It will take days to fully empty the city, but we're moving as quickly as we can. I'm afraid it's going to affect the harvest. We simply don't have the room in the country, not when every spare acre is dedicated to crop growth. But I've had my people convert two of the fields into a camp for the evacuees. It's not ideal, but it'll do until we solidify this situation."

Athena shifts. "Any change from Hades?"

"No. His word stands. He won't bring down the secondary barrier until the Thirteen are in agreement and we have an effective plan to repel the invaders. Seeing as how we're zero for two with those, I don't see him being a part of these conversations anytime soon." This from Aphrodite. I wonder where they get their information from. I didn't realize they were close with Hades, but maybe it has something to do with his wife. He might not play the political games, but Persephone is all too aware of their necessity. It wouldn't surprise me to find out she's been quietly in contact with several members of the Thirteen, her mother included, to do what it takes to ensure that the city is protected as much as possible.

Ares looks like she wants to shoot to her feet and only barely manages to resist the urge. "I don't understand what Circe's *doing*. It's been days, and she hasn't moved or attempted communication. If she's going to invade, why hasn't she done it already? If she's going to threaten us, she has to make contact to do that."

"It's rather brilliant." Athena doesn't say it like it's a compliment. More like it makes her furious. "The entire damned city can see her squadron just floating there, threatening us. The longer they do it, the worse the fear will become. She's softening us up, just like she's been doing from the beginning. First with that damned family, then with the murder of the last Theseus and her pet assassins continuing to rile up the general population. It might not be textbook, but it's close enough. She's ensuring that when she sets foot in Olympus, there will be as little fight as possible."

"She'll find plenty of fight from me and mine," Ares practically growls.

"Not without a vote for war," Artemis snaps. "Which you didn't have the majority vote on last night and sure as fuck don't today."

Athena ignores her and keeps speaking. "Fear is a useful tool and Circe obviously knows how to wield it. Don't underestimate that." She pushes to her feet. "Now, as lovely as this meeting that has accomplished nothing has been, Demeter and I have an evacuation to oversee and people to call back. We might not have forces, but if we can conscript citizens—"

"We need a vote for that. As Artemis so helpfully pointed out, we don't have it. Unless one of you who voted against war have changed your mind?" Zeus speaks for the first time since demanding a report. When no one speaks to say they'll change their vote, he nods. "In that case, we evacuate everyone. I don't give a fuck if some of the people try to volunteer. They're civilians and should be treated as such. Get them out of here. Ares, I want you to start patrols. Work with Poseidon to set up some kind of schedule to supplement his sentries along the coastline. When Circe finally does move, I want to hear about it the moment it happens, not when they're knocking down our doors."

"If I—"

He keeps speaking over his sister. "Maybe at *that* point, the people in this room will stop prioritizing petty politics over the good of the city."

Ares looks like she wants to fight with her brother but finally nods. "I'll see it done." She rises, and she and Athena leave the room together, shoulder to shoulder. They'll be getting in contact with me later for the sentry schedule apparently. I look around the room, but there's no peace to be had. Artemis glares at Zeus as if she'd like nothing more than to just shove him through a window. Aphrodite and Hephaestus speak in low voices. Dionysus appears to be taking a nap.

I guess the meeting is over. I haven't formed much of an opinion on our new Hephaestus—aside from xe being more capable than Theseus was in the position—but xe was right. There had to be a more efficient way of communication that didn't require all of us to travel to Dodona Tower.

My gaze catches on hazel eyes and stops there. Hera jerks her chin slightly, a clear command. I rise and walk out of the room, taking the elevator down one floor to where her offices are. From what I hear, she doesn't spend much time in them, preferring the orphanage she's recently renovated, but the door unlocks under my hand. I don't have to wait long for her to arrive.

"The evacuations aren't enough. You have to know that."

I nod slowly, but can't help pointing out, "We'd be doing more than evacuating civilians if you'd voted in favor of war." I'd like to believe that getting the people out of the city is enough, that we might have a way to be victorious if we aren't worried about civilian casualties, but the longer this goes on, the more I wonder. Circe has outmaneuvered us at every available opportunity. I can't imagine that now that we're in new territory, with Olympus facing a threat from outside our walls for the first time in the city's history, we'll suddenly turn the tables on her. It's possible Icarus has information that might undermine her, but it's even more likely that we're past the point when information will actually matter.

We're about to have a fight on our hands.

And we can't even get organized enough to *vote* on meeting that fight head-on. Circe will be at our gates—if we *had* gates—and the Thirteen will still be squabbling.

Hera moves to the window and peers out before lowering the blinds. "I spoke to Circe. She wasn't willing to discuss terms over the phone, but she will in person. Tonight."

I knew she intended to call, but somehow hearing it makes everything so much more real. I'm already shaking my head before she finishes speaking. "No. Absolutely not. It's a trap, and if she gets her hands on you—and the babe in your belly—then she has all she needs to bring Zeus and the rest of the city to its knees once and for all. You can't do this."

"I'm not doing it alone. You're coming with me. We're going to take a small boat out halfway between the ships and the shore. She'll come with only one person as escort. It's a peace talk, Poseidon. It's possible she wants something we're willing to give up. We won't know until we actually *talk* to her—and that's exactly what I intend to do."

I can't tell if she's right or if she's leading us down a road of pure destruction. Hera hates Zeus. I'm nearly certain that she hates this city as well, with the exception of her family and a few select others. What she may be willing to give up in order for Circe to spare the ones she loves is not the same thing as what I or any of the other Thirteen would be willing to give up.

I have a feeling if I tell her no, she'll just find a way to do it herself, and then there will be no witnesses to whatever *that* conversation entails. I have to go. And I have to ensure she walks out of that meeting alive and unharmed. *Damn it.*

I sigh. "When?"

"Midnight. There's not much of a moon, so we should have plenty of privacy."

Plenty of privacy for Circe to murder us. I don't say it. Hera isn't a complete fool, for all that she's deeply motivated by rage. She knows the risks, and she's decided they're worthwhile. So be it. It's not as if I have another choice or even a better plan. It's even possible that I'm wrong and what Circe wants is something that I'll be all too happy to give up.

And maybe, someday, pigs will fly. It's about as likely.

ICARUS

POSEIDON HAS BEEN GONE FOR HOURS. AT ONE POINT, around two in the morning, I checked the hallway to see if there was a possibility of escape, and there he was, his big body sprawled out across the open space. Protecting me? Ensuring I didn't flee? Impossible to say. All I know is that I slept soundly from that moment on, waking in the late morning to find my door still unlocked and the hallway unguarded.

I won't secure my safety if I keep hiding in my room. It's time to take the offensive.

I'm waiting for Poseidon the moment he walks through the front door. He looks tired, his head low and his shoulders bowed. That ceases the moment he sees me. He narrows his eyes and stops short. "What are you doing down here? You should be in bed."

"I'm feeling much better. Or at least better enough to get restless."

He remains unconvinced. He looks around as if expecting one of his people to pop out of the woodwork. There's no one around.

There hasn't been all day. I am not entirely certain that I couldn't have walked right out the front door and taken my chances in the city itself. I was tempted to try, but the reality of the situation is that I have very few resources currently—and no exit out of the city. I'm trapped as much as the rest of the Olympians, and that means I need someone to protect me.

Someone powerful...like Poseidon.

It seemed a reckless concept last night, but I've had plenty of time to think about it. He's my best shot. I just need him invested enough in my safety to step between me and any threat that arises. The best way to do *that* is to bring feelings into the mix. Starting now.

I smile in the face of his unease and spread my arms. "I was thinking we could share another meal."

Instead of appearing charmed, he just seems more suspicious. "Where's your shirt?"

"Some overzealous person decided to stab me a bunch of times through it. I hardly had a suitcase when you hauled me out of the bay. I don't have any other clothes."

"You were wearing a shirt last night."

"Was I?" I shrug. "It got blood on it." It's, strictly speaking, the truth. My cuts are mostly scabbed over, but one of them bled a little while I slept.

He frowns harder. "You need clothes. *More* clothes."

It's kind of cute how single-minded he is. "I'm not about to argue, but the fact remains that I don't have any without blood on them and I have no way to get some."

He looks around as if racks of clothing will suddenly appear just because he wills it. I'm not entirely sure he's wrong. He's fearsome when it comes to certain things. I even believe him when he says that none of his other people will touch me. A guarantee most leaders couldn't make. No matter how loyal people are, tumultuous emotions make them act without considering the potential consequences. Because of the moves my father made in service of Circe's war, there are plenty of extreme emotions to go around. I might even sympathize with Polyphemus, if he wasn't intent on carving up my chest.

The silence stretches between us, growing strained and awkward. I motion to the door leading outside. "Shall we eat?"

"I suppose." He cautiously follows me across the lovely little paved walkway to the main house. He's so tense, as if he's ready to jump forward and catch me should I stumble. But that's a fanciful thought. Poseidon might have taken care of me, but he doesn't ultimately care *about* me. I can fight for that to change, but it's entirely possible he'll still throw me to whichever enemy requires the sacrifice of my life—especially if it means his people have a better chance of living.

It's what *I* would do. You can't be loyal to everyone, so you have to choose wisely.

I've set up a haphazard seduction in the kitchen. In another time and place, there would be candles across every surface, soft music playing in the background, and delectable desserts designed to be foreplay. Best I can tell, though, Poseidon only keeps what's strictly necessary on hand. I suspect whoever his cook is buys a week's worth of ingredients and then cooks them all into meals that can be reheated for him and the revolving number of his people who stay in the guesthouse.

As such, I only found one half-burned tea light, a dusty bottle of wine, and some lasagna ready to be reheated. It's hardly my finest work, but the shock on Poseidon's face makes me wonder if anyone's ever done something like this for him. Surely they have. He's handsome and powerful and shows every evidence of not being a complete monster. He should be beating prospective spouses off with a club. And yet in all our research of the Thirteen, he's never been publicly attached to anyone.

"What is all this?"

I grab the first plate of lasagna and slide it into the microwave. "Dinner, obviously."

"That's not what I mean, and you know it. Why are you going through all this effort? It's not necessary. You're as safe as it's possible to be in Olympus right now."

It's really cute that he thinks so, but if he's not lying to me, he's far more naive than I would have thought. I'm not safe. All it will take is Zeus demanding my head, and there's not a whole lot Poseidon could do. He's one of the other legacy titles, so theoretically he could push back and actually be successful, but why would he? He owes me nothing. At least…not yet.

A few minutes later, we have two steaming plates of lasagna in front of us and I've managed to wrestle out the cork of an expensive bottle of merlot so I can pour us two glasses. Poseidon is still staring at the food as if he expects it to be poisoned, but before I can decide if I should address that, he takes a tentative bite.

I wait while he eats for a few minutes, allowing him to settle in and relax. A little. This man doesn't seem to relax completely…ever. There's no reason for that to make my chest feel funny. Just because he's a palatable enemy doesn't make him any more of an ally.

I sit back and sip my wine, determined to see this plan through. "I thought we could play a game."

"A game." He sets his fork down carefully and appears to give me his full attention. "Now we get to the heart of why you've gone through all this effort. There's no point in making it a game. Be direct and ask for what you want."

Be direct? The very idea is laughable. If I tell him I intend to seduce him so he'll be emotionally compromised and therefore keep me safe, he's liable to haul me back to the guesthouse and lock me in again. Better to circle around until I can come at this from an angle I'm sure will give me the advantage.

I smile and take another sip of my wine. It is quite good, full-bodied and dry on my tongue. "My only aim is to get to know you better. You're something of an enigma, and since you're my captor, I would like to learn everything I can about you. I propose we ask a question for a question. I have information that you want, I guess, for all the good it'll do you. And I'm curious about you. It's win-win from where I'm sitting."

"A question for a question." He seems intrigued for a beat, but then he shakes his head. "No matter what you say, I can't guarantee you'll be honest. There's no point to this game."

At this juncture, I have no reason to lie. Withholding information will just convince him I know nothing that's useful. I'm not certain my information *is* useful, but the time for secrets has long since passed. It sailed away with my sister. Maybe if I'd been honest with her from the beginning, we wouldn't have reached that point where the choice was to potentially watch the only person I care about in this world be cut down or to sacrifice myself so she has a chance at happiness. Secrets have a way of breeding complications.

"I'll be honest. Pinkie promise." I hold up my hand with my pinkie extended. He stares at it as if I just offered him a snake. I can't help but laugh. "Come now, Poseidon. You must know a pinkie promise is the most honorable of promises. It's horrible luck to break one. I wouldn't risk it."

"You're making jokes at my expense now."

"In fact, I'm being uncharacteristically serious. Come on. You know you want to ask me questions. Here's your chance." I wiggle my pinkie finger at him.

He reluctantly reaches out and loops his thick pinkie finger around mine. I shouldn't be startled at his calluses, but I am all the same. One of the Thirteen who actually works? Color me surprised. I release him and pick up my wine again. "In the spirit of charity, I'll even let you ask a question first."

He studies me long enough that I wonder if he's changed his mind. Then he shakes his head and takes a sip of his wine. "Do you really think seducing me is your pathway to freedom?"

I blink. Did he just...? I give a nervous chuckle. "Is that what you think I'm doing?"

"I'll remind you that you promised honesty. Are you already throwing your pinkie promise out the window?"

Damn it. In all my years of using seduction as a technique to gather information, I've never had someone call me out so explicit-ly—or so early in the process. Denying it will get me nowhere and it'll mean an end to this game.

I force a casual shrug, keeping my body language loose and

relaxed. "Is that so wrong? If you're concerned about power dynamics, just know I would have seduced you the moment I saw you regardless."

"You've seen me two times in the past at parties in Dodona Tower." He holds up two fingers. "We've never so much as spoken."

Well, he has me there. "My father kept me under tight control. I was hardly free to pursue sexual encounters of any flavor. Believe me when I tell you that, yes, I clocked you, and I've wanted you from the moment I saw you."

It's even the truth. Poseidon has an unrefined handsomeness that makes me want to dig my fingers into him. He's not like the perfectly coifed peacocks from the Aeaea court or even like the rest of the Thirteen. He doesn't play games. I should have taken that into account when I proposed this one. "But in the spirit of perfect honesty, yes. I do think seducing you will pave the way to safety, if not freedom. I couldn't ask for a better protector than one of the Thirteen's legacy titles."

"I already promised you my protection. You don't need to bring sex into the equation in order to ensure it." He's glaring as if being invited into my bed isn't a godsdamn gift.

Getting riled up isn't the pathway forward. I swirl my wine lazily. "Maybe not, but it certainly keeps things interesting. I think it would be fun. That's all the reason I need to do it."

"No." Poseidon pushes to his feet, towering over me. I can't help but rake my gaze over his body. He seems to favor jeans and T-shirts that hug his chest and round stomach, clothing with nothing loose to be caught in machinery or whatever the fuck it is he does. A working man, so to speak. I bet he looks excellent with dirt smudges on his brow and sweat glistening on his skin.

I don't exactly mean to lick my lips, but I'm only human. And no matter what other motivations I have, lust is always a good reason to jump into bed with someone. There's lust aplenty when I look at this man.

"I answered your question. I want you to answer to mine."

He doesn't sit. His body is tense, as if he's about to bolt out of the room. In all my estimations and plotting, I never expected Poseidon to be skittish. But then, a lot about him has surprised me in the last twenty-four hours. He finally gives a jerky nod. "Ask."

There are a thousand possibilities, and even more angles, to take to get what I want out of this. But the question that springs to my lips is one of genuine curiosity. "When I pulled your hair, your knees buckled. Does pain get you off?"

His face flames a deep crimson like I've come to anticipate. He looks away and starts up that tapping of his middle finger against his thigh. This man must be terrible at poker. The moment he gets even the slightest bit agitated, he starts fidgeting. Or maybe it's not actually fidgeting. Maybe he's stimming. That would make a lot of sense, now that I think about it.

"I...don't know." Each word sounds like it's forced from his thick throat. "I've never experienced pain in the bedroom in the way you mean."

I open my mouth to ask a follow-up question, curiosity sinking its teeth deep within me, but he's already on the move. He stalks to the doorway, his words trailing behind him. "This game is over. Go back to the guesthouse and don't leave. I can't guarantee your protection if you do." Then he's gone, the door slamming behind him. I swear the actual walls rattle with the force of it, but for all that, I don't even flinch.

Did Poseidon just *flee*? From *me*?

POSEIDON

MY SKIN IS SO OVERHEATED, IT'S A WONDER I DON'T burst into flames. I asked my question of Icarus on instinct alone, sure I was overstating things and that he would deny the accusation immediately. I wouldn't have believed his denial, but to hear him baldly state his intention to seduce me? I should be disgusted. I should be furious. I should be putting as much distance between us as possible. I'm doing the latter...but it feels like running away.

Because I *am* tempted.

He's nothing like my previous partners. That should mean it's easy to put him from my mind, but the truth is the exact opposite. I can't stop thinking about him. He's irreverent and uses charm to lie as easily as breathing, and yet...

What kind of strength must it take to survive someone like Minos? To snatch up a gun and hold it to *my* head, to sacrifice himself so his sister could escape? It's one of the bravest things I've ever witnessed. I may not have said it quite that way to him, but it's the truth. Most people wouldn't have done that.

Not to mention…he's incredibly attractive. Almost upsettingly so. Icarus is lean in an almost delicate way, his light-brown skin smooth and unblemished, his wavy, dark hair perfectly styled at all times—somehow even now, while existing in my household without so much as a spare set of clothes.

On that note…

I pull out my phone and call Orion. It takes only a few minutes to get them on the task of acquiring clothes for Icarus. At least enough to get him by until I can… Wait, what am I thinking? It's the height of impropriety for me to take him shopping for clothing. We're on the brink of a fucking war and I'm worried about doing things that might put a little bit of light back into his dark-brown eyes. Icarus only kissed me once, and yet I'm seduced in exactly the way he intended me to be. What a fool.

My reprieve comes later that evening in the form of Hera arriving to be ferried out to her ill-fated meeting. At least she's dressed appropriately to be on the water. She has fitted dark jeans tucked into tall boots and a thick, deep-blue coat that covers a good portion of her body. Her long hair is tucked back into a stylized design that looks almost like a crown. No doubt that's intentional.

Her brows wing up when she catches sight of me. "A little eager, even for you, to be waiting outside for me." Her gaze flicks over my shoulder to the house behind me. "Unless your darling little captive is giving you more trouble than you've admitted?"

"Let's go." I'm a smart man, but I know better than to get into a war of words with someone like Hera. She'll have me admitting things I have no intention of speaking aloud. If she thinks my priorities are suspect when it comes to Icarus, she may pause in her attempt to murder her husband and try to take Icarus from me.

That, I won't allow. Which is probably just further confirmation that he *should* be taken from me because I'm not thinking clearly. I don't care. I'm not ready to let him go.

Fuck.

I lead the way to my SUV and open the door for Hera. She settles in the front seat as I round the vehicle and climb behind the wheel. Thankfully, Hera doesn't bother to make small talk as I head down the long drive to turn toward the shipyard.

I haven't been there in days, and the absence is an ache of loss in the pit of my stomach. Not just for the familiar space but for what it represents. I miss my normal days; I miss knowing exactly what will happen at any given hour. There's been far too much excitement for my liking, and it won't slow down anytime soon.

Polyphemus waits by the small boat that we'll take out to meet Circe. His lone eye is lowered, intentionally not meeting my gaze. I'll have to talk to him tomorrow. It doesn't matter that I'm still furious at him for hurting Icarus. I'm not sending him away, which means I have to settle this so he can move on. So we all can. In the morning, I'll take him aside and reassure him that he still has a home here.

I clap him lightly on the shoulder and nod. "Thank you. We'll be back shortly. Wait here." I don't want any witnesses for whatever comes next. If it's a trap, then Hera and I will pay the price for our arrogance alone.

Hera steps down into the boat, and I follow her significantly less gracefully. She doesn't speak until I've started the engine and guided us away from the dock and onto the open water toward where Circe's five ships linger. "It's rather impressive how loyal your people are. They truly love you, don't they?"

There's no reason to think her question is a threat, but I bristle all the same. "What do you think you're going to accomplish with this meeting tonight? If the rest of the Thirteen find out—"

"But they won't find out, will they?" Her words go hard, her tone unforgiving. "Our intentions are the same, Poseidon, even if our methods differ. I need my family to be safe, and if that means I have to break every vow I've made and sacrifice a large number of lives, then I'll do it in a heartbeat."

I've heard her husband say something similar. I don't say as much, though. She won't thank me for the comparison, and she sure as fuck won't thank me for pointing out that she and Zeus are remarkably well matched. I can't leave her words unchallenged, though. "Our intentions are *not* the same, Hera. I'm not willing to sacrifice *anyone*."

"So you say now." She shrugs, her gaze going distant. "But when it comes down to your people or all the rest of Olympus, it won't be much of a choice at all." She turns to face the direction we're traveling in, effectively ending the conversation.

The salty air of the wind whisking the mist into our faces fills my lungs and relaxes a tight muscle between my shoulder blades. We might be driving to our certain deaths, but at least I'm out on the water again.

Out here, even in the relative shelter of the bay, I'm reminded of how small my life really is. My people find the feeling disconcerting, but for me it's a comfort. The sea doesn't care that I'm one of the Thirteen; it will crush any arrogance I have as easily as the next person's. I respect the destruction water and weather can come together to create, but I don't fear it. There's almost always warning and time to prepare, to minimize the damage.

The same can't be true of people.

The relative peace of the moment is over far too soon. "We're here." I ease off the throttle and allow the boat to coast to stillness. Or as close to stillness as we can manage while ensuring the waves don't wash us back to the shore. It's too dark to see the ships blockading the bay, but I can feel their presence like a weight pressing down on my shoulders. There's no true freedom on the water right now. There won't be until we end this.

The faint sound of a motor declares Circe's arrival. Squinting into the darkness, I'm shocked to find she's held to her end of the bargain. There are only two people aboard the small vessel cutting through the waves in our direction before slowing to pull up next to us.

I get my first look at Circe—or my first look since that ill-fated wedding to Zeus. She wears the years well. Even in the darkness, I can see her straight spine and proud shoulders, her face a pale oval as the boat gets closer, her short brown hair seemingly impervious to the wind. There're new lines at the corners of her mouth and eyes, but she's no less beautiful than she was all those years ago. Her companion has their hood pulled forward and is bundled up with enough clothing that it's impossible to tell anything about them.

She and Hera stare at each other, each appearing to weigh their enemy. To Hera's credit, Circe is the one who speaks first. She crosses one long leg over the other. "I'll admit, I was surprised to hear from you. It's enough to make one wonder how you got my number to begin with." Her gaze flicks to me and then back to Hera.

"That's the least important part of the conversation we need to have." Hera's voice is cool and even, showing no sign of the strain she has to be feeling. We sit in the presence of the person who has orchestrated so much pain and suffering in our city. People have died because of the plans Circe put into motion. More will die before this is over. But none of that is evident on Hera's face. "You've been sitting out here, so obviously you wanted someone's attention. I chose to give you mine."

"We had bets on who would reach out first." Circe examines her nails, long and painted some dark color that I can't divine with so little light. "You weren't even on the list. Bravo. A Hera with gumption and ambition and no small amount of ruthlessness. You've surprised me."

"If you were paying attention, I wouldn't have." Hera's voice goes hard. "I'm prepared to deliver you Zeus in exchange for you not sacking the city."

Circe throws her head back and laughs, the sound musical and light and downright joyous. It's completely at odds with the current situation, and it makes me shudder. When she finally controls herself, her laughter trailing off into little giggles, she presses a hand to her chest. "My, you certainly are full of surprises, aren't you?"

"That's what you want, isn't it? My Zeus isn't the one who caused you so much pain, but he'll do in a pinch."

"Darling, you have to learn to dream a little bit bigger." All amusement disappears from Circe's voice. "The entire power structure of Olympus is responsible for the harm I endured."

Hera huffs out a breath. "The entire power structure of Olympus has caused harm to a lot of people. You're not special. There's not much to be done about it."

"Maybe not for you. Personally, I mean to shatter it into a thousand little pieces and then rebuild it from the wreckage into something that doesn't serve only thirteen people, each more corrupt than the last." She smiles slowly. "Even you, who would offer up your husband to the enemy."

Hera is silent for a beat, two. "You can't have Olympus. If you invade, the people will fight you to their last breath and you'll inherit nothing but an empty, barren piece of land. And then, right when you're at your weakest and exhausted from the battle, the outside world will finally realize the barrier that kept our city safe and separate no longer exists. They'll come and they'll take what few resources are left."

Far from being taken aback by Hera's words, Circe seems downright delighted. "How are you going to fight me when you can't even manage a vote to go to war with me?"

I tense. How does she know about *that*? It's a silly question, and I have my answer as soon as I think it. Circe is Olympian. More than that, she's obviously studied us and the laws, no matter how archaic. She knew about the assassination clause. Of course she knew we'd have to vote to go to war—and how unlikely it is to get a majority vote among the Thirteen.

She...planned on it.

"If you weren't the slightest bit worried, you wouldn't have accepted this meeting with me. You don't seem like someone who likes her time wasted. You're looking for a contingency plan, so let's stop pussyfooting around. Why don't you tell me what you're *really* willing to accept in order to create peace?"

"You know, Hera, I think I like you. Keep that phone on you. I'll be in contact." She motions at her person near the engine and they power up. Within seconds, Circe is whisking away, disappearing into the darkness.

I turn to Hera. "What the fuck was that?"

"I told you my husband has to die, you agreed to *that*, and now you're going to falter when you discover the means?" She turns and looks in the direction where Circe disappeared. "Regardless, I was right. There's something she wants and she recognizes that a full-out battle benefits no one. She'll let me cool my heels for a little bit to assert her dominance, and then she'll give me her real terms. That's when we move."

I reluctantly start the engine and turn us back toward the shore. "More like she knows how incompetent the Thirteen are when the group of us are together." I shoot a look at Hera. "Why don't we tell Zeus to call another vote and this time you vote *for* war? That would *really* surprise Circe."

"Poseidon, I need you to understand something." She finally turns back to face me, her hair coming free of its braid and whipping around her with the speed of our movement. "There is nothing I wouldn't do to protect my family. *Nothing.* So you can stay by my side and ensure your people are protected in the bargain, or you can stand in my way and I'll cut you down first. Do you understand me?"

She's not saying anything that truly surprises me and yet I'm shocked all the same. I knew Hera was ruthless, but this isn't something as simple as killing a spouse she never wanted. She's talking about significantly more devastation. I have no doubt she means what she says, which means I need to stay by her side and do my best to temper whatever plans she's about to come up with. It's the only way to ensure as many people survive as possible.

I exhale slowly, tension winding tighter and tighter through me. "You're being intentionally difficult. We may not have a navy, but at this point, Circe only has five ships. Why are you wasting time with plotting when there's a clear solution?"

Hera shrugs, appearing completely unconcerned with how she continues to complicate my life unnecessarily. "You might be right, but if there's a proper war, then everyone will expect the Thirteen to be at the front of things. That's how it's supposed to be. My mother, my brother-in-law, right there with targets on their foreheads. Eros will be right there, because as much as Psyche gets frustrated with our mother, she will want her protected. Charon, Eurydice, Orpheus. All three of them will be conscripted to the battle for Olympus. I might not give a shit if that little asshole Orpheus dies, but Eurydice does."

The feeling in my chest gets worse, the pressure more intense. "The people you care about aren't the only ones who matter. *My* people are more likely to be on the front lines than anyone in your family, regardless of what tradition would state for the Thirteen."

"Precisely." She says it so clearly, as if she's led me to this point on her own. As if I haven't been aware of it from the beginning.

"There is no 'precisely' about it. The longer we delay, the greater the chance of more people we care about dying. You're not part of the solution. You're part of the problem!"

"Poseidon." Even over the whistle of the wind and the sound of the waves, her patronizing tone sets my teeth on edge. "Whatever gave you the impression that I'm trying to be part of *Olympus's* solution?"

I could shove her over the edge right now. We're still a good distance from shore, but not so far as to ensure she couldn't make the swim. It wouldn't be enough. I'd have to hold her under, have to muscle her beneath the surface until she stopped struggling. Until she drowned.

I've never killed anyone before. I've gone to great pains *not* to kill people. When Icarus tackled me into the water, I could have ensured I would be the only one to emerge alive. The stakes are so much higher now.

"Are you thinking about murdering me?" she asks me carefully, her body tense.

Is it possible to drown with air in your lungs? It certainly feels like I'm drowning right now. "It wouldn't matter if I did. With you dead, your mother still wouldn't vote for war. We wouldn't have majority." The impossible situation presses down on me, harder and harder. There's *nothing* I can do to fix this. No matter how hard I fight or how thoroughly I compromise my morals, it seems like I only manage to make things worse.

If Hera died, that would fracture what's left of the Demeter–Zeus alliance. It would ensure Hades never comes to another meeting with the Thirteen. It would make a shitty situation even more impossible.

I *can't* shove Hera over the edge and leave her to drown. I can't do anything at all. Just like always. No matter how much power I supposedly have, I'm just as helpless to the whims of the Thirteen as I've always been.

I can't fucking breathe. Getting closer to land only makes the sensation worse. I grab the edge of the dock and pull the boat close. "We're done after this. I want no more part of your schemes."

"Oh, Poseidon." Hera steps onto the dock, laughter trailing in her wake. "You don't get to decide that. We're done when *I* say we're done."

ICARUS

I STILL HAVEN'T MANAGED TO FALL ASLEEP WHEN THE DOOR to my room flies open and Poseidon appears. It was only a couple hours ago that he fled my presence, but he looks almost like a different man now. His eyes are too wide and he immediately starts pacing from one side of my bed to the other. "I need you to tell me something."

I sit up and rub my knuckles across my eyes. It's hard to focus, which means I was closer to sleep than I realized. My thoughts feel muddied and sluggish. "What's wrong?"

"Have you…used pain in your past sexual encounters?"

A bolt of pure heat sears me, blazing away the last cobwebs of not quite sleep. I force myself to take several deep breaths and to think. He's not coming to me in a flurry of lust. He's running from something. That shouldn't matter—this is what I wanted, after all—but…it does matter. A lot. "Poseidon, before I answer your question, I need you to answer one from me. Are you okay?" I'm slightly horrified by the words coming out of my mouth—even more so by the fact that I *mean* them.

"No," he says simply. "I'm overwhelmed and I don't know what the right choice is, and I can't think. Or I'm thinking too much. I don't know." He shakes his head roughly. "I just need some space, a little bit of peace. I'm sure things will become clearer after that."

I'm no stranger to using sex as a form of escape. I facilitated it in many of my partners over the years. When they start coming to you for escape, that's when you have them in the palm of your hand. I suppose it's a gift of sorts, but I've never cared enough about my lovers—or them about me—to see it as such. With this man, though, this near-stranger who I barely know? It feels like unearned trust. Guilt sprouts in my chest. "I don't know if that's a good idea."

He stops short and pivots to face me. For a moment, he looks more like the man I've started to get familiar with. The one who studies me as if he can reach inside my brain and map my very thoughts. "Earlier, you said you intend to seduce me. So seduce me." He swipes his hand through the air. "I'm saying yes, Icarus."

Unease still filters through me, but this is an opportunity I can't afford to ignore. Or at least that's what I tell myself as I climb out of bed and pad barefoot to stand in front of him. There's a strange feeling in my chest, almost hidden beneath the odd guilt. Something almost like appreciation? No, that's not quite right. He's obviously in some measure of distress, and he came to *me* for a solution. It indicates a trust I haven't earned. A trust I have no intention of earning.

But turning him away feels wrong.

I reach out, stopping short of making contact with his body. "If you're serious about this, then there are a few fail-safes that need to be put in place."

"I don't care about any of that."

He truly *is* desperate. My guilt starts to fade, replaced by a sensation I have no name for. Surely I'm not feeling protective of my captor? That would be absurd. It would make me the worst kind of fool. "It doesn't matter if you care or not. Fail-safes are what *I* need in order for us to move forward."

He opens his mouth as if he might keep arguing but ultimately shakes his head. "Of course. Whatever makes you feel the most comfortable."

It's a testament to the kind of person he is that he's still thinking about my comfort instead of his. He might be in my room, offering himself up to me on a silver platter, but if I told him no with any amount of surety, he would turn around and walk away. That knowledge, more than anything, settles any doubt in my mind. "First, we're going to talk."

"I don't want to talk."

"It's a short conversation. I'm sure you'll survive." I take a step back and marvel at how he shadows my movement, maintaining the careful distance between us but not allowing it to increase. My next inhale makes me feel more like my normal self. "Tomorrow, we'll have a full discussion on what your limits look like. But for tonight, there are two things I need from you. First is for you to pick a safe word. Are you familiar with the concept?"

His hands open and clench rhythmically at his side. "I am easily twice the size as you are, Icarus. I could stop you anytime I want."

"Probably." I shrug. "But I won't touch you again without a safe word. It's required for this kind of play, and whether you're strong or not, I need the assurance that you'll use it. You might be something of my enemy, but that doesn't mean I want to harm you."

He frowns at me as if I've said something revolutionary. Which part? Us being enemies? Or that I don't want to harm him? My chest pangs at the idea that maybe his past lovers haven't taken care of him. That maybe they took advantage of this big man and his too-big heart.

Finally, he gives a jerky nod. "Trident. It's as good a word as any."

"That will do." A thrum of excitement goes through me. This is truly happening. It's something I want for calculated purposes, but it's also something I just flat-out want. Ever since I kissed him, ever since his knees fucking *buckled* from the tiniest bit of hair pulling, I've spent more time thinking about my captor than I have about escape. He's so reactive. I have to wonder what else he'll react to, what else I can do to draw out those delicious whimpers. I'm at a buffet of delights and I don't know where to start first.

I take a slow breath and try to marshal my thoughts. "The second question I have for you is, what do you need from me? Be explicit, Poseidon. I want no confusion between us."

His exhale shudders through his entire body. "I don't want to think anymore. I don't want to worry anymore. I don't want to keep pretending I have the answers. Even if it's only for a little while." He sinks slowly to his knees before me, his amber eyes desperate. "Hurt me. Fuck me. Do whatever you want. As long as I don't have to think anymore."

My mouth works, but no words come out. That's hardly any guidance at all. The amount of trust he's putting in me, even if he is larger, is absolutely absurd. I could harm him. I could fucking *kill* him. And it's almost as if he'd welcome it. I knew I was playing a dangerous game when I embarked on this attempted seduction, but Poseidon just raised the stakes and then offered me his throat.

I'm not certain I could ever deserve his trust…but there's a small, quiet part of me that *wants* to.

I force myself still. There's a proper way to do things, and it's not falling on him like a ravenous beast. That would be fun for both of us, but it's not what he's asking me for. I draw in a careful, steady breath. Well, a mostly steady breath. "Take off your shirt and pants and then return to your knees."

His relief is written all over his handsome face. His shoulders sag, and he scrambles to his feet and hurries to obey my command. His shirt and pants end up in a pile at his feet, and he dips his thumbs into the band of his underwear, but I shake my head. "Leave them on." I should be taking advantage of everything he's giving me, but there's still a part of me hesitating.

Poseidon sinks to his knees and places his hands on his meaty thighs. He truly is a specimen to be marveled at. He's so fucking thick in every part of his body that I just want to take a bite out of him. His freckles extend down his broad chest and over his barrel stomach, accompanied by a smattering of hair the same color as his beard. I've never found freckles so fascinating before, but I want to use them to write my name and tattoo it across his chest.

Wait. No. Damn it, *no*. This isn't permanent. He doesn't care about me, and I certainly don't care about him. We're captive and captor, and he should have *me* on my knees, begging. To stand before him like this, with him watching me with pleading in those amber eyes, is beyond comprehension. What is he thinking?

But he's asked me for escape, and escape is one thing I know how to do.

"Place your hands on the footboard. Don't move them." I watch as he shifts awkwardly to the foot of the bed to follow my command. He's tall enough that he's not fully bent over, but it will still work just as well. I move to his side and now, only now, do I allow myself to touch him. I trail my fingers down his spine. He tenses in response, but when I simply keep stroking him gently, his head eventually falls forward, baring the back of his neck to me.

He has freckles everywhere. I don't know why I find that so charming, but I sure as fuck do. I want to trace the path of them with my tongue, with my fingers, with other things. Not tonight. Maybe not ever. I can't afford to be focused on the future, not when he's relying on me.

He's big enough, strong enough, that it would be nice to have a flogger or a paddle, but he's also new at this, so an open hand will do. I shift closer and stroke down his back to the top of his underwear. His muscles flex against my fingertips. Gods, he's shaking and I've barely touched him. "I'm going to spank you now."

His whole body shudders at my words. "Please. Do it."

I take a moment to allow myself amazement that this man apparently hasn't engaged in kink when he's obviously primed for it. I don't know what it means that I'm his first. A surge of possessiveness nearly takes me to my knees. Another feeling I have no right to. Poseidon is my enemy. I have to keep reminding myself of that fact. If there was a choice between me and his beloved city, he would throw me to the wolves without hesitation.

But he's here now. Trusting me to give him what he needs. Opening himself up and exposing all his vulnerable bits.

The overwhelming urge to spank him until he wears my bruises for days afterward, to mark him as mine, shudders my breath out. I don't know where that came from, but I'm not about to indulge it. He's not mine. He never will be.

Except for right now. For tonight.

"Remember your safe word. Use it if you need to." I hook my fingers into the band of his underwear and pull it down over his round ass. Freckles here, too. *Gods.* Before I can sink to my knees and take a bite out of him for real, I bring my hand down on the top of his ass. I don't try to hit him with all my strength; this is more a test of what he's looking for. Of what he needs.

Even knowing that he asked for this, even knowing that he's fully consenting, I'm still shocked to my core when he lets out a moan I feel in my bones. A moan *I* caused. *Holy fuck.*

I press one hand to the center of his back, where I will be able to feel every bit of his reaction to every blow. Then I bring my free hand down on his other ass cheek. There's a trick to this, to the steady pacing, not so quick to rush things, slow enough that he can feel the full sting and blossoming of pain from every strike, so that he has a chance to protest if he needs to.

But he doesn't. Every time I spank him, he lets loose one of those delicious moans that I want to eat with a spoon. I keep going, alternating sides and rhythm so he can never quite anticipate or brace against the bloom of pain. His ass reddens beautifully, drowning out the freckles there. It makes my mouth water and my cock hard. I can almost—*almost*—feel exactly how good it would be to sink into him, to have the heat of his reddened ass against my pelvis as he clenches around my cock.

Sometime around the dozenth strike, he starts shifting as if he can escape the pain, pushing against the bed as if he's not sure he wants to retreat or arch his back and offer me better access. Through it all, he keeps moaning, his head hanging limply between his broad shoulders.

Finally, I can resist it no longer. I sink down and bite him on the upper curve of his ass. Not as hard as I want to, nowhere near hard enough to break the skin, but he jerks and makes that whimpering sound I've been craving since our kiss in the kitchen. I press my forehead to the small of his back. Measuring his little shudders and shakes. "Poseidon."

"Yes?" His voice has gone soft and slow, the way submissives often do when in the middle of a scene. If he's not fully in subspace, he's damn close. "Icarus? What do you need?"

I smile despite myself. Trust him to be the kind of man who asks me what I need when *he* came to *me* in desperation. *Does he ever put his needs first?* The thought staggers me. It threatens to make this moment impactful in a way I don't want. I can't be trusted to hold him with care. I can't be trusted to hold *anything* with care.

And he…deserves that.

Fuck. I kiss my bite mark. I shouldn't be doing this. Now's the time to stop things and bring him down, to hold him long enough to ensure he's okay and then flee. Except I don't.

I kiss his heated skin again. "Are you only here for pain? Or do you need pleasure, too?"

I hold my breath as he whimpers again. Addiction. That's what this man threatens to be. I've kissed him once and given him a relatively light spanking, and it's everything I can do not to push for more, not to take *everything*.

"Pleasure, too," he finally grinds out.

My selfish monster of a heart hoped he'd say as much. He just gave me the excuse to do what I want to. Without moving from my position, I trace over the band of his underwear with my fingers to the curve of his stomach, and carefully lower the fabric past his massive, hard cock.

Now, we can really start having some fun.

POSEIDON

I NEVER THOUGHT IT COULD BE LIKE THIS.

Can't think clearly enough to define what *it* is in this scenario. Sex. Pain. Peace. It all applies.

I'm here on my knees, my ass one agonizing screech of pain, my cock so hard that one faint touch might send me over the edge. But the awful pressure that threatened to crush me has eased. My thoughts are slow and peaceful, almost so peaceful as to be nonexistent. There's no space for overthinking or overanalyzing when each contact his hand makes against my bare skin sends a wave of agony through me. How can I worry when he has me so well in hand? He plays my body as if I'm an instrument under his command. I'm not so sure he's wrong.

I'm not someone who worries over much about the gods, but if religion were like this, maybe I'd actually be interested in participating.

Icarus pulls my underwear down to free my cock, and suddenly this is all too real. Pain hasn't been something I've shared with past lovers. Either they weren't interested, or I wasn't, but now I wonder what I've been missing out on. If it could have always been like this...

Icarus pulls my underwear tight, the band digging into the base of my cock and making me moan. "Stay with me, big guy."

What little thought I was able to gather in that moment scatters like marbles. I can't breathe, but it's nothing like the horrific sensation out on the water with Hera. It's more that I don't *need* to breathe, not with Icarus commanding me. The only thing I can manage is a faint, "I'm with you." My voice is slow and almost sleepy.

"Good." He sets his teeth to my shoulder and bites down. I shudder and my hips jerk as pain blossoms like the prettiest flower I've ever seen. And still, my thoughts remain perfectly at ease, almost sedated, which doesn't make any sense, and yet I'm experiencing it all the same.

"You can take some more."

It doesn't seem like a question, but he doesn't move, so maybe he's waiting for a response? I gather what's left of my wits and answer him. "I can take some more."

He keeps his tight hold on my underwear, keeps the pressure on the base of my cock, and then he resumes spanking me. Each strike sends another wave of pure pain through my body, cleansing me. I have every intention of staying silent and enduring, of simply floating in this bliss. Even if it hurts. Especially if it hurts.

But he delivers a particularly vicious blow and—"I'm going to fail them." Each word feels wrenched from my chest, a confession that I would never have allowed myself to speak. And yet I keep going. "There's no way out of this. No matter what games Hera and the others orchestrate, we can't fight the sheer numbers Circe has. We can't even align long enough to vote to go to war and protect the city, which is *our only purpose*. I've failed. We've all failed. The people who depend on me—on us—are going to die."

Icarus shifts and then his hand is on my ass, kneading and squeezing. "Oh, I don't know about that." His touch is painful, but somehow it's soothing at the same time. "You're an amazing leader. I'm sure you'll think of something." For once, no sarcasm or false charm clings to his words.

I choke out a laugh. "I let Hera meet Circe and further whatever game she's playing, only to find it's at the expense of Olympus instead of to help the city. Hardly the amazing leader you claim."

"Hmmm." He presses his hand to the center of my back, a steady weight that allows me to deepen my breathing again, to release the fear threatening to ruin this perfect moment. "I'd say you're doing the best you can with the circumstances you find yourself in."

"The best I can." I choke out a laugh. "How can you say that? I'm holding you captive."

"Yeah, you are. But you're also on your knees for me, so I think it all evens out." He goes back to kneading my ass, spreading my cheeks and then pressing them together. His intention is vividly clear. "If we enjoy each other long enough, I'd like to take you here. Not tonight, though."

His voice is rougher than normal, nowhere near as eloquent. But I can picture what he says all the same. Him filling me, our bodies thrusting together in a rhythm as old as time itself. "I want that," I grind out.

"Then I suppose you'll have to earn it." He drapes himself over my back, the fabric of his pants agonizing against my tender ass. I moan as he wraps his fist around my cock and gives me the contact I've been craving. Icarus allows me no time to brace. He strokes me roughly, almost too fast, but I've been primed from the moment he first struck me. Even as I try to fight the orgasm gathering in my balls and tensing every muscle in my body, I might as well try to fight the tide. I'm equally as successful. Pressure gathers in the base of my spine, my balls drawing up, and then it's too late to do anything but submit.

I moan my way through an orgasm, hips jerking as I fuck into his hand. He gives me a few more strokes, each gentler than the last. "You did well, big guy." He kisses the back of my neck and wraps his arms around my chest as much as he can. "Now, you are going to stay perfectly still while I go find a washcloth. Then we're going to get in bed and you're going to let me hold you through the adrenaline crash. Got it?"

He could have told me that the sky was green and the sun will never rise again, and I would've given him the same answer I give him now. "Got it."

"You're precious." Icarus kisses my neck again. "Don't move." He rises on unsteady feet and walks to the bathroom. Only a minute or two later, he returns with a warm rag and sets about cleaning me up. Truthfully, there's not much mess, certainly not enough to require the prolonged stroking and soothing, but I enjoy the gentle swipe of the wet cloth against my skin.

It takes me two tries to get to my feet, even with him urging me along. My head feels strangely floaty and my muscles are too loose.

I don't know if I've ever been this relaxed in my life. Later, I'll worry about this addictive sensation coming at the hands of this man. In this moment, there's no space to worry about what that means. I can only feel gratitude that I'll be able to sleep tonight. Probably.

Icarus pushes me onto the bed and follows me down, tucking himself against my side and pressing another kiss to my throat. He laughs softly. "Your beard is scratchy. I like it."

Tentatively, I wrap my arms around him and, when he doesn't protest or move away, gather him close. There's something about him that feels larger than life when he's standing there being charming. It's almost startling to realize how slight he is. How perfectly he tucks under my arm and lines up with my chest.

I...like it.

He strokes me gently, his fingers trailing over my chest, my stomach, then moving to my arm. "Next time, there needs to be a little more negotiation ahead of time. If you were anyone else, I don't know if I'd give a fuck, but you're too damn *good*. I don't want to harm you."

He calls me too good, but there's no way to look at our current position, mostly naked in his bed, and come to any conclusion but that I abused my power just as thoroughly as the rest of the Thirteen do. He's my captive. My enemy. Strange how those words feel more like a lie every time I think them. You're not supposed to fuck your enemy, not even in Olympus.

"I shouldn't have asked this of you." But even as I say the words, I gather him closer. Gods help me, but I'm glad I came here. He offered me a gift I didn't know how to ask for.

"You're a good man, Poseidon." He says it without lifting his head, allowing me the illusion of privacy as I blush in response to his words. "And you're right on one count—Circe won't be dissuaded. But..." He clears his throat. "But maybe there's something I can do to help you strip her of some of her allies. It won't save the city from invasion, but a smaller invading force has to help the odds, right?"

I try to think through the slog my thoughts have become. "How could you possibly do that?"

He's silent for so long, I think he won't answer me. That's okay. This evening feels almost like a fever dream already. I'll ask again in the morning.

Just when I'm on the edge of sleep, Icarus eases away from me. My eyes snap open. It's everything I can do to let him go and not pull him back to sprawl on my chest. I have to respect this silent request for space. It's the least I can do.

He sits up and drags his hand through his curly hair. "I was going to use this information to blackmail them to protect me from Circe's rage and transport me back to Aeaea, but it's obvious freedom isn't in the cards for me." He shakes his head. "Most of the generals who will be sailing with Circe are people whom I've shared a bed with. As a result, I have plenty of blackmail—information I know they would rather betray her for than allow to get out into the world. If I utilize it, there's a decent chance I can convince some of them to abandon her. I just need to know which of them she brought with her. Like I said, it's not going to stop the invasion, but it might give Olympus more of a fighting chance."

I stare at him, trying to divine the thoughts behind his perfectly smooth mask. "If you do that for us, it will mean that you won't have any cards left to play after this is all over."

"Yeah." He shrugs, not meeting my gaze. "I've kind of made my peace with the fact that I'm not going to survive this. There's no reason for all that hard-won blackmail to go to waste."

There're so many things wrong with what he just said. I hate his fatalistic view of the future. I hate even more that I'm not certain he's wrong. The only reason Zeus hasn't come to visit our prisoner is because he's distracted with Circe squatting on our horizon. Eventually he'll remember Ariadne and the Minotaur left someone behind. A year ago, Zeus wouldn't kill someone unless he absolutely had to. Now, I'm not so sure. He might very well decide Icarus serves no purpose except to be a knife at our back and that he needs to remove the threat once and for all.

I won't let it happen.

I clamp my jaw shut to keep the words inside. If I tell Icarus that now, he'll think I'm only saying it because I want the information in his pretty head. Or that it's only the orgasm and pain making me silly and romantic enough to issue promises I have no intention of keeping. He has no reason to trust me. To trust anyone.

I silently vow to myself that I will see him come out of this alive and well, and I'll give him whatever money he needs to start a new life. *Someone* should escape Olympus, after all.

If I hadn't been at the marina, he might have managed it on his own.

But I need those secrets he holds. I need to give the city as much of a fighting chance as we can possibly manage. There are too many lives on the line. "We'll talk about it in the morning."

Icarus frowns down at me. "I'm not really the sleepover type."

He's trying to withdraw from me, to put up barriers between

us. I should allow it. It's the right thing to do. I don't; the thought is abhorrent to me. I want to grasp at him with greedy hands, to hold him to me. But why would he want such a thing from *me*?

"Come here." I don't mean to say it, don't mean to hold out my hand in a physical plea for closeness.

He huffs. "You're going to get the wrong idea and end up getting your heart broken."

Maybe. Probably. It's a risk I'm willing to take. It feels wrong to leave him like this, alone and in his room, and so I won't. Not unless he specifically asks me to...but I suppose I should give him the opportunity to tell me to leave. He puts on a good front, which means I can't guarantee he actually trusts this balance enough to advocate for himself. "Do you want me to leave? Just say the word, and I will."

"You're fucking ridiculous." He rolls his eyes and flops down next to me. "Stay. It's too late for you to go wandering the halls. You're liable to fall down a set of stairs, and then I'll be left in the tender care of your people, and we both know that's a death sentence for me."

His words have the ring of truth. I hate that. But it doesn't stop me from gathering him close and letting the steady beat of his heart lull me to sleep.

ICARUS

FALLING ASLEEP WITH POSEIDON WAS STRANGE. WAKING up alone should put me right back into familiar territory. It's what I'm used to, after all. There's absolutely no reason for the odd ache in my chest. I take a leisurely shower, but it only eats up an hour of what promises to be a long and boring day. By the time I'm done and dressed in a set of clothes that belong to someone taller and thicker than me, my stomach is making loud and unhappy noises. I try the door and, once again, the knob turns easily against my palm.

No one leaps out to stop me, so I carefully retrace my steps to the front door. The house feels empty in a way that makes me shiver. Surely if there was danger, Poseidon would have locked me in or let me know. My stomach grumbles again, deciding for me. I push through the front door and follow the path to the hulking main house.

Every step, I expect to be accosted, but no one leaps from the bushes to tell me to get my captive ass back to my room. It's

a relief to step into the main house and walk into the kitchen...
until I see *her*.

Hermes sits cross-legged on the kitchen island, a giant bowl of
marshmallow cereal cradled in her lap. She pauses, a spoon halfway
to her mouth, and studies me. "You look pretty well for a captive."

Against all odds, I find myself blushing. I'd like to think she
didn't know what Poseidon and I were up to last night, but in our
short acquaintance, Hermes has always seemed to know more than
she should. The Olympians treat her as if she's one degree removed
from magic itself. I suspect it's something far more mundane—
excellent surveillance, a connection to whatever system Olympus
relies on for its cameras, and a twisty brain in that gorgeous head
of hers.

I can't help glancing over my shoulder, wondering what Poseidon
would think of her presence. There's absolutely no way they're on
good speaking terms, not after everything that's happened. Not after
she *brought down the barrier*. Personally, I haven't seen her since
the party my father...

Just like that the reality of him being gone crashes over me. I still
don't know if I'm relieved or grieving or something else altogether.
I haven't had the space to untangle my complicated feelings about
his death. I suspect I won't have that space anytime soon. It seems
to defy belief that sometimes I forget he's dead.

I stumble to the fridge on sheer instinct. Showing weakness is
never an acceptable option, but doubly so when in the presence of
this woman. My father's secret informant. It's still up for debate on
which one of them came out on top in that little agreement. Except,
I suppose it's not. He's dead.

As for her? The barrier has come down and Circe is at Olympus's figurative gates.

I pull out a container labeled as breakfast and pry the lid off. I'm not even certain what I'm looking at—some kind of hash maybe? It doesn't matter. I'm starving and I need to keep my hands occupied while in the presence of Hermes. I shove the whole container into the microwave and turn to face her. "What are you doing here? I would think you'd be cozying up to Circe now that there's not a barrier between you."

There's a tiny twitch at one corner of her lips. Grimace or smile? Impossible to say. She dips her spoon back into her bowl. "Come now, my boy. You must know that things are always more complicated than they seem. Circe and I aren't exactly on speaking terms."

She has to be lying. I eavesdropped on her deal with my father, and later Ariadne hacked into his computer and got secondary confirmation: Hermes agreed to sponsor my father so that the family could come into Olympus for the Ares trials, then she sold him her house and lent her presence as an element of respectability, such as it is. All along, she knew he intended to set Theseus and the Minotaur after members of the Thirteen, killing them to trigger the assassination clause then take their titles. For that alone, I suspect most Olympians would label her a traitor. And she did it all in the name of getting more information about my father's benefactor: Circe.

Why do that if not to seek her out? It doesn't make sense.

I stare at Hermes until the microwave dings, startling me out of my confusion. "Then why go through all this trouble?" Without her help, my father would have had a harder time getting into the city and digging his roots in so deep. No doubt Circe had backup plans in place, but that doesn't change the fact that Hermes made it *easy*.

She waves her spoon at me. "Normally, I would remind you that I'm a lady and a lady never tells, but we're in the endgame now." She tilts her head to the side, her braids sliding over one thin shoulder. Truly, she is one of the most beautiful of the Olympians. She's a Black woman somewhere in her thirties, or possibly older, or maybe younger. It's really hard to say because her features are so youthful. She's worn her hair in a number of styles since I've met her, but currently it is in box braids that hit the middle of her back. It leaves her high cheekbones and generous lips on full display. She's stunning.

"The endgame," I repeat slowly. "But *why*?"

"You're from Aeaea."

I blink. "You know I am."

"Mm-hmm." She takes a bite of her cereal and chews slowly. "You like the way they run things there?"

It's an effort not to tense. Of course I don't. I grew up in relative privilege, but the cost was so damned high. It's still nothing compared to what the Minotaur experienced, to what Theseus and Pandora survived. I might not like any of them all that much, mostly due to my father's favoritism, but I'm not a complete fool. I know their stories are just three of many. "No."

"That's how I feel about Olympus." Her deep-brown eyes are shadowed with the past—or maybe the future. "Just because something's always been this way doesn't mean it should continue to always *be* this way." She shrugs. "Sometimes you have to blow up a few eggs to make an omelet."

I don't point out that that isn't how the saying goes. I'm too focused on the fact that I'm apparently having a frank conversation with the Queen of Secrets herself. "But you're one of the Thirteen. You're one of the most powerful people in the city. If you don't like how things are run, then change it."

"Been there, tried that, bought a shitty T-shirt. The corruption goes too deep." She surveys me. "You should get out of the city, sooner rather than later. Traitors to both sides don't tend to have long lifespans."

"I'm aware." I'm so focused on her, I don't realize Poseidon has joined us in the room until he's glowering from the doorway I entered through a few minutes ago. He crosses his arms over his chest, seeming to fill the space even more. I glance at his face and shiver. He's fucking *furious*.

Hermes tenses, almost as if preparing for flight, and then makes a visible decision to relax. Her brows rise and she takes two bites of her cereal while he glares at her. She doesn't rush, and I can appreciate her audacity even if the tension in the room becomes so thick, I want to part it with my hands just to get some relief.

Poseidon is the one to speak first. "What are you doing here? Zeus has been looking for you. Everyone's looking for you."

"And here I am. You found me. Well done, you." She lifts the bowl to her lips and drinks the milk. When faced with that look on Poseidon's face, I might piss myself in fear—and that's being relatively assured he intends *me* no harm. I doubt Hermes can say the same. She's been labeled an enemy of the city, a traitor, guilty of treason. At least according to MuseWatch.

From what she just said, it's all true.

Poseidon watches her closely as she leans over and sets the bowl in the sink. He's doing that thing where it's as if he can reach past the carefully curated external expressions and delve right into the thoughts of a person. I don't know if that's really a skill he has, but it certainly feels like it when I interact with him. "You haven't been missing in action for so long only to come here for food. You have your own house—several of them. Why are you *here?*"

"Oh, that." Hermes hops to the floor and stretches, her fingertips reaching toward the ceiling. I'm always shocked to find that she barely comes up to my shoulder. Her energy fills the room every time I've ever interacted with her. Something in her back pops and she gives a sigh of relief. "Much better. Now, where were we?"

Poseidon leans on the doorframe, and I could swear I hear the entire house creak in response. "You were telling me what you're doing here and why it appears you've committed treason."

"'Treason' is such a strong word." He makes a sound shockingly close to a growl, and she shifts to put the island between them. "Now, now, Poseidon. I came here because you're the most reasonable of the Thirteen. I expect you to *be* reasonable. On the other hand, you are keeping the delicious Icarus captive, and if I'm not mistaken, there's the scent of sex about you. What a horrible abuse of power."

"*Hermes.*"

"Fine," she says flatly, all charm disappearing between one beat and the next. "You can't trust Circe, no matter what she promises you in late-night meetings on the water. She won't rest until this city burns and every member of the Thirteen and the legacy families are dead. While we're on the subject, you shouldn't trust Hera, either. Those two are more similar than is comfortable."

Poseidon narrows his eyes. "I have a question for you, and I want you to answer honestly. Are you the reason the barrier fell when it did?"

I jolt. How did he make that leap? The barrier in Olympus has been failing for a very long time—something like thirty years. It was always going to come down; Circe made sure of that. Before Zeus attempted to murder her on their honeymoon, she somehow managed to steal a key component that kept the barrier in place. Ever since then, it's been slowly weakening. Faltering.

Hermes taps her fingernails against the counter in a rhythm that I almost recognize. "I made a promise to someone. Several promises, in fact. The barrier was coming down regardless. It served my interest that it came down when it did."

"What interest?" For the second time since I met Poseidon, his voice raises in anger. He slashes a hand through the air. "Because even now, while you claim to be telling me the truth, you're still talking in circles. Everyone in this fucking city talks in circles. None of you ever say what you mean. So, for fucking once, *tell me what you mean.*"

She shifts back on her heels; she's going to bolt. A quick sweep of the kitchen makes her intended exit clear—the small window over the sink that's cracked to let in the late fall air. I move before she can, sliding my body between hers and the sink. Now, if she wants to get to that window, she has to go through me.

Hermes glances over her shoulder at me and glares. "I thought we had an understanding, Icarus. That's just rude."

Poseidon slams his hand against the doorframe. "Leave him out of this." He leans forward like he's going to vault the island if she doesn't speak up. "Answer the fucking question."

She tilts her head to the side, and I can't see her face from this angle, but it seems like she's studying him just as closely as he studied her previously. "I want what I've always wanted—what's best for this city."

"Ten people were killed in the explosion that brought the barrier down. I highly doubt they agree with you."

"Probably not." She sighs. "But if you'd stop reacting and *think*, you'd come to the same conclusion I—and others—have. This system is broken and the barrier was allowing the system to stay broken. If it didn't come down, then nothing was going to change. Things *have* to change, Poseidon."

His mouth works, and I can tell that part of him agrees with her, even if he doesn't want to. He clears his throat, his tone lowering but becoming no less angry. "What makes you the best person to make this decision?"

"I'm the only one who has the audacity to actually get shit done. Well, me and one other. Consider us an army of two. You and Hades and the few who actually want change just sit around and wring your hands while the very people you're supposed to be protecting are harmed by the very system that you benefit from. I'm not willing to do that. Not anymore." She takes a deep breath. "Join us. You've watched the Thirteen play at being gods in this city for too damned long not to recognize the cost. Help us change things."

"No." He shakes his head slowly. "You might be right that things need to change, but we need to focus on Circe. The rest of it can wait until that threat is dealt with."

"I had hoped you would understand. Oh well. I told her you wouldn't listen, but she insisted."

"You told *who—godsdamn it!*"

She doesn't wait for him to finish questioning her. She spins and punches me in the stomach. It happens so fast, I don't have time to brace for it. I crumple like paper. I hit the floor on my side, curled up with my knees to my chest. Fuck, that hurts. Worst of all, I don't stop her from leaving. I don't even slow her down. I don't see her jump over me and shove through the window, but I hear it slam open and feel the wind of her passing. I failed.

"Icarus. Icarus, talk to me." Poseidon crouches next to me, his hand rubbing soothing circles on my back. "Did she reopen one of the cuts?"

"No. Wind…knocked out…of me."

"Okay." He exhales shakily and keeps rubbing my back. "Try to relax. Your breath will come."

As if his words summon reality, my body slowly unclenches and my lungs allow air to move through them. I gasp in a breath and start to sit up, but Poseidon shifts his grip to my shoulder, keeping me on the floor. "Slowly." He helps me sit up and urges me to lean against the cabinets.

"I kind of hate her," I wheeze.

"I kind of do, too." He gives my shoulder one last squeeze and rises to shut and lock the window above the sink. It's a foolish thing to do, more to comfort us than anything else. Hermes has long since proven that she can get in and out of nearly any residence. I used to think that was pure rumor, but it's obvious that it's true. Fuck, she was fast.

Poseidon slides down to sit next to me, his shoulder pressing against mine. After several beats, I finally force myself to speak.

"What do you think about what she said? About Circe and Hera and Olympus and the rest?"

"I don't know. I might not like her methods, but she's not wrong about the system being broken." He taps his middle finger against his thigh, his expression distant. "But I don't see how *this* helps the city. The barrier protected us from the outside world. It ensured foreign nations couldn't meddle and use us. Now it's gone and Circe is poised to invade. People are going to die. A lot of people. How can that be a good thing?"

That's the question, but I don't have the answer—or at least not an answer that's comforting. "Maybe Hermes means to take the city for herself. Maybe that's how she'll break the system."

Poseidon sinks down to sit next to me, his big shoulder pressing to mine. For just a moment, I can almost believe it's us two against the world, rather than simply a captor and his captive, sharing a moment of mutual misery.

He sighs. "That's what I'm afraid of."

POSEIDON

I WANT NOTHING MORE THAN TO SIT ON THIS KITCHEN floor all day, Icarus's shoulder pressed to mine and his now-steady breathing centering me. Being Poseidon has never been easy, but it feels like the walls are closing in now more than ever. There're no right moves, only wrong and worse. I don't have any answers, and I don't know the right questions to ask to find them. In short, I'm fucked.

But there are too many people depending on me. I can't afford to sink into depression and hopelessness. I have to *move*. I've already wasted too much time. I heft myself to my feet and give my body a good shake. "Come on."

Icarus stares up at me and I have a hard time understanding what I see in his dark-brown eyes. It's not fear, not horror, but there's something I can't quite define. Finally, he accepts my hand and allows me to carefully lift him to his feet. "Where?"

If I were smart, I would send him back to his room and lock him in for safety. I would set someone I trust as guard at his door to ensure no one gets any ideas similar to Polyphemus's. But the thought of letting him out of my sight makes my chest hurt. "We're going to the shipyard. I have to meet with my people. We might not be officially at war, but we're still the first line of defense."

Icarus straightens his shirt, his expression concerned. "Before, you agreed to go along with Hera's plan to deal with Circe."

"Yes."

"But now you're going to...what? Double-cross her? Poseidon, that's suicide." He follows me out of the kitchen, so close that he's nearly stepping on my heels. "What the fuck do you think you're going to do? Circe has an actual navy out there. It's a small one, but still more than you have."

That's just another question I don't have an answer to. The people under my command are sailors—at least some of them. But there's a wide gap between knowing how to navigate a ship and knowing how to use one in a fight. We're not a navy, and I'm sure as fuck not a naval general. I can do my best to prepare them, do my damnedest to ensure we're ready as the front lines to protect the city, but in my heart of hearts, I'm certain I'm going to get every single one of them killed. For nothing.

Circe will still invade before the Thirteen can get their shit together and vote on war and unification. Even more people will still die. We just won't be around to witness it because we'll be the first people she cuts down. Even if Hera manages to work out some kind of deal, it won't extend to me and mine. That's just how she operates, and I have a feeling that's how Circe does, too. Hera's priority is her family. I don't hold it against her, but it's so fucking shortsighted I want to scream my frustration. Now Hermes is in the mix, no longer to play court jester, revealing just how dangerous she's been all along.

We're too fragmented, everyone looking out for their own interests. We don't stand a chance. Maybe we never did.

I open the front door and step aside so Icarus can follow me out. I don't realize that I haven't answered him verbally until he wraps his hand around my bicep. He tries to tug me to a stop. I'm distantly aware that I could just keep dragging him down the street, but I allow him to halt me.

"I mean it, Poseidon. Maybe it would be better if you made your own deal with Circe. If your people stood down, she'd spare them."

"You can't guarantee that."

He looks like he wants to do just that, but huffs out a breath instead. "Okay, she'd *probably* spare them."

I rotate to look at him. For once, there's no apparent lie on his face, just a worry that makes my chest twinge in response. Or maybe he's a better liar than I realized... "Are you that worried about me? You hate me."

"Oh, that." He waves it away as if our being enemies is something to discard so easily. "You're not altogether terrible, but if it'll make you feel better, call it selfish interest. Circe holds no love for me, not after my father and family failed her so spectacularly, and I intend to use my blackmail material to remove some of her. Maybe if she's rushing past us, she won't stop to cut me down in the process."

The words are correct, at least for the playboy spoiled brat that Icarus has portrayed since arriving in Olympus. And yet...I don't believe him. He wasn't speaking out of self-interest. He was worried about *me*. I don't know how to feel about it, so I push the sensation kindling in my chest aside. "Even if I were willing to do something so dishonorable, if Circe is as smart as you say—and she's shown every evidence of being exactly that smart—she would agree to my deal and then double-cross me the moment she made landfall. To do anything else would be to leave a potential dagger at her back."

Even if she *would* take the deal, I...can't. Throwing all of the city to the wolves in order to save myself and the small group of people I'm personally responsible for feels wrong. Damn it. Not for the first time, I acknowledge that ignoring my inner moral compass would've allowed me to go much further in Olympus. But it's not who I am. It will never be who I am.

"Well...yes. Her immediately murdering you and everyone under you is definitely a possibility, even if you make a deal." Icarus sighs and drops his hand. I try very hard not to miss the contact of his fingers digging into my muscle. He sighs again. "We're fucked."

"Not yet." Even if I privately agree with him, I refuse to do so verbally. It feels too much like giving in. My people are depending on me. Hope is already a nebulous thing, and giving it up without a fight means our deaths are a certainty instead of a probability.

Apparently I *can* lie when my moral compass calls for it.

I lead the way to my SUV and hold the door open for him. He raises his brows but for once makes no comment. He hauls himself up into the passenger seat. As I circle around the front of the vehicle to the driver's side, it strikes me that so much has changed in forty-eight hours. I can't allow myself to think about what happened in the bedroom, both the pleasure and the release of the pressure that seems to follow me around every moment of every day. Ever since I was forced into the title of Poseidon, I've had the weight of my corner of the world on my shoulders. There's no one to share that burden with, and even if there were, my people depend on *me*. I'm the one who bears the title. Not someone else.

It never occurred to me that I might find something resembling a safe space with a partner. My past lovers have been about lust, no small amount of loneliness, and occasionally desperation—but never whatever this is. They all cared for me in their own way, the same way I cared for them, but I never felt *cared for*. Not in the way I did last night with Icarus.

I never should have put him in that position. He's depending on me for his very survival, and I abused that power. I grip the steering wheel and stare out the windshield, guilt lashing me. "I'm sorry."

Icarus is far too clever by half. He twists to face me and pokes my shoulder. "No, we're not going to do that. The paladin act is very adorable but not when you use it on me."

"It's not an act." Sometimes I wish it were. It would be nice to discard it when the pressure gets to be too much.

"Yes, I'm aware." He pokes me again. "If I had told you to leave the bedroom the moment you walked in, what would you have done?"

I manage to tear my attention from the horizon to look at him. Fuck, he's beautiful—and furious, his perfect brows drawn together and his eyes intense. I clear my throat. "What kind of question is that? I would've left. To do anything else—"

"Exactly." He pokes me a third time. "So unless you want *me* to apologize for taking advantage of you when you were in a vulnerable emotional position…"

I shake my head sharply. "No."

"Perfect. Then let's stop this bullshit about apologizing for something neither one of us regrets and go deal with the siege Circe is laying on the city. Then we can figure out what Hermes is actually planning and deal with that, too." He shifts his touch against my shoulder, gripping it, his fingers digging into my muscle once more, but this time with a specific intention.

I stare at him, unable to look away. How can he rivet me with just a single touch, a slight shift of tone? I don't understand it and yet I respond to it instinctively.

Icarus smiles slowly. "And then, once all the boring and tedious responsibilities are taken care of, we can come back here and I'll take you to bed properly."

Take me to bed properly. I'm both terrified and elated to discover what that means. Last night rocked my world off its axis. Another night like that and I might not recognize myself in the morning. Impossible to say if that's something I should dread or welcome with open arms.

I put the vehicle into gear and drive toward the shipyard. By the time we arrive, I still don't have an answer to how I feel about his offer. Or rather, how I think I should feel. The truth is that I want nothing more than to turn the SUV around and haul him back to the house to have the promise of his words fulfilled. But that's unacceptable. I have responsibilities. Not to mention, if we're about to be at war—are *already* at war, no matter what the ridiculous vote says—then there's no telling if I'll actually make it home tonight at all.

Orion meets us at the shipyard headquarters, waiting for us the moment I step out of the car. They look as tired as I feel, the lines bracketing their mouth deeper than normal. "No updates."

They turn smoothly to fall into step next to me and Icarus as we head toward the stairway leading up to my office. "Aside from the meeting you had last night, there's been no movement from any of the ships." They don't ask me for details, which is just as well. I still don't know what to say about it.

If Circe decides to take Hera's offer, I don't know that I can stop her. I might not even know she's accepted it until I'm up to my neck in blood. The thought leaves me cold. I never should have taken her out there. I never should have let her have access to Icarus and, by extension, Circe's phone number. *Fuck.*

Normally I'm at my office for several hours every day, but there hasn't been a normal day in far too long. It looks much the same as when I left it a few days ago, sparse and utilitarian and matching my needs perfectly. The desk is large and sturdy, the chair equally so, the computer old but serviceable. The wall behind where I sit holds a paper calendar with various shipping schedules marked in carefully color-coded highlighter. The only real decorations I have are a few prints of Olympus's rocky shorelines by a photographer I've liked since I was a kid.

It's the polar opposite in almost every way to my uncle's house. I can't help glancing at Icarus, searching his handsome features for his reaction to this space that is more *mine* than anything else he's seen so far. He studies everything with open curiosity. I look away before disappointment can filter across his handsome face.

"Have any ships been able to get through?" I ask, determined to focus on the problem before us and not Icarus.

"No."

Damn. That's what I was afraid of. Thanks to myself and

Demeter, it will take some time before Olympus's citizens feel the pinch of the blockade, but it *will* happen—and sooner than I'd like. I drop into my seat and slowly tap my finger against my thigh as I try to sync my breath with the contact. I don't know what to do. I'm not equipped for this. Other than keeping watch...

I glance at Icarus, but while Orion might be more open-minded than Polyphemus, surely they would draw the line at me asking a known enemy for advice. Better to save any questions for when we're alone.

Icarus sits on one of two chairs across from my desk and crosses one leg over the other. He glances at me and then appears to give Orion his full attention. "Do you have the ship names?"

Orion waits for me to nod before they answer. "The *Swine*, the *Scylla*, the *Canens*, the *Moly*, and...the *Penelope*."

I jolt. "Did you say the *Penelope*?"

"Yes." Orion nods their head. "It's the flagship, the one Circe returned to after meeting with you."

Penelope is a common enough name in Olympus, but there's something there, something tickling the back of my brain, a memory I can't quite place...

"That's new," Icarus murmurs, distracting me. He twists to face me, and I can see the wheels turning behind his eyes. "Do you remember how I told you that I have information on a number of people in Circe's inner circle?"

"Yes."

"Four out of five of the ships belong to those people. If I'm able to divert them from supporting her, you'll have significantly better chances."

None of my ships are warships. There must have been a time when Olympus didn't have the barrier because there are old cannons in some of the towers that bracket the bay. They're coated with rust and ancient enough that I have no idea how they work outside of theory. Even so, our odds are better if we have only a single ship to face. We could load up one of the smaller boats with explosives and ram her. I'd prefer not to do something like that, but desperate times call for desperate measures. Even if we didn't attack the *Penelope* directly, we could run the blockade and get ships in and out. Probably not without losses, but some would manage it.

I glance at Orion, who's absolutely stoic in the face of this prospective plan. Even so, I've worked with them long enough to know they don't trust Icarus. They have no reason to. I'm not sure *I* do, but I can't afford to pass up any possible edge. "Have our people continue their watches. If any of the ships move, I want to know about it. In the meantime, I'll see what I can do."

They open their mouth, seem to think better of whatever they were about to say, and nod shortly. "Consider it done." Orion hurries out of the room, closing the door softly behind them.

I lean forward and brace my elbows on my knees. Part of me can't believe I'm doing this, attempting this, trusting *him.* I finally say, "That blackmail information you have must be particularly damning if Circe's generals would consider leaving her at this moment."

"Oh, it is." Icarus smiles slowly. "I just need a way to contact them."

Surely you don't trust this man after a couple days in his presence and one outstanding orgasm? Surely you're not that much of a fool.

The voice might be my uncle's, but it strikes right to the very heart of me. I was never particularly good at Olympian games, and that's even truer since becoming Poseidon. In those first few years, I was outmanipulated by the rest of the Thirteen and those around them over and over again—until I stopped playing the game entirely. That's the only way I could if not win, then at least minimize losing. "They're not going to turn on her based on your say-so."

His smile dims. "No, they won't. Which is why I have plenty of evidence to support my information."

Betting the entirety of Olympus on Icarus's word is a terrible idea. I can't do it. "I'll think about it."

His smile vanishes completely, and my chest aches at being the cause of it. It's on the tip of my tongue to take my words back and tell him that I *do* trust him, that I'll get him a computer and whatever else he needs, but he speaks before I have a chance to walk back my words. "Sure, Poseidon. Whatever you need."

ICARUS

THERE'S NO REASON FOR POSEIDON'S LACK OF TRUST TO sting. He's shown every evidence of being a smart man, and a smart man would never trust someone like me. Someone who was, until a few days ago, an enemy to him and his people.

But it *does* sting.

As I follow him through the day, witnessing the way he interacts with his people, that awful feeling in my chest only grows. He shows every evidence of being a good person. He knows every single one of his people's names. As we make the rounds, checking on the stations they've set up to keep watch on Circe's people, he pauses to ask them about family members and friends, about spouses and children, to inquire on the health of sick people in their lives. So many little details, all stored in that impressive brain of his.

And they love him for it. It's there in the way their eyes warm when they catch sight of him, the way their spines straighten as if they want to ensure they make him proud. It's certainly there in the way their distrust for me blossoms when they catch sight of me at his back.

I didn't know you could be a leader like this.

There's plenty of shame inside me as I marvel at that realization. The rest of the Thirteen rule by an ever-shifting combination of fear and ambition and even lust. Hermes wasn't wrong. It's fucked. The leaders back on Aeaea mostly just rule by instilling fear. Fear and power, the combination that sends the masses to their knees.

But not Poseidon. Again, I wonder at how he came to take this title. I highly doubt he had anything to do with the death of his uncle and cousins, but even in my short time here in Olympus, I've heard about what kind of man his uncle was. He fit right in with the Thirteen, using his position to abuse and terrify those under his command—and even those who weren't. To have him gone, replaced by this man?

Honestly, I'm surprised no one has slipped a knife between his ribs. It seems like offering the possibility of a different way of ruling is something the rest of the Thirteen would want to discourage. Permanently.

It's what my father would've done. It's what he *had* done, more than a few times over the years. Oh, he kept quiet about it. He had his reputation to protect, after all. He might have chosen to rule by fear, but that didn't mean he wanted to be disliked. It's a strange conundrum, but he danced at the knife's edge with legendary skill.

Now the only place he's dancing is his grave. My thoughts slow. Did he even get a grave? I have no idea. It didn't occur to me to ask.

"Poseidon?"

He steps away from the pair of people he's been speaking to in low voices and crosses to me, his expression concerned. "Is everything okay?"

It's a testament to my conflicted feelings that I don't laugh in his face. Nothing's okay. It hasn't been okay for a very long time. I'm not certain it'll ever be okay again. But this is Poseidon. He's not trying to be irreverent or sarcastic; he genuinely wants to know. Gods, he truly is too good.

It's almost enough to make me second-guess my plan to seduce him until he's emotionally compromised and chooses to keep me safe, to stand between me and any threat that will inevitably come. Almost. But my self-preservation is too strong. I thought I didn't care if I lived or died, but apparently the drive to live is too strong. I always was a coward.

I swallow hard and fight against the instinctive desire to shy away from whatever answer I'm about to receive. "What happened to my father's body?"

He frowns. "He's in the morgue. There hasn't been time to figure out a proper burial process, and Theseus wants nothing to do with the entire situation, but it didn't feel right to ask you when things were still..." He motions vaguely.

"When I was still captive?"

"Yes, that." He shifts closer and lowers his voice. "Obviously, sending him back to Aeaea isn't an option currently, but if that's something you want to do, we'll see about preserving him until we can make it happen. If Olympus is—"

"I don't care," I cut in. Strangely, it's even the truth. "He was a monster, and not even a redeemable one. The only reason he died is because he tried to kill me, and my sister defended me. So no, I won't be carting him back to Aeaea, regardless of whatever his wishes might have been. Toss him in the dumpster for all I care."

He frowns. "You don't mean that."

"In fact, I do." *I think I mean it.* My chest is a tangled mess of emotions I don't dare name. I should hate my father. I should not be mourning a man who was willing to pull the trigger and end my life. The one who made most of my life a fucking agony. Ariadne insists there was a time when he was a good father, but I think that's just a fiction she clings to because the truth is far too bleak for my sunny sister. Our father has always been a monster. And while maybe he offered her kindness initially when she was still a good, obedient daughter, I never had that privilege.

I disappointed him the moment I was born too small, too weak. I spent my entire life trying to twist myself into a form that he would approve of, only to discover that there was no approval. There never would be. I couldn't train out my very existence, and *that* was the thing my father most objected to. Me.

The wave of understanding is quickly followed by another of rage, so strong that it makes me quiver. Somehow, in all this, I didn't realize how angry I am. I would've never come to this fucking city if I hadn't been dragged along in service of my father's ambition. Maybe my life wasn't great back on Aeaea, but at least I was free. At least Ariadne was free. Now look at us.

Well, she actually is free this time. That's no small miracle, and I hold that kernel of relief next to my heart. It doesn't do anything to combat the mess that I am, but maybe in the future it will.

"Icarus...he's your father."

"Did you cry when you put your uncle in the ground? Your cousins?" The question snaps from my lips without me having any intention of speaking it.

Poseidon rears back as if I slapped him. "What's that supposed to mean?"

"An uncle isn't a father, but a monster is a monster. So I'll ask you again—did you shed a tear when you put your uncle in the ground?"

He stares at me for so long, I'm sure he won't answer. Or, worse, that maybe he'll pick me up and toss me into the surf I can hear crashing against the rocks below. But those are the actions of another man, not Poseidon. I really should know better by now.

"No," he says slowly. "I didn't shed a tear for my uncle or my cousins. We weren't close, which would be reason enough I suppose, but the truth is exactly what you stated—he was a monster."

I don't ask him if he killed his family. That may be the quietest rumor that's ever run through Olympus; my father's reports say it died out a very long time ago. Anyone who's spent five minutes in Poseidon's presence knows that he's not the type of person to coldly murder an entire family, no matter how monstrous. It was pure shitty luck that the illness that swept through that household was fatal.

Or maybe one of his uncle's many victims decided to take matters into their own hands. More power to them.

"Exactly. And I won't cry over my father." Probably. But if I do, I'll be damned before a single person witnesses it. He may have believed me weak my entire life, but I'll die before I allow that weakness to be witnessed by others. Not again. Never again.

Poseidon inhales slowly and then exhales just as slowly. "I have three more stops to make, but if you want to go back to the house—"

"No. I'll come with you." If my thoughts are this tangled while in his presence, they'll only become worse when I'm alone. I know from experience that they tend to grow thorns and claws and fangs, all the better to tear into me and heighten my anxieties about everything that could and will go wrong. It's why I've never been on good terms with sleep. There was a time when I could use sex to exhaust myself enough to sleep properly, but I haven't had that luxury since arriving in Olympus.

For a moment, it seems like he might argue, but he finally shrugs and leads the way back to the SUV. It takes us about an hour and a half to get through the last three stops, and they proceed just like the previous ones. It's a wonder that Poseidon's people don't fall to the ground and worship at his feet. They certainly follow him around with stars in their eyes. Maybe it would make me sick if I wasn't in danger of doing the same.

It says something about the level of damage my father scarred into me that I'm still seeking approval in all the wrong places. I should be angling for a way to escape, to follow my sister to freedom, and yet I'm standing here with my hands in my pockets staring at a giant, redheaded man whose approval I'm willing to twist myself in knots for. And yeah, I want to fuck Poseidon too, but for once the lust is almost secondary. I don't understand it. Maybe I really *am* grief-addled. It's been said to happen.

When it's finally time to head back to Poseidon's residence, I climb in the passenger seat and twist to face him. "Why do you keep that house? You obviously hate it."

He freezes. "What are you talking about?"

"It's your uncle's house, right? You inherited it when you inherited the title. But if I don't miss my guess, it's been relatively untouched since you took it over. You haven't changed a single damn thing, have you?"

He still hasn't looked at me. "Do you have a point that you're trying to make?"

Oh yeah, I've definitely struck a nerve. "My point, as you so sweetly put it, is that you're not going to relax if we're not in an environment where you feel comfortable. I can't relax if you're not relaxing." It's not, strictly speaking, true. Somehow, though, I think he won't bend to my will if I tell him I'm deeply curious about what a home crafted by Poseidon might look like. He's an enigma of sorts, and I can't help wanting to pick him apart and see how his brain works.

He leans back against his seat and taps his finger against his thigh—a sure sign of his agitation. But I don't retreat, and I don't take my words back. I simply wait for him to work through the puzzle I've presented.

Finally, he says, "Truth be told, most days I stay the night in an apartment in the shipyard. I work long hours, and the commute to the house feels like too much at the end of an exhausting day."

This might be the first lie he's ever told me. But I understand lies of the heart, so I don't call him on it. I simply settle back into my seat and buckle my seat belt. "That sounds much more relaxing than that big, echoing house. Let's go there."

He shoots me a stern look. "If you're thinking of escaping, it won't work. The shipyard is more intensely manned than anywhere else along the coastline right now. Especially with the sentry stations I've set up. You'd be caught immediately."

He's so damn *cute*. "Good thing I have no intention of escaping."

"You...don't." If anything, he looks even sterner. It makes a delightful shiver shoot down my spine. "Icarus, we said no lies."

"Technically, that was only for the game of questions." I continue before a bruised look can take up residence on his handsome face. "But I'm not lying. I wasn't thinking about escaping even a little when I suggested we go to your apartment."

He hesitates long enough that I have no doubt he's playing through several scenarios. Apparently none of them satisfy, because he finally says, "Then what *were* you thinking about?"

"Sex." I say it bluntly just to see his reaction.

Poseidon doesn't disappoint. His blush is visible even in the intermittent passing streetlights. "I— What— You—"

"I'm deadly serious." I lean over and press my hand to his cock and my mouth to his throat. He jolts in surprise, but makes no move to dislodge me. I smile against his skin. "My intentions, if you must know, are to strip you down, beat you until you go limp and make that delicious whimpering sound, and then fuck you until you forget your own name. How does that sound?"

He swallows hard and his cock goes rigid beneath my palm. When he finally manages to speak, his voice is hoarse with wanting. "That sounds good. Really good."

POSEIDON

I FEEL LIKE I'M IN A FEVER DREAM AS I UNLOCK THE DOOR to the little apartment I keep over my office. This is a mistake, and normally I do everything I can to avoid making blatant mistakes—the ones I accidentally commit are enough—but that doesn't stop me from holding open the door and allowing Icarus to precede me into the space.

"It was originally an office, but I converted it." I don't mean to speak, but nerves have a way of getting the best of me where this man is concerned. This apartment is just as sparse as my office, a king-size bed on a simple frame, a nightstand, a small table with a coffee maker and two chairs, and a door to the bathroom. It's… pathetic. Sad. "This was a mistake. We can—"

Icarus turns to me and grips my chin. The contact startles me into silence. He's shorter than me, slight, but in that moment, I quiver in his grasp. His deep-brown eyes flick over my face. "Did you change your mind? Or are you just embarrassed because you think I give a fuck about your decorating skills?"

Warmth flares in my cheeks, and I know even without access to a mirror that I'm blushing fiercely. "I'm embarrassed."

"Don't be." His tone isn't exactly hard, but it leaves no room for disobedience. "We need to have a conversation before we move forward. I would like you to sit down so we can talk."

Historically, when one of my past partners wanted to sit down and talk, it was a prelude to the end of our fling. Somehow, I don't think that's the case this time. Curiosity crawls through me, and I nod slowly. "Okay."

"Good boy." He releases me and turns away, as if he didn't rock my world to the core with two little words. My head feels barely connected to my shoulders as I pull the door shut and flip the lock. By the time I take the seat he commanded, he's perched on the edge of the bed. He's already moving easier than he was earlier today, his wounds obviously well on their way to healed.

Icarus studies me. He's a man with many faces. Charming and weak and strong by different measures. Dominant and fickle and even more I haven't been exposed to. Which one is the real him? I have no business wondering, but I wonder all the same.

His gaze falls to my thigh, and I realize I've started tapping my fingers there. My flush deepens but he doesn't comment on it. Instead, he props his hands on the mattress behind him. "How familiar are you with kink? The terminology, the power exchange, et cetera."

"Familiar enough." Difficult not to be when people use Olympian parties to share stories that make me blush. For all the importance the upper society puts on chastity and purity, it's a paper-thin covering for giddy indulgence.

"Good." Icarus nods. "Before we go any further, I need to know your limits."

"Isn't that what the safe word is for?"

"More or less." He shrugs. "But the goal isn't to force you to end the scene. The safe word is a nifty brake for when things dance too close to the line, or you have an unexpected reaction to something you thought you might want, or a thousand other scenarios. I may be a villain to Olympus, but I have no desire to be a villain to you."

We're just talking, but my heart picks up at the possibilities laid before me. "No lying."

He blinks. "What?"

"Don't lie to me. I..." The confusion on his face finally registers as I let my voice trail off. My throat threatens to close. "That's not what you meant by limits, is it?"

He recovers quickly; I'll give him that. Icarus shrugs. "It might not be on a traditional hard-limits list, but I don't see why it can't be on ours. I can't be perfectly honest at all times, but I *can* promise to be honest in the bedroom." He leans forward a little, his expression sharpening. "I would very much like to know what I can do to you, Poseidon. What you *want* me to do to you. You liked the spanking. Are you interested in different kinds of pain?"

"Yes." The word bursts out like the worst sort of confession. "All kinds."

"Poseidon." There's a strange mix of censure and pride in the way he says my name. "We're being honest. Let's walk through the list. Flogging?"

"Yes."

His lips curve. "Paddles, canes, that kind of deep impact?"

There's not enough air in the room. "Yes," I whisper. I want it. I want everything.

"Mmm." He surveys me critically. "Knives, branding?"

I'm so caught up in the possibilities he presents, I almost say yes before I catch myself. If I demand honesty of him, I can do no less than give it myself. As if I'm even capable of lying. "No. Maybe. I'm not sure."

"Wax? A delicious little burn without the consequences?"

I shiver. "Yes."

"Good." Icarus still doesn't move. I desperately want him to stop talking and start *doing*. I've negotiated ahead of sex before, but it's usually more about what happens outside the bedroom instead what happens inside it. Finally, he says, "How do you feel about bondage, big guy?"

I open my mouth, but nothing comes out. It takes me two tries to find the answer. "Yes."

"That's a good start." He slowly pushes to his feet. "And when it comes to the sex itself?" Icarus drifts closer, his gaze intense. "Can I take your ass, suck your cock?" He lowers his voice. "Do you want to take *my* ass, suck *my* cock?"

This time, I can't speak at all. I just nod, my skin so hot, it's a wonder it doesn't burst into flames. If he doesn't touch me soon, I might simply melt into a puddle at his feet. I don't understand what he's doing to me.

Finally, *finally*, Icarus slips his hand to the back of my neck. "It's a shame we don't have all the time in the world." He continues before that statement can sting. "But we'll make do with what we have."

I command scores of people and possess one of the most powerful titles in Olympus, but I still stare up at him with something like wonder. "We will?"

"Yes." He tugs on my hair, sharp enough to hurt. "On your feet, big guy."

I rise slowly. My legs hardly feel like my own and my body moves as if a puppet on strings of Icarus's making. He smiles up at me. "Now, stand perfectly still."

His hands go to the front of my shirt, but I still don't understand his intentions until he begins unbuttoning my shirt. It takes everything I have to keep my hands at my sides and not try to help him. I could be naked in moments under my own supervision. Icarus, on the other hand, takes his time. His knuckles brush my chest with each button he frees. It's agonizing. I never want it to stop.

He reaches the bottom of my shirt and parts the fabric. "You really are a masterpiece." He trails his knuckle down the line of hair that descends from my navel to the band of my jeans, and then reverses course, moving up the curve of my stomach to spread his hand over my pec...over my heart. His smile gains an edge of cruelty. "Your heart is racing."

There's no point in attempting to dissemble. There hasn't been since the beginning of this. "Yes."

"For me."

"Yes." He's barely touched me, and yet I'm shaking like a leaf. It's never been like this. I didn't know sex *could* be like this. "Icarus...please."

He ignores me and nudges my shirt off my shoulders, trailing his fingers down my arms in winding patterns until I'm shivering and shaking. And I still have my fucking pants on. He lifts one hand and presses a kiss to my palm. "I'll tell you a secret."

I want all his secrets. Not just the ones that will benefit the city. *All* of them. I manage to clamp my mouth shut before saying as much. He already has so much power over me—too much, most people would say. I can't give him more.

But I want to.

He carefully unfastens my belt. "Pleasure can be even more painful than a beating when conducted with the proper patience."

"What?" I stare at him, my mind sluggish with desire. "You're not going to hurt me?"

"I *am* hurting you, big guy." He grips the front band of my jeans, brushing my cock, and I nearly go to my knees. Icarus jerks me closer and leans down to press a kiss on the center of my chest. He's barely touched me, and I'm about to come in my pants.

He sinks to his knees before me. The sight of him kneeling should trigger some dormant dominant feeling, but there's no illusion about who's in control. He takes his time undoing my jeans and then tugging them down my hips and thighs, one inch at a time.

Which is right around the time he realizes I still have my boots on. Icarus hums a little under his breath and wrestles them off with a faint laugh. It's awkward and should feel odd, but it does little to dampen the spell he's woven around me.

Once I'm free, he tosses my boots over his shoulder and urges me to step out of my jeans. Then he runs his hands up the outsides of my legs to grip my hips. My cock is so hard, it's threatening to escape the band of my underwear. He makes that sexy little humming noise again and drifts his fingers over my length. "Big guy indeed."

"You had your hands on me last night," I manage to grind out.

"Yes." He grips the band and tugs it down, pressing it against my cock as he does. "But I was caught up in the moment and didn't have a chance to properly appreciate you." He stops with my underwear at the base of my cock, so tight that every bit of me fizzes. "You're magnificent."

"Don't."

Icarus raises an eyebrow. "Don't what?"

It's difficult to think with my heartbeat pounding along my hard length. Difficult to think with him looking at me like that, slightly impatient and yet indulgent at the same time. I drag in a breath and try to think clearly enough to form proper sentences. "You don't have to say stuff like that."

"I know," he says simply. "But I *want* to. Why does it make you so uncomfortable to be complimented?"

My mouth works, but no sound comes out. I swallow hard. "Can we talk about this later?"

"No." His tone goes hard. "Answer the question, Poseidon."

I desperately don't want to. There's no escaping him, his touch, his gaze, his dominance. Even as I look up to the ceiling, I can feel him. "I know who I am—what I am. I know that you hate me, even if you desire me. I asked for honesty."

"Look at me."

I'm helpless to do anything but obey. The cruelty on his face is gone, replaced by something I have no name for. It's intense, though. Icarus sits back on his heels but doesn't release me. "I promised you honesty in the bedroom, and I'm being honest when I compliment you."

"Icarus—"

"No, you're going to listen." It should be absurd to have this conversation with him on his knees and my cock out. Somehow, it's not. He tugs my underwear down a few inches, and then a few more. "You're so fucking sexy, it drives me to distraction. I like your combination of strong and soft. Your freckles make me wild. And…" He leans forward and drags his tongue up the length of my cock. "I can't get enough of your taste." Icarus looks up at me, his deep-brown eyes luminous. "I can't wait to eat you right up."

ICARUS

I THOUGHT I'D EXPERIENCED SOMETHING RESEMBLING power while playing bedroom games with Aeaea's most influential people. It's nothing compared to the feeling filling me now, with Poseidon standing over me, his heart in his amber eyes. Little tremors work their way through his body. I need to get him on his back soon, before he collapses.

I wish I had a whole dungeon's worth of toys to use on him. I want silk sheets, enough lube to drown in, and nothing but time. I don't have any of it.

Speaking of... "Do you have lube and condoms here?"

He swallows visibly. "Yes. Nightstand."

I stroke my thumb up the underside of his cock. "If I tell you to get ready for me, do you know what I'm asking?"

Another of those surprisingly sweet swallows. He's so nervous, I'd think he was a virgin if I didn't know any better. But he essentially is, isn't he? He's never had *me* before. Never played games of pain and kink. The realization kindles something hot and fierce in my chest. I don't understand it, so I tuck the feeling away to examine later.

"I know what you mean."

I push to my feet, my knees creaking a little. The carpet is thin in the apartment, the floor probably concrete beneath it. Definitely not made for kneeling for any length of time—something to keep in mind for Poseidon. He doesn't move as I lean in and capture his bottom lip between my teeth. I bite down, drinking in his groan of pleasure. It's all too tempting to keep going, to kiss him and drag him to bed, to forget what I promised him and revert back to my default as a selfish lover.

It's strange that I don't want to. I kiss him quickly and make myself step back. "Good. Go handle that."

He seems a little dazed as he turns toward the bathroom, wobbling a little with each step. I lick my lips at his bubble ass. We're racing the sun—we might have all night, but sunrise will come too soon. I don't move until the bathroom door closes.

Only then do I exhale and drag a shaky hand through my hair. I'm somewhat limited on what I can accomplish for him without toys, but all that does is allow for delicious inventiveness. I pace from one side of the room to the other three times before I realize what's driving the frenetic movement.

Nerves. I'm fucking *nervous*.

Last night was different. There was no time to worry that I might do something wrong, that I might disappoint him somehow. But for all that it was absolutely a full scene, it was a short one. Tonight, he's looking for something more involved. *I'm* looking to give it to him.

I turn and study the bed. It has a simple headboard that looks a little too much like I imagine a jail cell would look—metal, square frame. I'll make it work. I don't have anything safe to bind him with, so I'll make him bind himself. That's a fun little head fuck.

As for the rest, I'll play it by ear and adjust accordingly.

My stomach flutters. I ignore it. Poseidon has nothing to compare this to. I just need to get him off harder than he's ever come before. Easy. Sure. I veer around to pull the bottle of lube and the box of condoms—both unopened—from the nightstand.

The bathroom door eases open and Poseidon steps back into the room. His entire body is flushed a cute pink that makes me want to redden his ass even further. He actually shuffles his feet. "I'm, ah, I'm good."

My heart lodges in my throat. It's tight and hot and I can barely speak past it. "Come here."

He pads across the room to me. With each of his long strides, my nerves settle even further. How could I possibly fuck this up when I have *him* in my bed? I press my hand to the center of his chest, stopping him before he makes contact.

Instantly, he goes still. The sensation of power fills me once more. It only grows as I back him to the bed and urge him to sit on it. He's completely unresisting, his gaze intense on my face. Anticipating my next order, verbal or otherwise.

There's a calculated way to go about things, but all my plans fly right out the window as I step between his thick thighs. I pull my shirt over my head and toss it to the side. My pants need to stay on for now, a reminder to go at a proper pace. I straddle him and smother the surprised sound he makes with my mouth.

Fuck, he really does taste good. The best thing I've ever had on my tongue.

His hands land on my hips, but I pull back enough to say, "Hands on the bed. Don't move them."

"*Icarus.*" My name is a plea on his lips. I fucking love it.

"You want to be my good boy, don't you?" I gently bite his bottom lip, purposefully keeping the contact just shy of painful. "You want to please me."

He shivers. "Yes."

"Then keep your hands on the bed." I barely wait for him to obey before I'm kissing him again, claiming his mouth as if I have any fucking right to it. As if I'm not setting us both up for heartbreak. I shift closer, grinding my cock against his. The jeans are too thick a barrier. It's almost painful for me and it damn well better be painful for him, but he just moans and sucks on my tongue. More and more and more, until I have to jerk away from him to prevent the pleasure from getting the best of me.

I stand on shaking legs and strive to get the dominance back in my voice, the snap of command instead of wanton need. "Bend over the bed."

Poseidon blinks a few times. It eases something deep inside me that he's just as caught up in the spell of this moment as I am. He moves before I have to repeat myself, lumbering to his feet and bending over the bed. This frame isn't as high as the one I sleep in back at the guesthouse; even bracing his forearms on the mattress, his hips are higher than his torso. Perfect.

I press my hand to the center of his back. "All the way down, big guy."

He groans and arches into my touch, but he obeys. Of course he obeys. Poseidon has been carrying around the weight of the world for all of his adult life. I can't imagine what it must feel like to hand over the control, just for a little while.

Maybe it feels as good for him as it does for me to *take* control. My life has been a never-ending spiral, dragging me along for the ride. Here, with him, in this moment, the ground finally feels steady beneath my feet.

I have the strangest desire to be worthy of the gift he gives me, of the responsibility he's so willingly handed over.

I ease back, stroking slow circles over his wide back. "If we ever get the opportunity, I want to map your freckles with hot wax." He shivers under my touch. "Would you like that?"

"Yes," he moans.

"Then we will," I say simply. There are Dominants who like to play true head-fuck games, but if given a choice, I'll always lean toward simpler measures. A few well-placed words can do as much as caning someone—and the echoes will stay long after a bruise has faded. I press lightly against the small of his back, and he responds by arching his spine, offering his ass to me. My mouth goes dry. I can't believe this is happening. "Your safe word."

"Trident." No hesitation. Only pure trust—trust I don't deserve. I've never fucking deserved it. I always mess things up, manage to disappoint the people I care about the most. It's easy to be perfect when you're just a forbidden bed partner and presenting a fantasy to someone who's only seeking that. This is *supposed* to be like those encounters, a seduction that ultimately benefits me. It...doesn't.

It matters.

I massage the muscles on either side of the small of his back, trying to buy myself some time. I'm not prepared to deal with the messy emotions sloshing about inside me. Not now. Not ever, if I have anything to say about it.

"Hands flat on the bed." I barely wait for him to obey before I bring my palm down on his bare ass. Yesterday I reddened his skin enough to release the ugly feeling riding him. Tonight, I'm going to leave my marks—as many of them as I can manage. I keep my hand on his lower back and alternate my strikes, warming us both up. A proper beating is a workout, and I'm out of shape.

Not that he needs much work. By the seventh strike, when I'm really getting a good rhythm and increasing my power, he's shivering and shaking and moaning. I'm not holding him down in any meaningful way. It's exceedingly cute how he starts to retreat from every hit but somehow ends up arching his back deeper by the time the pain blossoms. "You are a *gift*," I murmur. I spank him again, the hardest blow yet, before he can argue with me.

"Icarus, *please*." Poseidon presses his face to the bed and then lifts his head. "I can't take anymore."

"You're doing wonderfully." I move behind him and squeeze his big ass, filling my hands with the curve of him. His skin is a deep red that's bordering on purple in a few places. He'll be feeling me through tomorrow, at least. I pull his cheeks apart and hold him like that, vulnerable and exposed to me. "Tell me how you want it."

"However...however you want to give it to me."

I close my eyes and strive for control. How the fuck hasn't this man been snatched up and locked in someone's dungeon? He's too sweet, too trusting. I could destroy him, and I have the sudden suspicion that he'd thank me for it afterward.

Not tonight. I have to do this right. If he's not going to take care of himself, then I'll do it for him. I squeeze his ass tighter, making him whimper. "That is not an answer, Poseidon. It's a cop-out."

"Icarus—"

Gods, but I love the way he says my name. I release his ass and give him a little slap. "Tell me. Explicitly. Use your words, big guy."

He makes that delicious whimper again and fists the comforter before he remembers my command to keep his hands flat. It's amazing how such a small movement makes me feel like I can soar.

Poseidon presses his head hard to the bed, every muscle in his back tensing. "I want you to..." He drags in a breath that feels sucked directly from my lungs. "I want you to fuck me, Icarus. I want it to hurt."

I have to close my eyes and count slowly to prevent myself from coming on the spot. Holy fuck. I... Gods. Focus. I just need to focus. Another night, another time, I'd give him the exact opposite, would go slow and soft and prolong it until we're both a mess. But trust is built one block at a time, and his honesty deserves the reward of giving him exactly what he had the courage to ask for.

"One last question," I murmur. "When is the last time you had someone here?"

He's silent long enough that it's clear he doesn't want to tell me. I'm not moving forward without an answer, so I simply keep stroking him while he wrestles against the impulse to stay silent.

Finally, Poseidon says, "Six months."

So long.

"Got it." I make myself stop touching him long enough to shove off my pants and grab the condom and lube. After a quick internal debate, I roll the condom on my aching cock and set the lube next to his hip. I'll need that in a moment.

But first, I fully intend to make Poseidon beg.

POSEIDON

I DIDN'T KNOW IT WAS POSSIBLE TO FEEL LIKE I'M FLOAT-
ing while also existing in pure bliss in my skin at the same time. My
ass pulses in delicious agony in time with my racing heart, spurred
on by Icarus squeezing me roughly. He hasn't even touched my
cock, and yet pre-come leaks from the tip and my balls are heavy
and ready to explode. Just from pain.

I didn't know it could be like this. Not even last night prepared
me, and he's still only using his hands. The fantasy of how exquisite
the experience could be with toys... I shudder. "Icarus, please."

"That's a start, big guy."

Every time he calls me *big guy*, my thighs shake. I'm so used to
being the biggest person in the room, to being careful around others
because that fact comes with a level of responsibility and a threat
I can never quite escape. But when Icarus uses that pet name, it's
almost indulgent, as if he's nodding to my size and strength while
knowing that *he* has *me* on my knees. He's the one who holds the
power.

I've never felt so free.

He kisses the small of my back and then moves down the curve of my ass, the softness of his lips a direct counterpoint to the pain still throbbing. It heightens the sensation, and I can't begin to say if it's more pain or if everything's transformed to pleasure. I don't have to have an answer for that right now. I just have to *feel*—and to obey.

Icarus bites me. Pain flares, overriding pleasure, and I moan. He licks the spot and I can feel him moving behind me. A few moments later, cool lube smears over my ass. Icarus spreads me wide, no less commanding for how softly he speaks. "I'll give you what you want, big guy, but you're going to promise me to use your safe word if it becomes too much."

I don't know if there's such a thing as too much. I'm drunk on the sensations he's given me, greedy in a way I've never allowed myself to be. I don't care what he does to me as long as it's *more*.

The head of his cock presses to my ass. He's not moving fast, but he's not giving me much time to adjust, either. I inhale and relax on the exhale, surrendering to whatever he chooses to give me.

He murmurs something comforting that I can barely understand as he presses inexorably into me. Slow but steady. Unrelenting. He's not a small man, either. The penetration is uncomfortable in the best way possible, a faint burning as he spreads me, eased with the generous application of lube. On and on and on it goes, until I have to concentrate on not tensing, have to focus on my breathing, have to...

His hips meet my aching ass cheeks. "Well done." He soothes me with his touch, stroking my back, my hips, my ass. "You're doing wonderfully."

I can't breathe. I certainly can't think. It's glorious.

Icarus leans down and bites my back. "Ready?"

There's barely air to answer, but he won't keep going if I don't; he's more than proven that at this point. "I'm ready," I say thickly.

He withdraws almost completely and pauses for a beat, giving me a chance to change my mind. As if that's even a possibility. I should be terrified of the strength of my need. Maybe tomorrow, I will be. Tonight, all I can do is *feel*.

The only warning I get is his hands tightening on my hips. Then he shoves forward, driving into me until his hips meet my abused ass. Pain and pleasure flare into an intoxicating mix inside me. "Oh *fuck*."

"That's it, big guy." His words are so soft, so caring, while he brutalizes my ass, thrusting into me hard enough to shove my body against the mattress. The jarring motion only sinks him a little deeper, allows us to be a little closer. Icarus strokes my back even as he claims me in a way I don't know if I'll be able to recover from.

I never want it to stop.

My body has other ideas. Even as I sink into the need and ache of him inside me, my balls draw up. "Icarus—"

"Come if you need to." His laugh has an edge of cruelty. "But don't expect me to stop until I'm finished with you."

His words push me over the edge. I try to move, but he presses down on the small of my back, pinning me in place. Or maybe it's his cock pinning me. All I know is that I can't even manage to thrust my way through my orgasm. The pressure sweeps over me, bearing me away. I cry out his name as I come, spurting all over the side of the bed.

Icarus laughs again. "Up. On the bed."

It's awkward and strange to obey when my limbs don't want to work and his cock is lodged deep in my ass. We manage. I sprawl on the bed and Icarus presses me down... And then withdraws completely. "Hey!"

"Roll over." He doesn't wait for me to obey this time. He's already gripping my shoulder and urging me to flip onto my back. At first, I think it's better this way, to be able to see his gorgeous face as he kneels between my splayed thighs, his dark eyes intense. But it's almost *too* good. There's no hiding from him like this. He doesn't give me a chance to try.

Icarus hooks his hands under my knees and presses them up, bending me in half. He maneuvers my legs to either side of my torso, making sure he's not pressing on my stomach. "Hold your legs."

I reach up with shaking hands and replace his, holding myself open for him. I've never felt more vulnerable in my life, and yet there's power here, too. It's there in the way he sits back on his heels so he can drink in the sight of me, in the way he bites his bottom lip as he stares at my chest, my stomach, my cock, my ass. As if he's cataloging every bit of me that belongs to him. At least in this moment.

He grabs the lube without looking away from me. "If you were mine, I'd tie you up like this. Keep you in my bed and ready for me." He leans forward and props one hand on my shoulder. "Don't let go of your legs."

I open my mouth to confirm, but he pinches my nipple before I can get the words out. It's a vicious move, reigniting the pain and overflowing the pleasure still echoing through me. I flinch away from him—except there's nowhere to go. I'm fully restrained, but *I'm* the one doing the restraining. I could release my legs at any moment. Except I can't. It would be disobeying his order...disappointing him.

Before I can fully reason my way through it, he pinches me again, adding a little twist that bows my back and draws a cry from my lips. "That's it, big guy. Breathe through it. You're making me so proud." His voice is kind and caring, completely at odds with the agony ratcheting from where he's still pinching me. "Just a little more... There you go."

The release hurts almost more than the initial pain. It radiates through my chest, my body, hardening my cock even though it hasn't been nearly long enough to recover from that last orgasm. I'm panting. Or maybe I'm not breathing at all. I can't *think*.

Icarus smooths his hands on my chest, lightly dragging his fingertip over my throbbing nipple. I shiver and he grins. "You truly are perfect. I wish..." His smile fades. "It doesn't matter. We'll have to make our time together count."

"What—"

He moves down and takes my cock in his mouth. Pleasure twists through me. I can't move. I can't do anything but shake. What is he *doing* to me?

He sucks me deep, not hesitating to take my full length, until his lips meet my base. I stare down at him, my brain filled with white noise. It's...peaceful even in agony. I don't have to worry that I'm doing something wrong. I don't have to worry about miscommunication. He's telling me exactly what he wants from me, is demanding nothing less than perfect honesty in return. More, that careful communication isn't dampening the mood. If anything, it's only increasing my desire.

I–I didn't know it could be like this.

I don't know how I'm supposed to do anything *but* this in the future.

Icarus eases slowly off my cock, the pleasure so acute, it melds with the echoes of pain. He grips me in one elegant hand and meets my eyes. "You had your orgasm, big guy. The next one belongs to me and I'm not generous. You're going to have to work for it."

"I—What?"

"Don't come until I tell you to." He doesn't give me a chance to answer, just dips back down and resumes sucking my cock. The motherfucker teases me, licking and sucking and, yeah, biting. I grip my thighs so hard, I'll surely have bruises tomorrow, and somehow that just makes the pleasure spike higher.

I can't stop myself from moaning. It doesn't even occur to me to try. "Icarus. Icarus, I'm going to… Icarus, *please*."

"No." The single word feels like he reached out and slapped me.

I whimper and shift, but there's nowhere to go. "If you don't stop—"

He nips my balls. Every muscle goes tight, and I lose all track of my ability to speak. He, of course, doesn't have that problem. He straightens and lightly massages my thighs, trailing down to my ass once more to spread me even further. "I'll stop when I'm ready, big guy. And you'll come when I tell you. Do you understand?"

I'm not going to last. I can't fucking count or recite facts or what-ever the fuck I'm supposed to do to keep from being so overwhelmed with the moment that I orgasm. I can't *think*. "Icarus," I moan.

"Don't disappoint me." His tone is almost forbidding as he spreads more lube over me and then presses inside once more. "Fuck," he breathes.

I almost come right then and there. That little word wasn't intentional; I'd stake my soul on it. No, that was an involuntary sound in response to the feeling of sinking deep into my ass. He feels even larger in this position, filling me to the point of pain—which only heightens my pleasure. "*Icarus.*"

His hands find the back of my thighs, pressing them even harder, bending me even farther. He drags his attention to my face. "Can you breathe okay like this?"

Breathe? What kind of question is that? I don't need to breathe when I'm flying. My mouth works, but no sound comes out.

Icarus eases back a little. "Talk to me."

If I don't manage to speak, this might stop. I have to close my eyes, have to inhale deeply through my nose, but even that doesn't help because all I can scent is sex and him. "I can't breathe," I finally whisper. "Don't stop."

He doesn't move, not until I drag my eyes open. Only then does he grin and press my legs down until my hips groan in protest. "Good boy. Now, here's your final command. Don't come until I do."

ICARUS

I WANT TO BLAME THE STRENGTH OF THIS PLEASURE ON the fact I haven't slept with anyone in a long time. I want to pretend that anyone would have me panting with need. I'm a fucking liar. It's not just anyone splayed out beneath me, their ass clenching so tightly around my cock I think I might die.

It's Poseidon.

It's *his* face gone flush and lust-drunk with what I'm doing to him, *his* giant cock bouncing against his stomach with every thrust of my hips, *his* freckles still driving me to fucking distraction.

Too much. It's too much to hold out. Not blowing my load before this is a godsdamned miracle.

I tighten my grip on his thighs and drive harder into his ass. Once, twice, a third time. On the fourth, I lose it. I grind into him, coming so hard, my vision flickers. Pleasure threatens to make me boneless, all the feel-good chemicals in my brain inspiring me to start spouting unforgivable words.

This is the exact feeling I've historically used to my benefit, teasing out secrets bed partners would never dare share if not essentially drugged on lust. I've just never felt it myself. Not on this level.

Now is the moment. I should roll off him, clean us both up, and cuddle just enough to get him through the crash after a scene. But I look down and the sight of his still-hard cock catches my attention. It makes *my* cock twitch.

Poseidon jerks. "No more," he moans.

"You should know better, big guy." I ease out of him and guide his thighs down, going slow in case any muscles spasm. "You practically threw a gauntlet at my feet."

"Icarus." His eyes are half-closed, as if he doesn't have the energy to open them. "I can't."

"You have thirty seconds to rest." I can't stop my grin at the way he moans and writhes, his legs coming up as if he can hide his cock from me. He's so big, so fearsome, so fucking *powerful*, and in this moment he's mine. It doesn't mean anything—it can't—but the knowledge has me feeling like I'm walking on air as I make my way to the bathroom and dispose of the condom. I take a few minutes to clean up, to glance at myself in the mirror.

The same face I've had since my body settled into adulthood. When I was young, I used to stare at mirrors and search my features for evidence of my father, of the strength he craved so intensely. Even when I was sure I found it in the line of my jaw, the curve of my eyes, it was never enough for him. *I* was never enough for him.

I turn away. He's dead and gone. There will be no reconciliation, no finally gaining his approval. It's beyond my reach forever.

Back in the bedroom, Poseidon is still curled on his side. I climb onto the bed and arrange myself at his back. I kiss the base of his neck. "Are you done?"

He stirs. "Are you?"

"That's not what I asked you." I could start stroking him, to weigh the scale in my favor. I don't. I simply wait.

He's silent for what feels like a very long time but probably isn't more than ten seconds. "I'm done when you say I'm done."

My heart swells in a really worrisome way in response to his words. He's given me his trust. I don't deserve it. There's only one person in this world who I'll never betray, and she sailed off to a happy future because of my sacrifice. I did more for my sister in staying behind than I could ever do at her side. At least this way I won't have another opportunity to disappoint her.

I only became aware of Poseidon a few months ago, and I've only begun to know him the last few days. He can't trust me. He shouldn't. At this point, I'm only out for myself, which means I'll turn on him and the city he loves so much the first chance I get.

I press my forehead to his back and hiss out a breath. "How are you so fucking *perfect*?" I don't give him a chance to answer before I have him on his back and his cock in my mouth. The saltiness of his pre-come has me moaning around his length. One last orgasm. We can both survive that.

Before, I gave him frenzy. I gave him pain. Now, there's only softness and pleasure so acute, he's gasping and cursing under his breath. I apply all my hard-won skills to make Poseidon come apart at the seams. Teasing, licking, nibbling, losing myself in the way my jaw starts to ache, in the sensation of his cock bumping the back of my throat.

"Icarus." Gods, I'll never get tired of the desperate way he says my name. His hands find my hair, tangling with my curls. "Icarus, I'm close."

I don't stop. There's a temptation to pick up my pace, to rush him through this, but if his last orgasm was intense, I want this one to be ruinous. I keep sucking his cock even as he digs his heels into the mattress and thrusts up into my mouth, my throat, so far gone that he's nothing but *need*.

He calls my name as he comes, his voice wondering and damn near worshipful. I swallow him down, victory making my blood sing. He's not mine—he can't be mine—but in this moment, I can almost see a different world, a different set of circumstances, where he *could* be.

I ease off his cock and crawl up to sprawl on his chest. Poseidon wraps cautious arms around me. His chest heaves, his breathing ragged and his heart racing against my ear. He makes a sound like he might try to talk, but I reach up without looking to press my fingers to his lips. "Not yet. I'm here. You're here. We have nowhere to be until morning."

Thoughts circle, predators keeping to the shadows, waiting for the opportune time to strike. They'll still be there in the morning—or, more accurately, in the darkest part of the night, when sleep eludes me.

I try very hard to just relax into the moment. To let the comfort of his breathing soothe me. To…

I jolt awake, my eyes flying open and my heart in my throat. The lamp on the nightstand is still on, the sky through the sliver of window still dark, but the clock reads three in the morning.

I fell asleep.

Poseidon's soft snores fill the room. He's still under me—I don't think we've shifted even an inch—his arms still wrapped loosely around my body. But we're covered in a blanket that I sure as fuck didn't orchestrate. I lift my head cautiously and look into the big man's face.

Gods, he's handsome. It's even more apparent when he's sleeping, his features relaxed, the stress of the world he carries around through every waking moment having been set down for a little while. *He could look like this all the time if he weren't Poseidon.*

The thought jars me out of the peace of the moment. He *is* Poseidon, and he's far too good a person to turn his back on his people, even if he's facing a losing fight. Being foolish enough to fall in love with such a man is a recipe for disaster.

What the fuck am I thinking? *Love?* He's a mark, plain and simple. Just because he's kinder than I expected and so sweet in his submission that he makes my teeth ache… It doesn't *mean* anything. It can't.

Even as I tell myself that, even as I extract myself from his soft grasp, guilt rises, so thick I can barely breathe past it. Everything about this feels so wrong, I might die. Not because it is wrong but because it actually feels so right.

My father is laughing on the slab in a morgue somewhere, safe in the knowledge that I can't even do *this* correctly.

I walk silently to Poseidon's discarded clothing and dig through them until I come up with his phone. The passcode is easy enough— I've seen him key it in twice. I know better than to look back, but I can't quite manage to stop myself. He's moved a little in my absence, one arm thrown over his face, his chest rising and falling in slow, steady cadence. The blanket sits low on his hips, under the curve of his stomach, and I want nothing more than to tug it lower and wake him up with my mouth. It's not dawn yet, after all...

No. This might be my only chance to ensure I can actually keep my word for once. I told Poseidon I would leverage my blackmail to drive away Deo and the other four generals. All I had to do was *ask* for the phone and I have no doubt Poseidon would have given it to me.

But then he'd be standing there to watch me potentially fail to do what I promised. I can't stand the thought of that.

I glance at the front door but decide the bathroom is a better bet. No matter how much Poseidon acts like he trusts me, at least part of it has to be a lie. Surely he has people watching the apartment, ensuring I don't kill him and try to take off in the dead of night. If he doesn't? Well, I can't afford to think about that right now.

I duck into the bathroom and close the door softly behind me. Then I dial one of the numbers I memorized before coming to Olympus.

Despite the hour, it only rings twice before he answers. "Hello?"

It's disgustingly easy to sink back into the plaything I was on Aeaea. My voice drops a little, smoothing out and gaining a flirtatious edge that I've almost lost since being in Poseidon's presence. "Deo, did you miss me?"

Silence as he considers hanging up on me. A sigh when he realizes he can't afford to. "So, you're still alive."

"The very picture of health." I lean against the bathroom counter and avoid looking into the mirror. I don't want to see whatever my face is doing. "I was just thinking about you and that delicious little thing I do with my tongue that makes you squirm."

He coughs. "Icarus, do you have a reason for calling? I'm kind of busy right now."

I bet he is. Deo is the owner of the *Scylla*. The ships and crew might not be moving as far as the Olympians can see, but I highly doubt they're just hanging out and partying out there. "Make time."

"Fuck. Fine. Hold on." Rustling, a faint murmur in the background, too low to identify anything about the person's identity. I doubt it's his wife, though. She wouldn't know what to do without her estate and a full staff of servants at her fingertips. No doubt she's enjoying her husband being away—it means she doesn't have to sneak her lovers into the house.

When he speaks again, he sounds significantly more awake. "Make this fast."

"Darling, you know better. I love to go *slow*."

He curses. "This was a waste of time. I'm hanging up—"

"No, you're not." I laugh silkily. "Has Circe discovered the coup yet?"

Deo inhales sharply. "We're engaging in a blockade of Olympus right now, so I highly doubt she's unaware of an attempted coup of the city."

"It's cute that you think you can bluff your way out of this." It never used to take this much effort to pretend. I don't know when that changed. I want to drop the act and allow harshness to sink into my tone, but it's safer to keep up the person he's familiar with. "We both know that you have no intention of allowing Circe to take Olympus while you sail back to the scraps you consider Aeaea." I hate even saying it. My island home might be just as corrupt as this city, but it's *home*. My people deserve better than Deo and his ilk.

Fuck, I'm starting to sound like Poseidon.

Deo clears his throat. "I don't know what you're talking about."

"We both know that you do. You and that vicious wife of yours plan to double-cross her the moment she's done all the heavy lifting for you. I wonder what Circe will say when she finds out. She's not the most forgiving type."

"You wouldn't begin to know how to contact her to tell her our plans."

"I never realized you were so naive. I have her number, Deo." I rattle it off to prove it. "But we both know Circe wouldn't take *my* word on anything, which is why I have plenty of evidence stashed."

"Evidence," he says slowly.

"Indeed." I roll my shoulders, fighting against the tension raising them toward my ears. "You didn't think I spent all that time with you because I liked fucking you, did you? I was compiling a case against you—well, you and all the others currently piloting your cute little ships. Isadora has been directing an extra ten percent off her profits directly into her pocket instead of Aeaea's coffers. Evander's penchant for wandering has resulted in *three* children, one of which he plans to name heir after his wife mysteriously dies." A problem since marrying her is what brought him all his money and connections. She's universally beloved by both the rich and the poor on Aeaea. "And Agatha... Well, Agatha's is most delicious of all. She's the one bringing in the drugs that are running rampant through the island and fucking up all your workers. Be sure to tell them I know all their dirty little secrets—and that I expect them to do what I ask in order for those secrets to stay *secret*."

Deo swallows hard enough that I can hear it over the phone. "That's a lot of conjecture."

"Conjecture that I can back up with files. Call your wife. I'm sure she can take a break between all her lovers to check that cute little laptop you think no one is aware of in your wine cellar. I sent a copy of all your correspondence, records, and money transfers to myself from that computer. One push of the button and I can forward it all the Circe."

"I'll call you back." He hangs up before I have a chance to reply.

I hiss out a breath and stretch my arms over my head. It won't take long for Deo to confirm the truth of my claims. I intentionally left my prints all over the laptop, digitally and otherwise. I wanted him—and the others—to know exactly who was responsible so they'd pay through the nose for my silence.

Almost exactly three minutes later, the phone vibrates in my hand. I take a deep breath, paste a smile on my face, and answer. "Deo, that was so quick. Be careful or I might think you're worried."

"The others won't believe your blackmail without evidence."

I laugh. "They have the same evidence you do. They simply need to check."

A pause. "Were you the one behind Michail's downfall?"

Not in the least. Michail was a nasty piece of work who even I wasn't brave enough to seduce. His lovers had a habit of disappearing—and of being far too young. He was found murdered in his bedroom, photographic evidence of his sins literally blood-soaked around his body. "A gentleman never tells, but..." I lower my voice. "It's not a good idea to cross me."

I let him chew on the problem I've presented, let him realize that he has no recourse. Even if they wanted to kill Circe to cover their respective asses, the others' sins are too far-reaching. There's no neat way out of the trap I've set. There was never meant to be.

He finally curses and then keeps cursing, threatening me in any number of creative and horrific ways. I wait him out. There's nothing he can do to touch me right now and we both know it. Better for him to get his frustration out of his system now, so he can think clearly.

Sure enough, it doesn't take long. A few minutes later, he says, "What do you want?"

"Darling, I'm so glad you asked." I keep the playful edge in my tone. "You're going to convince the others to see things my way. Once you do, on my signal, you'll all sail back to Aeaea and never return."

He snorts. "You're asking the impossible."

"Am I? Circe didn't hold a gun to any of your heads to come here. Your greed did that for you. Leave her to fight her own battles. Really, Deo, I'm just giving you the excuse to do what you already want to. Leave Circe to be murdered by the Olympians, and step into the power vacuum her death will cause—and you don't even have to get your hands dirty to do it."

He's silent for several beats. "I'll talk to the others. Do I call you back at this number?"

And have Poseidon answer? "I'll contact you in a day or two. Have good news for me when I do. Otherwise..." I let the threat hang just long enough to make my point. Then I hang up and brace my shaking hands on the counter of the bathroom.

Fuck, fuck, fuck. I really did it. I've played all the cards in my hand. It's possible that Deo will attempt to call my bluff. If he does, I'll have to figure out the most strategic way to proceed. I hope it won't come to that, though. I'm giving them the excuse to do exactly what those selfish cowards always do—look out for themselves first, often at the expense of others.

I close my eyes and concentrate on getting my breathing back under control. It never used to be this difficult to play the game. I don't like the implications of what it means, so I refuse to examine them.

I have to play this game to its conclusion…even if it kills me in the process.

POSEIDON

I WAKE UP THE MOMENT ICARUS LEAVES THE BED, LIE there silently as he digs through my clothing to get my phone, and stare at the ceiling for the entirety of the time he's in the bathroom. Long enough to damn Olympus entirely. And yet I can't make myself get out of bed.

Why the secrecy? Why wait until he's sure I'm asleep to make this move? It's hard to make my brain, still sluggish with sleep and remembered pleasure, come to any other conclusion. He's doing something he doesn't want me to know about. Betrayal coats my tongue, ruining the happiness that had been bubbling up inside me.

I don't want to know that he just gave me one of the best sexual experiences I've ever had and barely waited for our bodies to cool before he stabbed me in the back.

Stopping him is what I should do, but what can he tell Circe— because who else would he call that he feels like he has to hide from me?—that she doesn't already know? That we're wholly unprepared for an attack? That we're evacuating as many civilians as possible to the countryside? That there's no chance the Thirteen will unite in time to vote for war? She's been watching us long enough to have planned for all of it. More, she grew up in Olympus. She has an insider's knowledge.

None of it matters. I'm making excuses because of the hurt kindling in my chest. I was never a child who played pretend, but apparently I'm an adult willing to close my eyes and block my ears as long as I keep one of the people who wants my city to burn in my bed. *Pathetic.* The word is dipped in poison and sounds so much like my late uncle that I flinch.

Icarus steps out of the bathroom and stops short. I can barely see him in the darkness of the room, but apparently he can see me clearly enough. "You're awake."

I guess we're having this confrontation whether I want to or not. "Yeah, I'm awake."

He moves to the nightstand and flips on the light. His hair is still tangled from my fingers, but I swear the circles beneath his eyes have gotten darker in the last few hours. "Listen, Poseidon, it's not what you think. It's—"

Three hard knocks on the door of the apartment cut him off. I search his expression, but there's only surprise there. Whoever is at my door, I don't think they're here because Icarus called them.

Which means they might be here to harm him.

I don't hesitate. I climb off the bed and shove him back into the bathroom. "Stay there."

"But—"

I slam the door before he can argue further and yank on my pants. I don't particularly like guns, so I don't have any in this apartment. I've never felt the lack until this moment as I grab a baseball bat, feeling like the worst kind of fool.

The door has no window in it, so I crack it open, angling my body to hide the view of the rumpled bed behind me. I'm so ready for a fight, it takes me several long beats before I recognize the man standing on my doorstep.

I blink. "Zeus?"

"Are you going to keep standing here are all night, or are you going to let me in? I've already wasted too much time tracking you down." Despite the late hour, he looks like he just stepped out of the office. His suit is perfectly tailored and doesn't have a single wrinkle, and his blond hair is styled just like it always is.

Shock has me falling back more than anything else. I deal with Zeus when I have to, and I work very hard to ensure I don't have to more than absolutely necessary. This one might be different from his father, but he's still Zeus. I can't trust him.

He steps into the apartment and closes the door softly behind him. Those cold eyes take in the place in a single sweep, and I have no doubt that he clocked every incriminating piece of evidence. The lube and condoms on the nightstand. The scent of sex in the air. The light under the bathroom door.

Zeus comments on none of it. He merely walks to my table and sinks into one of the two chairs, as regal as a fucking king. "We need to talk about Circe."

I exhale in a huff. "It's three in the morning. What could you possibly have to say about Circe that hasn't been hashed and rehashed in the countless meetings we've held?" I shake my head. "No. This is ridiculous and an overstep, even for you. You shouldn't be here. Get out."

"You're right. The meetings have accomplished nothing but wasting everyone's time. Circe will be actively burning the city to the ground and the Thirteen still won't vote to go to war."

I open my mouth to tell him to get out when the details finally register. The differences. Zeus has always been a cold bastard, even when he was still called Perseus, but somehow he's even colder right now. There's absolutely no emotion in his voice. He's talking the same way a person would about the weather they couldn't care less about. It's eerie.

I glance at the bathroom door, but Icarus is apparently smart enough to stay out of sight. Or maybe he's using this opportunity to make more calls. I push the suspicion away. There's only Zeus and me. "The vote is the only path forward. If not that, then what's your solution?" I ask carefully.

He reaches into his suit jacket and pulls out a gun. I tense, expecting him to open fire, but he sets it carefully on the table... pointing in my direction. "There's no more time for squabbling and power plays. There's no uniting the Thirteen with reason. So we're going around them."

"We?"

"Yes." He taps his finger on the barrel of the gun, and I can't stop my flinch in response. Zeus ignores it. In this situation, his late father would have been preening and showcasing a bravado bordering on mania. Not this Zeus. He's just as cold and contained as the moment he walked through my door. He meets my gaze. "The only question I need answered before moving forward is where your loyalty lies: with me and Olympus...or with my wife?"

Suddenly, there's not enough air in the room. "What did you say?"

He doesn't move, doesn't lean forward, doesn't do any of the traditional movements that telegraph threat into body language. He just looks at me. "You heard me."

"How did you...?" It's not the important question, but it's the first one that I manage to voice in the strained silence between us.

"I know what the rest of the Thirteen—and the city itself—thinks of me." His lips shift into something that's almost a smile. Almost. "A fool with too-large shoes to fill. The Thirteen step carefully around me, but only when they're in my presence. You don't think I keep track of where they go and who they talk to? You think I'm not monitoring *my wife?*"

It could be a bluff, but I don't think so. From my understanding, Zeus and Hera might have a privately contentious relationship, but it's mostly just posturing and icing each other out. He has no reason to think that she'd go to such lengths to plot against him. Even so... "How much do you know?"

"We're wasting time." He doesn't shift the slightest bit. "I'm aware of the little games she played with Ariadne and the Minotaur—and of the plot to ensure my death. And I'm aware that the original plot might have failed, but she still has her aims."

I almost ask him if he's aware that she's pregnant, but ultimately it doesn't matter. I'm still not even sure if it's the truth. I can't read Hera particularly well, and it hasn't been nearly enough time for evidence of the pregnancy to be visible.

I move slowly to the table and sink into the other chair. "Are you here to kill me?"

"No." He shakes his head. "For better or worse, we need you. Your people won't follow me, and you have no immediate family to pick up the title. It would fall to the eldest of Triton's daughters, and that's a mess I don't relish dealing with."

I can't help my wince. Triton is another cousin, though he's once removed from the line, which means the title passed to me even though I'm younger. He's only been dead a short time, but not having him constantly attempting to undermine me fills me with enough relief to feel guilty. He kept his seven daughters under lock and key for most of their lives, with the exception of the youngest, who slipped through the barrier and took off for Carver City. That was a few years back, I think, and it means that *she* now has more life experience than the rest of the sisters combined. They're not bad girls, but they're so sheltered they have no idea they'd be walking around with a target attached to them if they were Poseidon.

"What I'm suggesting," Zeus continues, "is that it's time for the legacy titles to do what we were meant to."

Alarm bells peal through me, but I fight to keep my expression controlled. I don't think I do a very good job of it. "There are Thirteen seats for a reason."

"That makes sense in times of peace. Not in times of war. We have to be decisive." He leans forward suddenly, making me flinch. "I'm not going to argue with you, Poseidon. I know my wife came to you with the same reasoning and you agreed with her. The difference is that she's only Hera and I'm Zeus. If we can convince Hades to join us, we have the power to protect the city."

Only Hera. I might laugh if the situation wasn't spinning wildly out of control. "Hades will never stand with you against the Dimitriou women."

"Not even if it protects his people? If the upper city falls, the

lower city stands no chance. Their barrier might appear to be holding strong now, but it won't hold forever. We both know Circe is too
smart to have left something like that to chance."

He has a point. I don't like it, but he does. I swallow hard. "I
can't fault your logic, but it's all theory. Ultimately, it doesn't matter
who holds the reins for Olympus because we're outgunned by our
enemies." I clear my throat. "And Circe will never bargain with a
Zeus."

"I'm aware." He taps his finger on the gun again, and even
knowing it's coming, I can't help flinching again. "My wife agrees
with you. She would bargain with our enemy to save herself and her
family. She'd open the gates and sacrifice every person in Olympus
as long as the people she cares about are safe."

He's not wrong.

Zeus continues, apparently not needing an answer from me.
"I'm not going to bargain with Circe." This time he does smile. I
really wish he didn't. It's disconcerting in the extreme. "I'm going
to kill her and every general she has fighting at her side. And then
I'm going to sink those fucking ships before they have a chance to
attack."

My mind races at the possibility of going forward with this plan
without the majority vote by the Thirteen. It's risky in the extreme,
but if we could pull it off... Without the ships, there is no attack. I
don't like the idea of the loss of life that will result, but I like even
less the potential loss of life in the city. At least the people on those
ships signed up to fight. They're soldiers, not civilians. Probably.

But... "You're proposing a coup."

"A *temporary* coup." He holds my gaze. "Athena and I have

an agreement. I'm not going to use this situation to set myself up as dictator."

There's so much going on beneath his words. I suck in a sharp breath and try to *think*. Athena is smart and savvy and ruthless to a fault. She's not going to give up her power to a coup willingly, not unless Zeus is being honest about it being temporary. "Athena is participating in this?"

"Yes."

I clear my throat. I've been embroiled in more plots in the last year than in the last fifteen combined. All because of Zeus and Hera. "What about your wife?"

"Let me handle my wife. She's none of your concern." He shifts slightly. "Just know that I'm never going to let this happen again, even if I have to kill most of the Thirteen and hand select their replacements. One way or another, we *will* be united once the threat of Circe is removed." He picks up the gun, not quite pointing it at me but the threat is clear. "So I'll ask you again—where does your loyalty lie?"

There's only one answer. There's only ever been one answer, no matter how my striving for it has taken me down strange and stranger paths. "I want what's best for Olympus."

"Glad we see eye to eye. We'll discuss the specifics later today. I'll text you the location." He moves toward the door but stops before opening it. "Bring your little captive with you when you come." He walks out into the night, closing the door softly behind him.

I stand and stretch carefully. There isn't a sliver of a chance that I'm going back to sleep now. I should be focusing on everything Zeus said—on his *coup*—but Icarus steps out of the bathroom, derailing my thoughts.

Just like that, his betrayal comes crashing back. "Give me my phone, Icarus."

ICARUS

I DON'T HAVE ANY STRONG SENSE OF ALLEGIANCE TO Circe, but fuck if she doesn't have a good point about the corruption in this city. She's all but literally knocking at Olympus's gates, and the people in power are all too busy stabbing each other in the back to do anything useful in response.

I might be doing a bit of stabbing myself, but it's not like I'm one of the people supposed to be running this place. And I *didn't* betray Poseidon, no matter what he obviously thinks.

Poseidon holds out his hand without looking at me. "My phone," he repeats.

My skin heats with shame even though I wasn't doing anything *wrong*. I pass the phone to him. "I wasn't betraying you."

"I didn't ask."

My shame gains new weight and intensity. He has no reason to trust me. And *I* have no reason to mourn the intimacy we shared in the bed only a few feet away. I could have waited to call Deo. I could have talked it through with Poseidon first. He knows I have blackmail that could help Olympus. *I'm* the one who told him about it. All I had to do was ask for the phone and I bet he would have given it to me, no questions asked. He probably even would have left the room and let me make my calls in privacy—or at least the illusion of it.

But I wasn't thinking about any of that when I snagged his phone and slipped into the bathroom.

Something flutters beneath my sternum. I know better than to fight to make someone see me when they've already decided they know everything they need to. I *know* better. But I still find myself saying, "I told you I had blackmail on Circe's generals. I couldn't use it unless I contacted them. So that's what I did."

He keeps watching me, but there's none of the warmth I've come to associate with him. I didn't even realize how much I enjoyed it until it's gone. I wait for him to condemn me or yell or tell me I'm worthless, but he simply waits.

This isn't a tactic my father ever employed. He was a volcano constantly on the verge of eruption. He might have been able to charm and coax people outside our household, but he saved the worst of himself for me. I suppose I shouldn't be surprised that it left scars, that I'm already tensing in preparation for Poseidon to cut me down to the bone.

As the silence stretches out, gaining a weight I swear I can feel against my skin, words spring from my lips, so quick I'm almost babbling. "It will take a little time for Deo to convince them to realize they don't have other recourse and that the best option is to do what I want. They will all need to independently verify that I actually *do* have the blackmail I claim to. But they *will* do what

I want and sail their asses back to Aeaea. Without them, it will be that much easier to sink Circe to the bottom of the bay like Zeus wants. It will be over."

He sighs, a nearly soundless exhale. "Icarus."

I hate how tired he sounds, how defeated. I want to fix it, but I'm at least partially to blame, which means I *can't* fix it. This is the moment when I retreat and realign to come at this from a different way. Poseidon's already proven that he won't hurt me—and that he'll stop anyone else from trying. I just have to be patient, to sit through this uncomfortable silence. There's absolutely no reason for the panic pulsing higher and higher as if it might expel itself right from my throat.

And then it does.

"Get on your knees," I snap. Desperation makes my voice hard. I can't stand this new distance between us, distance I'm responsible for. I have no right to this man, but I'm a selfish asshole and I'm not going to let that stop me.

"Trident." He speaks the word softly, but it rings through the room like a bell. Poseidon straightens slowly, towering over me. "If you want to apologize for stealing my phone and going behind my back to make those calls, then apologize. But you're not going to use sex to override my anger at you. It's not fair."

I stumble back and sit on the edge of the bed. It feels like he just sucker punched me. "But I'm helping," I say weakly.

"I understand that you've operated a particular way your entire life. I even understand why, having dealt with your father for the last few months." He bends down and snags his shirt from the floor. "I don't expect you to trust me."

"Then—"

"But if I am not going to put expectations on you, your reactions, and your feelings, then you're going to give me the same respect." He pulls the shirt over his head and gets to work stepping into his boots and lacing them up. He's so calm, and I can't stop shaking. I'm not afraid of Poseidon...but I *am* afraid of him locking me out.

I don't mean to hit my knees before him; I'm certainly not trying to reverse the failed order. It just sort of happens. I stare up at him, my heart beating so hard that it makes me dizzy. Or maybe that's the panic continuing to spiral through me and outward. "I'm sorry. Poseidon, please. I'm so sorry. Don't walk away from me."

He slows and stops, his brows drawing together. He searches my face and I'm too upset to try to hide what I'm feeling from him. It's strange to watch him process it because he *is* processing it. I knew Poseidon studied other people, but this is the first time I've seen him blatantly catalog someone's features and expression and come to a particular conclusion.

He sinks slowly down to crouch in front of me and take my shoulders. "Icarus, breathe."

"I am...breathing." Sort of. My chest is too tight. I can't think. I don't know what's happening to me. I've been upset before but never like this. "I'm sorry."

"I know." He massages my shoulders lightly, his amber eyes concerned. "I'm sorry, too. I'm not angry only at you, and it's not even fully anger. I dislike curve balls and Zeus just threw a particularly violent one. I'm upset." He kneads the tight muscles where my neck meets my shoulders. "Inhale through your nose. Hold it. One, two, three. Now exhale slowly. Again." Over and over again, he talks me through the simple act of breathing. Something I've been doing since birth but suddenly forgot how to do.

I don't know how long it takes before the rushing in my brain eases. It could be seconds. It could be hours. But eventually, the strength goes out of my body and I slump forward. Poseidon catches me easily, sweeping me into his arms and rising. "Keep breathing, Icarus."

"I don't know what's wrong with me," I whisper. The pressure is still there in my chest, but at least it's loosened enough that I *can* breathe.

"Panic attack." He sits on the bed, his back to the headboard, and arranges me on his lap. "It happens."

"Not to you."

He huffs out a pained laugh. "Yes, it does. Not exactly like that. I tend to shut down."

Shut down.

Just like he did earlier.

There's a proper response to this, but I'm too fucked up to figure it out. "Oh," is all I can manage. "Did I mention that I'm sorry?"

"Yeah." He rests his cheek against the top of my head, his steady breathing soothing me even more effectively than his careful coaching had earlier. I don't think he'll keep going, preferring to retreat behind that wall of silence that I shouldn't have pressed him to break, but he eventually says, "I don't know what to do. Zeus's plan isn't a bad one, for all that it's reckless enough to break the Thirteen. Hera is still determined to bargain with Circe, but I don't see how Olympus comes out on top of that. It's more likely that the people who will pay the price will be the ones who least deserve to."

I allow myself to sink into him, to relax little by little. "Circe won't bargain. I don't know what she told Hera, but she won't accept anything less than the ultimate destruction of Olympus." I know her story as well as anyone, so I don't exactly blame her for hating the city that let her be hurt even before it believed she died and moved on as if nothing had changed. The city that watched impassively as the same thing happened to her predecessor *and* the woman who held the Hera title after her. Three Heras, all rumored to be dead by the last Zeus's hand, and no one did a single damn thing to try to stop it. If I were her, I'd want to burn this place, too.

I certainly have similar thoughts about Aeaea when I go to a particularly vengeful place.

I don't hold any great love for this city. It's been kind and cruel to me in turn, and it shares equal responsibility as Minos in abusing my sister. I shouldn't care one way or another what happens to the people here. I'm not like Ariadne, too good for this world, determined to minimize casualties in every way she could manage. I'm the selfish sibling, the indolent one looking for his next pleasure to numb the pain of never being good enough. If anything, a full-out battle should give me the opportunity to slip my captor and escape to keep my promise to Ariadne.

And yet...

If the city falls, Poseidon will fall with it. He doesn't have a navy, but he's not one to lead from the back. He'll fight even though he's not a warrior, and he'll die in service of a war he doesn't even believe in to protect the innocents he feels responsible for. All while the rest of the Thirteen argue and politic. I've only known him a short time. The thought of him dying shouldn't bother me—but it does. Deeply. Which means there's only one play.

"Zeus is right. At least partially." I speak without raising my head, feeling my way through the reasoning. "If I can convince Circe's generals to abandon her, Athena and her people should be able to sneak aboard and assassinate her and whoever else of value is on her ship without too much risk." I almost tell him to just sink the ship after that and be done with it, but a little voice in the back of my head warns of unnecessary death. It sounds a lot like Ariadne.

I clear my throat. "But before you sink it, you should allow the crew to surrender. Aeaea is different from Olympus in a lot of ways—but it's the same, too. When our people decided not to turn the island into a tourist destination, it started the long death of our industry. I still don't think it was the wrong call, but if people don't leave after secondary school, then there are only so many routes available to them—especially if they don't have a family business to step into. The navy is the main route."

Poseidon strokes a hand down my back. "I can't risk our people by—"

"I'm not asking you to risk anything. If you're already on the ships, you can evacuate them and send them to the nearest port that isn't Olympus. Without Circe in the mix, they won't be in a rush to fight." I'm asking for extra steps, extra effort, and it's not like I know any of those people, but it still feels...right. And not just because Ariadne would want it.

He keeps rubbing my back while he ponders it. It's tempting to push him for an answer, but I stay silent and let him work through it. Ultimately, I can only argue. I can't actually make the decisions that will change anything for anyone.

Finally, he says, "It's not a bad suggestion, and lessening casualties means it's less likely we'll be dealing with another revenge-fueled invasion in a decade or two. I can't promise anything, but I'll see what I can do." His lips brush my temple. "Thank you for suggesting it."

I tense instinctively, ready to keep arguing, but then the meaning of his words wash over me. He's agreeing with me. Not making promises, but then Poseidon isn't the type of man to promise anything he can't actually fulfill. The success of this plan depends deeply on Zeus's support, which I suspect won't be easy to get.

But Poseidon listened. He…found value in my input. I reach out and tentatively grip his big bicep. "Poseidon?"

"Yeah?"

"Are you still angry with me?"

He huffs out a laugh and what little tension was left in his body dissipates. "No, I guess I'm not."

Thank the gods. I shift, earning a muted groan from him. "We still have another hour or so until sunrise."

"That's true."

I smile a little at how deep and gravelly his voice goes. The world still feels slightly unsteady around me, but the man holding me is a rock in the midst of a storm. I don't know how to tell him how sorry I am for hurting him, how much I appreciate the fact that he actually *listens* to me without rejecting my suggestions out of turn. I've never had to say anything like that before. Historically, I'm usually fighting for my life just to avoid being the biggest disappointment.

I know how to show him, though. I'm very good at it. "I can kiss you?" The sentence flickers a little, becoming one that I don't dare speak aloud: *Can I keep you?*

I know better than to ask. The answer is always the same.

No.

Never.

Why would you ever consider that I'd want to be kept by a fuckup like you?

For the first time in my life, I want something different. Something...more. Too bad the person inspiring that feeling is the same one who will kick my ass to the curb the moment this conflict with Circe is over.

POSEIDON

ICARUS IS BREAKING MY HEART. I WANT TO SHAKE HIM until some sense rattles into that beautiful head of his. I want to walk away and never look back because that's the only way to prevent myself from falling harder for him. I want...I want everything to be okay.

He'll see anything but a kiss as a rejection, no matter how I intend it. There's no right answer, and that makes me want to crawl into a quiet, dark space and hold perfectly still until the world makes sense again. I press a light kiss to his lips and retreat before he can deepen it. "We need to sleep."

"But..." His voice trails off and he ducks his head. "Yeah. Sure. Okay."

"Icarus." I wait until he looks at me. It takes a while. Only then do I continue. "I'm not angry at you. I'm not disappointed. You're doing what you think is best, and I'm not even sure you're wrong. Just...give me a little bit, okay?"

He swallows visibly. "Sure. Of course. Anything you need."

It's horribly awkward as we lie down next to each other. He can't quite bring himself to move away from me, but he's not doing that careless sprawl he was earlier. I finally haul him over my chest, keeping my eyes closed so I don't see rejection on his face.

Except he doesn't reject me. He's only tense for a single breath before he goes completely lax. It doesn't take long before his breathing evens out in true sleep. I still wait a little longer before I relax. Understanding his motivations and actions doesn't mean I fully trust him. I'm not a complete fool, no matter what the other Thirteen seem to think.

My heartbeat finally calms and my thoughts lose the numbness that always signals complete overwhelm. Too many surprises, too fast. I was already worried about the situation with Hera spinning out of control, and now Zeus is in the mix as well with a fucking *coup*. The ridiculous thing is that I don't trust either of them to hold the same priorities I do. If push comes to shove, *both* Zeus and Hera will choose their family over Olympus as a whole. I'd bet my life on it.

The question remains which of them is the better bet to actually protect the city.

I still don't have an answer when sleep finally takes me. Or when I wake up to early-morning light streaming through the window and Icarus sprawled next to me, one arm outstretched as if reaching for me.

I tense, but he doesn't immediately open his eyes and his breathing remains even. It feels a little strange to watch him while he sleeps. He's removed all the bandages on his chest but one, and the cuts have scabbed over, even with the...energetic physical activities we indulged in last night. Still, I should have considered that he was still injured when we started talking about safe words.

"You're staring." Icarus speaks without opening his eyes.

I don't jolt, but it's a near thing. "Yeah, I guess I am."

I know what he's going to say even before he opens his eyes. "I'm sorry about last night."

"Yeah, me too." It's the truth. He didn't act outside the range of expectations. There's no point in being mad at a dog who bites when they've been kicked their entire life. Icarus has no reason to trust me, so the fact that he's telling me what little he is should be counted as nothing less than a miracle.

My phone vibrates on the nightstand. I don't exactly lunge for it, but I move fast enough that it's probably clear I want to get out of this conversation. Any relief I might feel is gone the moment I read the text.

Zeus: Be here in an hour. Hades has agreed to meet.

He doesn't send an address, just a screenshot of a map with a spot circled near the river just south of Juniper Bridge. Hades might be attending this treasonous meeting, but he's not taking any chances by coming farther into the upper city than strictly necessary. The fact that he's showing up at all defies belief—or maybe it just highlights the fact that he's as worried that *his* wall will fall as the rest of us.

"We have to go." Even this early, it will take the better part of the hour to get across the upper city to that spot. I haul myself out of bed and make quick work of dressing and brushing my teeth and dragging my fingers through my hair. My beard gets a little more attention, with some of the clove oil that Orion gifted me for my birthday. It's only when I step back into the bedroom that I realize Icarus hasn't moved. I frown. "What's wrong?"

"Are you sure you want me there?"

I blink. "Yes. If I didn't, I would have told you to stay here."

Icarus huffs out a rough laugh. "Gods, you really would, wouldn't you? You don't do anything you don't want to do."

"*That* isn't true. I do lots of things I don't want to do." Top of that list are parties with the Thirteen and all the legacy families. I don't like parties on principle; they're too loud, too crowded, and too filled with agonizing small talk. "Get dressed. We need to leave in two minutes."

For once, he doesn't argue. He just slumps into the bathroom and, two minutes and thirty seconds later, reappears in the same clothes he was wearing yesterday. Because he has no changes of clothing yet. Orion has probably picked up some clothes for him by now, but those would be back at the house.

I barely pause to text Orion that I'll be gone for a few hours and then we're in the SUV and heading south. Despite my concerns for the potential traffic, the upper city is a ghost town, even in the city center that's usually bumper to bumper with morning commuters. The colors seem almost muted, but that might be the overcast day.

I half expect Icarus to ramble on the way he seems to when bored, but he stays perfectly silent during the drive, his attention tracking on the buildings and streets of our route.

It gives my mind time to wander, though there was only ever going to be one destination for my thoughts. Circe. I might have forgiven Icarus last night, but I still don't know who he called or what blackmail might be strong enough to make Circe's generals abandon her on the brink of invasion. Getting that information should be the highest priority—and it *is*. But…I worry about him. About what comes next, about what he's risking for a city that hates him. I think he really doesn't believe he's going to survive the coming conflict.

Fuck that. I'm determined that he will. The world would be a dimmer place without Icarus in it. I refuse to allow it to happen.

I'm still deliberating on our current disaster when we arrive at our destination. The River Styx's current is unforgiving, so people don't tend to swim in it, even during the summer months. Halfway through October, the small, rocky beach is empty except for Zeus himself, standing as if the cold, early-morning air doesn't touch him.

He only looks over when Icarus and I are a few feet away. His icy-blue gaze flicks past me to Icarus. I can't begin to guess what Zeus is thinking. He's about ten years younger than me and even though I've seen him at Dodona Tower parties since he was a teenager, I've never been able to get a good read on him. He doesn't have tells like normal people do.

I glance at the river, the thick fog amplifying the shimmering barrier between upper and lower city until I can't really *see* the lower city. If I were a fanciful person, I could almost imagine that we're completely cut off from the world here. That nothing can touch us. A lie, no matter which way you look at it.

"He'll be here," Zeus says, answering my unspoken question.

Next to me, Icarus shivers. I mentally curse myself for not thinking to make him get a coat, and I shrug out of mine. He makes a sound of protest as I drape my jacket around his narrow shoulders, but I ignore it.

When I turn back around, it's to find the barrier's shimmering flicker as a small boat coasts through it. I'm familiar with the experience—before the greater barrier came down, it was the job of every Poseidon and their family to ferry resources into the city. I've done it myself countless times and yet I'm still not sure how the technology identifies me with a nonintrusive scan. It appears the secondary barrier is identical, except it's keyed to Hades's bloodline instead of Poseidon's.

He's not alone, but I didn't expect him to be. Charon sits at the near-silent motor, a white man nearly as large as I am with dark hair and a personality that discourages people from fucking with him. He guides the boat onto the shore and Hades steps out smoothly. It's been a couple weeks since I've seen him, but he looks much the same as ever, a white man nearing forty. There're the beginnings of gray sprinkled through his dark beard and new lines at the corners of his dark eyes, but ever since he married Persephone, something unwound in him. I'm glad for whatever happiness those two have experienced.

They're both people Olympus failed—more victims of the previous Zeus's monstrosity. He murdered Hades's parents in a house fire. And he would have married Persephone against her will—and likely killed her as well, eventually.

All while the rest of us did nothing.

Hades takes in Icarus huddling in my coat, nods at me, and focuses on Zeus. "Well? I'm here."

The last Zeus would have drawn this out, would have lorded

over his hated enemy. This one just nods. "We all want the same thing, and we're all dealing with the sins of the past that we inherited. The Thirteen was set up for a specific reason, but the founders couldn't have known we'd end up here. Thirteen is too many prideful personalities to make an effective war council, and that's even if we could get the majority to vote to go to war, which has proved to be impossible."

Hades slips his hands into the pockets of his long coat, expression carefully blank. "Did you call me here to make proclamations about things I already know, or do you have something actually useful to say?"

"Your wall won't stand against Circe indefinitely. If the upper city falls, the rest of Olympus won't be far behind." Zeus holds his gaze as he goes in for the kill. "When Circe is done picking her teeth free of the rest of the Thirteen, she'll turn on you…and your children. She won't risk another legacy title rising to defy her."

Hades doesn't flinch. This obviously isn't news to him. He meets Zeus's eyes steadily. "I'm aware."

"We don't need the rest of the Thirteen. We're the three legacy positions, and there's power in that. We don't need to bother with the rest of them—Athena excepting—to remove the threat Circe represents."

I've heard the spiel, but it still makes me look around to ensure no one is listening. What Zeus proposes is as much treason as what Hermes is up to.

From the way Hades lifts his brows, he agrees with me. "Your father must be dancing in his grave to see how well you follow in his footsteps."

"You're saying that as an insult, but I couldn't give a fuck what that man wants." Zeus doesn't flinch, doesn't raise his voice. "I want what I've always wanted: what's best for Olympus. We can argue semantics if you'd like, but it's a waste of time. The others can't see it through their gilded walls, but *you* can—both of you can. Circe has the capability to destroy us, and she'll do it if we don't get to her first."

As unconvinced as I remain, I can't help saying, "He's made a deal with Athena. If he doesn't hand back power after the attack…"

"She'll kill you?" Hades gives a sardonic smile. "That's a polite little fiction to get us to go along with your plans."

"If you think Athena would permanently consent to losing her status and her power, then you don't know her." Zeus crosses his arms over his chest. "I understand your stated condition, and I'm asking you to make an exception for tonight so we can remove the threat of Circe once and for all."

Hades turns and looks out into the fog, his expression contemplative. None of us speak as he thinks through this tangled mess. I already know he's come to the same conclusion I have when he turns back and says, "I suppose you have an actual plan."

"I do. Poseidon can get us to the ships, and Athena's assassins can take out the leaders, but we need your people to help with the rest. Once the crews realize the ships are sinking, they'll panic and try to swim for the city. I don't want a single one of them to make it."

Icarus is so tense next to me, he's practically vibrating. I can feel him looking at me, imploring me to say something. To spare what lives I can. I clear my throat. "Not the crew."

Both Zeus and Hades turn to me, nearly identical blank expressions on their faces. "What?" Zeus says.

"Not the crew," I repeat. "We kill Circe and the generals if we have to, but not the rest of the crew. My people can ferry them to the nearest port outside Olympus." Zeus opens his mouth as if he's about to argue, but I'm already pressing forward. "In addition to that, there's a chance that the information Icarus holds is enough to ensure some—if not all—of Circe's generals will abandon her. We're going to try that first before we murder our way through five ships' worth of leaders."

Hades raises his brows. "That must be particularly interesting information."

Yeah, it must be, but I haven't the slightest clue what it entails. It's something I should have asked Icarus before coming here, but I was too unwilling to break the silence. I turn to Zeus. "Those are my terms. I agree that this is the best way to deal with Circe. The rest of the Thirteen won't move quickly enough to stop her from terrorizing the people who remain in the city or attempting to starve us out. If we can remove the threat in one fell swoop, then that's the most logical step to take, regardless of it requiring a coup. But the fact remains that *Circe* is the driving force behind this invasion. There's no reason not to explore all our options to ensure as many of *our* people come home as possible."

"Cut the head off of the snake and all that," Hades murmurs.

For a moment, it seems like Zeus might argue, but he gives a short nod. "We can't afford to wait long."

Hades considers us. Finally, he says, "I'll lend my people, but there are several conditions. The barrier between the upper and lower city stays up, and I'll only ask for volunteers. I won't order my people to cross the river and help an upper city that thinks we're shit on the bottom of its shoe."

"We're one city, Hades."

"Maybe once upon a time. No longer."

"We could be again."

Hades shakes his head. "No, we can't." He extends his hand. "But I'm willing to commit to your coup for the space of a single attack. After that, if you don't step down, Athena won't be the only one you have to worry about."

Zeus smiles tightly and shakes his hand. "Noted."

They both turn to me. I don't like this. It feels wrong to break the rules, no matter how archaic some of our laws are. I'm honestly surprised there's not some cleverly hidden bylaw for a situation such as this. The fact that there *isn't* seems to suggest that the founders of the city were just as worried as their descendants are about the legacy titles abusing their power.

They should be worried.

"One night, one battle." I reluctantly shake first Zeus's hand and then Hades's, sealing our fates.

"We need to act fast." Hades turns away. "Three days, no more. Figure out the details by then."

If Zeus is remotely alarmed at the idea of putting this plan together and into action within seventy-two hours, he doesn't show it. We have to gather the people, arrange the groups, decide on the best time to approach... The sheer magnitude threatens to overwhelm me.

Zeus speaks, bringing my circling thoughts to a shocked standstill. "Three days is too long. We move tonight."

Tonight? *Tonight?* I'm already shaking my head. "What you're asking is impossible. There's no way we can manage it by tonight. You're going to get people killed."

"It has to be tonight." He doesn't say it like he's lording the decision over me, more like he's resigned to a truth the rest of us haven't discovered yet. "The Thirteen don't trust me, and half a dozen of them have spies watching me closely. No matter how close we play this to the chest, word will get out and Artemis and the others might move to stop us. We have to finish this tonight."

Hades hesitates but finally nods. "As loathe as I am to admit it, he's right."

I want to keep arguing, but Zeus has brought *Hades* around to this impossible plan. If he's right and this is our chance, then I'm honor bound to uphold my third of it. I clench my fists at my side in a rhythm that does nothing to soothe me. "So be it."

We stand in silence as Charon pushes the boat back into the water and Hades steps gracefully aboard. Within seconds, they're gone, disappearing into the mist. The only indication of their passing is a slight ripple in the lights of the barrier.

"We have a lot of work to do and not much time to accomplish it." Zeus speaks without looking at me. "I'll convey our plans to Athena. You have until we launch to confirm those ships are leaving—or their lives are forfeit."

So cold as he orders the deaths of others. I clear my throat. "You agreed not to kill the crew."

"If they surrender, you can play the hero and ferry them to safety." He shrugs. "If they don't? Then the order stands." He finally turns and starts for the parked cars, but he pauses when he comes even with Icarus. "I'll kill you myself before I allow you to betray us." He keeps moving, taking the steps up to the parking lot easily. Within a few seconds, his car starts and he's gone, leaving us alone.

"You know, I never understood why people found this Zeus scary." Icarus shivers. "I get it now."

"Come on." I don't exactly intend to put my arm around his shoulders and tuck him against my side. It just sort of happens, and then it feels so good that I don't want to put any distance between us.

We walk to the SUV and I hold the door open for him. It's only when I'm in the driver's seat that I'm not sure what to do. I need to get my people ready, but ultimately that's a small ask. We *are* ready. Every one of my people is a sailor to some degree. We have anti-scanning gear, though we don't make a habit of using it since I became Poseidon, and enough small craft that we should be able to get Athena's and Hades's people to the ships without being caught. We have the easy part of the plan...as long as it goes well.

If it doesn't, I'll be sending my people to their deaths.

ICARUS

I'VE MET BOTH HADES AND ZEUS PREVIOUSLY, BUT THERE was something about witnessing them standing with Poseidon, making war plans, that really drove home how different they are from me. A direct approach, decisive even, for all that it's in service of a coup. A simple plan to slide beneath the radar and kill everyone who makes decisions, and then hand back all that power before anyone realizes they've stolen it in the first place.

It might even work.

What do I know of war? Nothing. Less than nothing. My skill set is better suited to the bedroom. But that doesn't mean it's not valuable. If I can pull my part of this off, it means Zeus's plan has a better chance of success. It means that Poseidon is more likely to be safe.

I don't know where that last thought popped up from. Except, yes I do, don't I? This man has snuck beneath my skin. It's actually hilarious, because Poseidon is so up-front that I don't think he's ever snuck anywhere once in his life. And yet here we are. The thought of being shut out by him sent me into a fucking panic attack, and in response he just held me until we both fell asleep. He's too fucking kind and it's going to get him killed.

I take a shaky breath. "Poseidon."

"Hmm?"

"I need your phone. Not yet, but this afternoon. By then, my marks will have had time to realize they don't have recourse." It's less time than I'd prefer to give them, but we're definitely in desperate-times-call-for-desperate-measures territory. "This will work." It has to.

He finally puts the SUV into gear and eases back out of the parking spot. "It's hurting you to do this. I'm sorry."

I blink. Of all the things I expect him to say, this wasn't even on the list. "What are you talking about?"

"Icarus." He doesn't look at me. "You promised not to lie."

Something cold and ugly squirms through me. I don't have a name for the emotion, only a deep desire not to be feeling it right now. I force a laugh. "Come on, big guy. I'm not lying. They can't hurt me. They never could hurt me. The worst I got out of the experience is some lackluster sex."

I expect him to laugh alongside me. To allow me to charm my way past his comment. To do anything but veer into a shadowy parking lot, still untouched by the rising sun in the east. He puts the SUV into park and twists to face me, expression severe. "Don't do that."

I don't know how to do anything else. I manage another laugh, this one a little too harsh to be believable. "Don't do what? This is who I am."

"Icarus." He reaches out slowly, as if he's not sure of his welcome, as if I'm not about to throw myself into his lap and start sobbing without even knowing why. When he finally makes contact, cupping the side of my face with his big, rough hand, I quiver in something that feels almost like fear.

His eyes are filled with devastating understanding. "You did what you had to do to survive."

I want to jerk away, but within the confines of the front seat, there's nowhere to go. So I do the only thing I know how. I lash out, aiming to make it hurt. "Oh, please. I might have been a poor little rich boy whose daddy didn't love him, but I never went without. I was never hungry or without shelter. What I did had nothing to do with *survival*."

"Didn't it?" Poseidon brushes his thumb beneath my eye and I'm horrified to realize a tear has slipped free. Where did that even come from? I don't have an answer by the time he keeps speaking. "How old were you the first time?"

"I don't see how that matters."

"Indulge me." It's no less a command for being softly spoken.

I swallow hard. "Sixteen, but it's not what you think."

He nods, his amber eyes completely free of the judgment I expect. People have bargained their bodies since the beginning of time, for safety, for money, for food. I did it for secrets I didn't even need. It's not as if they paved the way to power. The most use I'll get from them now is saving the lives of strangers who wouldn't piss on me if I were on fire.

Apparently there's no way but forward. I curse myself for the awful feeling in my stomach that I can't quite dispel. "Look, no one made me do anything. Maybe at first I was looking for love in all the wrong places, but I figured out the game pretty quick. I always planned on getting out, Poseidon, but I didn't want to do it with *his* resources."

He strokes my face again and leans forward to press a kiss to my forehead. "I'm sorry."

"Don't. Don't do that."

"Do what?"

"Act like I'm someone to be pitied. I made my choices, and they're going to save this fucking city. I don't need this weird song and dance of comfort." When he leans back, I expect him to be shut down. Or be angry. Or be anything but still brimming with that deep understanding. "Stop it," I whisper. "Stop being nice to me."

"I don't know how to be anything else."

That's what I'm afraid of.

When the threat Circe represents ends, so does Olympus's need for me—and by extension, Poseidon's need to keep me captive. If I even *am* captive anymore. I don't think I can exactly waltz out of here and go wherever I want, but I'm hardly being kept under lock and key.

I know better than to hope. Allowing hope means setting myself up for devastation. I sit back and close my eyes. "I promised my sister I'd meet her in Brazil. I try really hard not to lie to her because I lie to everyone else. Something—someone—has to be sacred."

He shifts, but he doesn't touch me again. Anyone else would start driving again to allow this uncomfortable conversation to fade away. He doesn't. Of course he doesn't; he's Poseidon, and Poseidon has never done anything that I expect him to.

Finally, he says, "Why Brazil?"

"It's on Ariadne's list of places she wants to visit, experiences she wants to have." It's like the strength goes out of my body when I talk about my sister. Or maybe it's the fact that I've never talked about her to *anyone*. My past lovers were essentially marks—the goal to get information, rather than give it. If I made small talk or told them things, those topics were easy and safe and didn't matter. They couldn't be used to hurt me. Not like the sister I love.

Poseidon doesn't say anything for so long, I finally give in to curiosity and open my eyes to find him watching me the same way I imagine someone would watch a feral animal they were trying to coax close enough to aid.

He catches me looking at him and smiles a little bashfully, color splashing his cheeks. "I'd like to hear about her if you're willing to tell me."

I try to analyze the request from different angles, to see how it could hurt me—could hurt *her*—but more than anything, I *do* want to talk about her. With him, specifically.

I wrap my arms around myself and huddle into the jacket he gave me without hesitation when he realized I was cold. It wasn't a move with the intention of getting something in return. He saw my need and he met it with no expectations.

This offer to talk about Ari is the same.

I take a deep breath. "My sister is the one with dreams. Ever since we were kids, she had her eyes on the horizon, on all the places the world has to offer. All she ever wanted to do was travel and inhale every experience. She's always been fearless like that. It didn't matter that it was unlikely to ever happen, that our father intended to marry her off to the first strategic match he could find. She *hoped*." I chuckle hoarsely. "Now look at her, sailing off with her pet monster to do exactly what she always wanted." She'll accomplish it, too. I have no doubts about that. She's already managed the impossibility of freedom, so what are the little details like money and papers?

"Brazil?" Poseidon prompts gently.

"Carnaval." My heart aches like it's rotting in my chest. Because this is just another promise I'm going to fail to keep. "It happens in February every year, a massive party and explosion of joy and color and music. Right up Ari's alley. But it's one of the places on her list that has a specific set of dates. Easier to find each other, I guess." Though that's not the full truth. If I escaped Olympus, I have my sister's phone number. She and the Minotaur have no reason to think anyone would bother tracking it, so she'll keep it in the hope that one day it'll ring and be me on the other end.

I hate that I won't get to experience freedom with her, that I won't be at her side as she visits all the places on the endless itineraries she created over the years. Sometimes when we were young, we would play pretend about the adventures we'd have in Egypt or Korea or New Zealand—endless places to visit and things to experience.

"I'm sorry," he says.

I turn to him in surprise. "What are you talking about?"

"If we'd been a little later, you would have been on that ship with her." He shakes his head slowly. "I'm not in the habit of making promises when I have no guarantee I can keep them, but I'll do everything in my power to ensure you see the other side of this—and have the resources to keep your promise to your sister."

I laugh. I can't help it. "Either you're the most fucked-up manipulator I've ever met—which is saying something—or you're too fucking good for this world." Before he can argue, I lean across the console and kiss him hard. He instantly melts for me, which just proves my point about him being perfect. The temptation to sink into the kiss is almost more than I can resist. But I do resist—because he needs me to. We have less than twelve hours to accomplish the impossible, and we're not going to manage that by me hauling him into the back seat of this SUV and fucking him senseless.

It's still a balm to my shattered soul to see disappointment on his flushed face when I finally lean back. I smooth my thumb over his bottom lip. "We have things to do."

"We…" He clears his throat. "Right. Yes. You're right." But as he gathers himself enough to resume driving, he reaches over to take my hand, lacing his big fingers through mine. I know I can't actually feel his heartbeat through the palm of his hand, but imagining it eases the last of my tension. Because I know this isn't manipulation. I'm beginning to believe he's not actually capable of it. This is just…him.

Poseidon. One of the most powerful people in Olympus and the only person I've ever met who seems to hate the idea of power. And still he manages to use it to be a force for good. Those under his command are safe and cared for in his blunt way. They don't fear him because they know he has their best interests at heart. He's a godsdamned unicorn.

And I want him more than I want air to breathe.

POSEIDON

WE MEET ORION AT MY OFFICE IN THE SHIPYARD BELOW the apartment we slept in last night. Icarus insists he doesn't need to rest, but he appears to fall asleep roughly three minutes later, slumped over my desk with his head pillowed by his arms. It makes my back ache to look at him, so I carefully scoop him up and lay him out on the threadbare couch in the corner.

Which is the exact moment Orion walks into the room. They raise their eyebrows at me but don't comment. It's just as well; I don't know what I'd say. I can't pretend I'm not starting to care for Icarus. It's inconvenient at best and disastrous at worst, especially with the information he shared this morning. I don't want to be the next in the line of people he's seduced while attempting to find safety. I want him to want me, full stop. A fool's dream.

I motion for Orion to take the chair across from my desk and then drop into my seat. "How many people can we spare without damaging the line of sentries?" It's tempting to pull everyone in, but that feels shortsighted. Circe hasn't attacked and we have no evidence that she's left the *Penelope* after the meeting with Hera, which means she's waiting for something. I originally thought it was an attempt to instill fear because she knew the Thirteen wouldn't unite to attack first, but now I wonder. Surely she's not giving us time to evacuate the civilians?

"Half, give or take." Orion leans forward and props their elbows on their knees. "I have them in three-person teams taking four-hour shifts."

Smart. It's a good way to keep them fresh and prevent sloppiness. I pinch the bridge of my nose and try to think past the exhaustion weighing me down. "Okay, pull a third of them back, one from each team." I lay out the basis of the plan, watching Orion's expression and body language all the while for some indication that they think it won't work.

Orion gives me no sign of doubt. They nod. "We'll need to know the numbers the others are bringing to be sure, but there should be more than enough boats to make it work. We only need one of our people on each. Smaller is probably better for this purpose. It keeps us maneuverable and stealthy."

"That's what I was thinking. Have Polyphemus ensure that there are jammers on every boat we take out. This won't work if they see us coming." It's tempting to keep talking circles around this, but until I have more information from Hades and Zeus on the numbers they're sending, until we know if Icarus's information is enough to make Circe's generals abandon her... There are too many factors. Better to wait and reconvene after sunset. "See it done, and then get some rest. We're all going to need it."

"Will do." Orion rises. Their gaze tracks to Icarus, but they don't comment on him as they turn and walk out of the office.

I want nothing more than to stretch out on that couch next to him, molding my body to his, and let sleep take me. But thinking about the evacuation reminds me that I haven't had an update about the overall situation in Olympus in over twenty-four hours. I take a deep breath and dial Demeter.

For once, she doesn't make me wait. "Hello, darling, how are you holding up?" Her voice is filled with warmth. I've never been able to tell if it's genuine or not.

The last thing I want to do is make small talk, but it's one of those strange societal expectations. The house might be on fire around us, but we still have to exchange pleasantries before we can get around to calling for a bucket of water. I clear my throat. "As well as can be expected. You?"

"I'm tired." She sounds almost honest in this moment, almost vulnerable. "It's been a long few weeks, and things promise to get more complicated before the end. I've only managed to get one of my daughters to listen to reason and evacuate, and even then she only did it to appease me. I'm worried."

It wasn't too long ago that Demeter and I were lovers. It started almost like friendship, and we were months into sharing a bed before I realized she intended to use sex to manipulate me, to get one of the legacy titles in her corner. She was never overt about it, but Demeter is one of the most ambitious people I know, and she rarely attacks a problem head-on. Our current Hera comes by her ruthlessness honestly.

So, no, I don't trust this apparent vulnerability, even if it would be reasonable for the current situation, even if I sympathize with a mother trying to get her daughters to safety. "I'd like an update on the evacuation."

"Of course." Papers rustle in the background. "We've got about sixty percent of people out of the city. Some are choosing to stay, but a lot of the rest don't have personal transportation, so we're having to ferry them in groups via bus. It all takes time."

No matter Demeter's faults, she takes care of the people of Olympus. It's how she got the title in the first place, winning an election by popular vote after the last Demeter passed in his sleep. I have no doubt she's doing everything in her considerable power to help. "Is there anything I can do?"

"You've been performing admirably."

"Demeter." I take a breath. I had no intention of asking her this, but I can't quite stop myself. "Why did you vote against going to war? I'd like an honest answer."

She's silent for a single beat. "I know what you and the rest of the Thirteen think of me, that I'm power-hungry and ruthless in my ambition."

"Aren't you?"

"Well, yes." She laughs a little. "But I do nothing without reason. If I'd voted yes, Zeus would have launched an attack before we were able to evacuate the city. More than that, even with a majority vote, the minority among the Thirteen are still more than capable of digging in their heels. We'd have instantly bit off more than we can chew, and the civilians would pay the price."

She's...not wrong. She'd also travel back to Olympus to stage a riot herself if she knew what Zeus, Hades, and I are planning. I sigh. "Circe won't be content to squat out there in the water forever."

"No, she won't. And we should all be worrying about *why* she's still out there."

It's nothing more than I was thinking earlier, but hearing it echoed in Demeter's voice has the small hairs on the back of my neck rising. I wanted to attribute Circe's hesitation to her giving us a way to remove civilians or to her arrogance about the Thirteen's constant squabbling, but it doesn't feel right. She's already created a tumultuous and unsafe environment in Olympus with her machinations, which has put civilians in danger, directly and indirectly.

"Demeter," I say slowly. "Post sentries around the borders of the civilian camp."

"You think she's going to send some of her soldiers to harm the civilians the same way she did Hades in the lower city."

"It's possible I'm being paranoid."

She chuckles. "Are you truly paranoid when our enemy has proven to be clever and ruthless?" She pauses for a beat. "We are keeping order in the camp, and that includes guards around the edges to dissuade anyone from taking advantage."

I release the breath I'd been holding. "That's good to hear."

"We both want the same thing, even if we're going about it in different ways. We'll figure this out and then we'll crush the bitch." Voices in the background. "I'm sorry, Poseidon, but I've got to go."

"Be safe."

"You too."

I set my phone down but pick it back up almost immediately. I don't like what Hera is attempting, don't like not knowing how far she'll go, but there's one part of this whole thing I don't understand, and I won't be able to move forward until I do. Before I can talk myself out of it, I call Zeus.

Like Demeter, he answers on the first ring. "Problem?"

I'll never admit it aloud, but it's a strange sort of relief to deal with Zeus during this time of crisis. *He* doesn't bother with wasteful small talk. "Before we move forward with tonight, I have a question, and I want an honest answer."

"A plan that will benefit all of Olympus."

I flush, but I've been dealing with the Thirteen for twenty years. I'm not going to fold over a sharp question, no matter how valid. "Yes."

He sighs. "Very well. Ask."

No going back now. "To hear you tell it, you knew of Hera's rebellion from the start and chose not to intervene until now. Why? Why did you allow Hera's plans to move forward?"

His silence reigns as the seconds tick by into minutes. I check and make sure the call hasn't dropped—or he hasn't hung up on me. Finally, he says, "Because I was the only one she intended to kill."

I don't want to understand...but I do. I laugh hoarsely, and then louder, the sound gaining a thread of hysteria. He waits me out, once again silent as I try to regain control of myself. My chest feels too tight, my brain not firing properly. What are we *doing* among the Thirteen?

"Are you done?"

Apparently I am. "You and she really are on the same side, aren't you?"

"My wife doesn't see things that way." He continues before I can ask another question. "It's a moot point. Her values have changed and she'll let the city burn to save her mother and sisters. I won't, no matter how little the city in question appreciates it. Are you satisfied?"

"Yes." There's no other answer. He's right. I agreed to Hera's initial plan to kill Zeus for the same reason—to save the city. Now that she's stepped over the line and her priorities have narrowed so dramatically, I can't continue to side with her. "We'll have your boats ready. If things go well, you'll only be fighting one ship's worth of leaders instead of five."

"We'll see." He hangs up before I can say anything else, which is just as well. There's nothing else to say. We only have to get the pieces in order.

I turn my chair to survey Icarus. His chest still rises and falls in a steady rhythm. Orion will deliver the clothing I requested in the morning. Until then, there's little to do but wait. I lean away and lace my fingers behind my back, popping my spine. I can't help the faint groan that slips free in response.

"There's room on the couch, big guy."

I smile even as I tell myself not to. "I thought you were asleep."

"I was." He yawns and rolls to his side, creating a tiny sliver of space that will certainly *not* fit me. "Come here."

I pause long enough to set my alarm on my phone and then arrange myself on the couch. Not next to him but pulling him up to sprawl on my chest. I like him like this, fitted perfectly against me, his weight a comforting pressure against my chest, keeping me firmly in my body. I stroke my hand down his spine. "Comfortable?"

"Yeah." He presses his face to my throat and inhales deeply. "Thank you. For...everything. I don't deserve your kindness, but I'll try to deserve it. I promise." His words go syrupy and slow toward the end, trailing off into a cute little snore.

I'm not sure he was truly awake through this whole conversation, but I hold his words close all the same. I kiss his temple and wrap my arms carefully around him. "We're going to get through this, Icarus. *You're* going to get through this. I promise."

No matter what it takes.

ICARUS

I'M SHOCKED I WAS ABLE TO SLEEP AT ALL, BUT WHEN I open my eyes, the light creeping in from the partially closed blinds is bright. It's well past noon now. Poseidon is already awake, typing one-handed on his phone. His other hand is pressed to the small of my back. When I move to slide off him, he releases me easily. My back aches, but not as much as I expected it to. Probably because Poseidon was my mattress for that little nap.

I've never slept with someone the way I sleep with him. It's not a simple sharing of a bed until the appropriate time to slip away. I sleep deeply. I'm pretty sure there's a drool spot on his shirt from me. What the fuck? I drag my hand through my hair and duck into the bathroom.

By the time I return, he's sitting up, still on his phone. I don't know if I'm supposed to go sit with him or... I cross my arms over my chest. "You shouldn't have let me sleep so long."

"You needed it." He appears to give me his full attention. "Zeus has garnered both Athena's and Ares's support—privately—so we're moving forward as planned. It's time." He holds out his phone.

I take it gingerly. It's tempting to duck back into the bathroom to make this call, but I've been cowardly enough. Over and over again in the last few days, I've shown Poseidon the absolute worst version of myself and he hasn't flinched away. What's one more?

Deo is the first number I dial. He answers quickly, likely waiting by his phone for this exact outreach. "We've considered your offer."

Offer. Interesting term for blackmail. As much as I don't want to show my ugly underbelly to Poseidon, I put the call on speaker and force a smile to my lips and a coquettish tone to my voice. "Darling, it means the world that I've been on all your minds. I hope we're in agreement about the right course of action."

Deo and the others have already made their decisions, but he's a stubborn bastard and the idea of plucking Olympus is tempting. "I could simply kill you, you know. Your father isn't the only one who has pet assassins."

I shiver. My father *isn't*, not *wasn't*. Circe and her people don't know Minos is dead. *That* is a clever move on Olympus's part. I glance at Poseidon, but he hasn't so much as twitched since this conversation started. He's watching me closely, but it doesn't feel like he's ready to launch himself forward if I do or say something to betray him. More like I've just revealed a new facet to him and he's analyzing it and fitting it into the puzzle in his head that represents Icarus.

"You could," I say breezily. "I still like the odds of my being able to push a button and send all this damning evidence to Circe and the rest of Aeaea before they can cut me down."

"How do we know you won't release the information anyway?"

"You don't." There's no point in pretending otherwise. There's no foolproof assurance I can offer, so I don't bother. "But I've managed to keep these secrets just between us for nearly ten years. You don't think I'm going to spill it out of spite, do you? You all weren't *that* bad in bed."

"Fuck you, Icarus."

"I already did, darling. I even have videos."

"You—"

"You're just going to have to trust me, Deo. Promise to sail away and never return, and none of this juicy evidence will ever see the light of day." He truly doesn't have a choice. Circe won't tolerate this kind of rebellion, and a good portion of the sailors on those ships are conscripts. They won't stand between him and someone out for his blood. He has to know that. This plan of attack only works if Circe and the Aeaeans have surprise on their side.

So why haven't they actually attacked?

I can't ask. Showing any kind of ignorance will put me in a position with less power. Deo and the others need to believe I'm unassailable.

Finally, he curses. "Fine. We'll do it. We don't have any other choice."

"You really don't. I want you to sail away at…" I glance at Poseidon and he holds up ten fingers and then two. "Midnight. It's suitably dramatic, but also late enough that Circe won't have time to pivot to a different defense. Douse the lights and take off."

"So be it. I'll text you when we're leaving." He hesitates a long moment. "Circe's ship is run by a skeleton crew. If you're quick and quiet, they won't see you coming."

He truly is helpful when he gets out of his own way. "I'll keep that in mind."

"Do whatever you want. Just hold off your damn attack until we're out of the way of crossfire."

"Good boy." The words taste foul on my tongue.

"Icarus, if you're fucking me over, I won't kill you," he says calmly. "I'll hunt down that sister of yours who sailed away a few days ago and slit *her* pretty throat."

It takes everything I have to keep my voice cheery. "It's been a true pleasure doing business with you, Deo. I'll be waiting for your text and watching for your retreat." I end the call.

I'm shaking and I can't seem to stop. I toss the phone onto the cushion beside Poseidon. "There. Done. All four of them will abandon Circe at midnight tonight."

Instead of appearing victorious, he just seems worried. "Deo's threats were...convincing."

"It goes with the territory." I shrug, though the motion is too tense to fully pull off. "If any of them really had assassins in Olympus, they would have already tried to kill me after the call last night. It's been hours, and even without MuseWatch reporting on my whereabouts, any assassin worth their salt would have figured out where I am. We haven't exactly been hiding."

"True," he says slowly, his amber eyes still worried. For *me*. "But that doesn't mean Deo didn't do harm."

I laugh. I can't help it. "You truly are too pure for this world or any other. Harm is a reality of life, Poseidon. The powerful harm the weak. It's how they stay in power."

He rises slowly. He's so fucking *big*. Last night was amazing— beyond amazing—and it did nothing to ease my attraction to him. I want to tie him down and paint my name in wax over his chest. I want to prick each and every one of his freckles with a needle until he's panting and begging and dripping his pre-come all over his stomach.

But it's not just lust; if it were, maybe I could control my reactions better. I want quiet meals while he decompresses from his day. I want him to show me around the shipping yard, to share all the things he very clearly loves. I want to spend my nights sprawled across his chest, feeling safer than I ever have.

I want…everything.

He proves just how good he is by pulling me into a hug that feels like maybe he really could press all my broken pieces back together with sheer determination and acceptance.

Dangerous thoughts. Dangerous desires. "Now what?" I speak against the soft fabric of his T-shirt.

"Now, we wait for sunset." He strokes a hand down my spine, obviously aiming to soothe me. I mostly don't hate that it works. "Are you hungry?"

Yes, but not in the way he means. I lift my head. "Poseidon?"

He goes still, instantly picking up on the change in mood. "Yes?"

"If we don't have anywhere to be, if tonight is going to be the big fight that frees Olympus and changes everything…" I lick my lips, my cock hardening when he follows the movement. "I want you again before it's over. Please."

He doesn't move away, but it's clear he's trying to think his way out of the lust slowly settling around us. "I know you seduced me for safety, Icarus. But you don't have to. I'll keep you safe. No stipulations. No demands."

Fuck, but he keeps saying things I don't know how to deal with. I blink past the way my eyes start to burn. "I know."

"You say that, but I…" He curses, but he doesn't retreat physically. "I don't hold a single thing you've done against you—no one should—but I don't want to be another person who harms you, intentionally or not."

"Poseidon, I *know*." I run my hands up his chest and cup his face, his beard scratchy against my palms. "I won't pretend I didn't initially seduce you because I thought it would compromise you emotionally and ensure you kept me safe, but…I care about you. It's too soon and not the right timing and I don't expect you to feel the same way, but—"

He presses his fingers to my lips. "I care about you, too."

"This will never work," I mumble. I don't know why I say it. He isn't offering to make anything work. Saying he cares about me is the bare minimum. It doesn't mean he's letting himself imagine a future that's impossible. Even if he declared himself in love with me and even if we are successful in removing the threat of Circe, Poseidon is a legacy title. He has a responsibility to Olympus to father a bunch of heirs and spares to keep that title going.

I can't believe I'm even thinking it. My cart is so far in front of my horse that it's out of sight.

As if he can hear my increasingly frantic thoughts, he shifts his hand around to cup the back of my neck and presses his forehead to mine. "Maybe it won't work; only time will tell. First, we have to survive tonight and whatever comes after."

I lean back and he allows the distance, just like he allows me to see the desire kindling within him. "How long do we have?" I ask softly.

"A couple hours. Hades and Zeus are coming to the shipyard to strategize at first dark. We'll launch close to midnight."

By sunrise, the fate of Circe will be sealed and Olympus will be able to start picking up the pieces. Zeus might demand my head, but I'm reasonably sure Poseidon will give me a ship and send me on my way before he has a chance to collect. Poseidon is honorable like that. But surviving, reaching my sister, starting a new life, all of it means leaving this man behind. Even if he wanted a future with someone as broken as I am, the Thirteen would never allow it. Neither would the city itself. One villain killed in the depths of the night before even reaching Olympus's shores won't be enough to make people feel like justice was served. They'll be out for blood.

But not today. Right now, it's only Poseidon and me in this little apartment. I drop my hands and take a step back. After the briefest hesitation, he lets me go. He watches me carefully as I walk to the door and flip the lock. "I want to outline something I'd like to do to you, with you. If you have any reservations at all, I want you to tell me."

That beautiful flush rises in Poseidon's cheeks. He clears his throat and shifts from foot to foot. "Okay."

It takes effort to maintain our distance, to not do anything to heighten the desire between us until I've laid out my proposal. By the time I'm done, his chest rises and falls with quick little breaths and his cock is a hard line against the front of his jeans. "Yes. I want that. Right now."

"Tell me your safe word."

"Trident."

"Good boy. Now, go get ready for me."

POSEIDON

IT DOESN'T TAKE LONG TO FULFILL ICARUS'S ORDER AND return to the bedside. He's been busy. He found a candle from some-where—I don't usually burn them because the scents irritate me—and has lit it on the nightstand...within easy reach of the bed.

He smiles slowly at me, his body loose and relaxed. "Strip for me, big guy."

The simple act of taking off my clothes is foreplay with this man. Icarus doesn't touch me, doesn't speak, doesn't do more than watch, and yet by the time I shove off my pants, I'm shaking. I take a moment to fold my clothes so they aren't in a pile on the floor and then turn to face him.

In the days since I've gotten to know Icarus, he's used charm and flirting to lie, to manipulate, to hide things from me. He's not hiding anything right now. His desire, his *care*, are right there in his deep-brown eyes, drinking in the sight of me. There's fear there, too; I'm not so far gone as to miss that.

I swallow hard. "We don't have to."

He laughs softly, bitterly. "You really do see too much. I'm not worried about this scene. I'm worried about the rest of the world on fire." He motions vaguely to the window. "Now come here, big guy."

Big guy.

I love it when he calls me that, especially with that almost indulgent look on his face. As if my size is just another part of me that he values as equally as the rest. Not a strong man to be feared. Not a fat man to be ridiculed. Just...me.

It should only require a single step to close the distance between us. It takes me three. I want what he outlined, want whatever pieces of me that he'll give. The thread of trepidation I feel only seems to heighten with every beat of my heart.

And then I stand before him, naked and imperfect and yet cherished all the same. How can I think otherwise when he's reaching out to drag his fingers down my arm, over my hand, to lace with mine.

I never understood the concept of someone having their heart in their eyes. It seems a terrible, bloody thing to behold. As I meet Icarus's gaze, get lost in the depths, I realize it *is* that...and so much more. There's tenderness and care...and even the possibility of love.

Or maybe those are the emotions blossoming in *my* chest.

He leads me around the bed and urges me down onto my back. I expect him to strip, too, but he merely climbs onto the mattress and straddles my thighs. All while still *looking* at me.

I shift. "Touch me. Please."

"All in good time, big guy." He shifts, using his thighs to press mine tightly together. It's such a small movement, but it slams me back into my body. I hadn't even realized I was slipping away. There's no danger of that now. Not with Icarus's touch drifting over my arms, my shoulders, my chest, my stomach. My blood seems to gather to his call, making everything sensitized and my skin feel almost too tight. In the past, that sensation has always been something I avoided, but at the same time, it feels different.

I don't want it to stop.

Icarus pinches my nipples. Hard. The pain happens so fast, it's as if my brain can't process it. I jolt and moan, my cock so hard, I'm suddenly afraid that I'll come without him touching me there.

"There you are," he murmurs. He pinches my nipples harder, making my back bow. I'm not certain if I'm trying to lean into the touch or get away from it. It's not as if he's holding me down; not with anything other than his will. "Too much?" he asks casually, as if he's not sending agony searing through me.

There's only one right answer, one true answer. "I can take whatever you want to give me," I gasp.

"You are a gift." His tone is a perfect contradiction to the pain making me twist and writhe against him. *This* is what I never expected, this tenderness even as he gives me the pain I crave, washing away every thought in my head. At least temporarily.

All the bad things waiting outside this apartment will still be there when we're done, but that doesn't change the way he offers me escape with his gentle words and vicious pain.

Icarus rakes his short nails down my stomach. "Hands on the headboard, please."

I blink at him, dazed enough that it takes a few beats for the order to penetrate. He waits me out, seeming pleased by his effect on me. I finally dredge up the concentration to force my body to move, shifting to grip the bottom of the headboard. I feel more exposed like this, even though I'm *not* more exposed than I was mere seconds ago.

"Very good." He leans down and sets his teeth into the curve of my pectoral muscle. It's not quite a bite, but my brain doesn't know that.

I moan and arch my back. "Icarus, please."

"Be careful, big guy. I might get addicted to your begging." He moves down my body, lightly biting along the curve of my stomach. It's not nearly as painful as the scratching and pinching, but it makes me jolt every time.

Until he reaches my cock…and bypasses it entirely.

I make a sound of protest and Icarus chuckles warmly. "What did I tell you before? There can be pain in pleasure." He shifts off my legs and pushes them wide. His breath ghosts over my length and then he kisses my inner thigh. "Patience is a virtue."

"Says who?" I sound almost petulant, something I've never been accused of. "Hurt me. Or suck my dick. Or—"

"Poseidon." There's no censure in the way he says my name, only amusement. Icarus squeezes my thighs. "It's cute that you think you can rush me."

Maybe it should be aggravating that I'm unraveling at the seams and he's perfectly in control, but it makes me feel safe. I can afford to lose control because he'll be there to catch me when I do. "I'm sorry."

"Mmm." He cups my balls, nearly sending me out of my skin. "You will be, big guy." And then he gives me what I thought I wanted—his mouth on my cock. He drags a messy kiss up my length and flicks his tongue against the sensitive underside of my head. Wet and slick and nowhere near enough.

The bastard knows it, too. He keeps kissing my cock lazily, winding me tighter and tighter. But it's never enough to push me over the edge. My world narrows down to the slow slide of his tongue, the softness of his lips, the barest hint of his teeth.

Icarus wraps his hand around the base of my cock and squeezes hard enough that I cry out. He pauses. "Too much?"

Too much? Is there such a thing when it comes to this man? Surely not.

He starts to loosen his grip. "Poseidon?"

"Not too much," I manage, my voice strangled. "Don't stop."

His only response is to suck my cock down—*finally*—until his lips meet his fist. He squeezes me even harder, the near-pain a perfect counterpoint to the slick feeling of his mouth. It's so good that my balls go tight and my vision blacks out.

But, even as I lose control, I don't come. I…can't.

"Icarus?" I rasp.

He eases off me enough to say, "Your orgasms belong to me, big guy. You don't come until I give you permission—and I haven't done that yet, have I?"

I swallow hard and then do it again. "No?"

"That's right. I haven't." He smiles at me, happier than I've ever seen him. It shines from his eyes. "Now, unless the next word out of your mouth is your safe word, don't interrupt me again."

ICARUS

IF THERE WAS GOING TO BE A MARK TO SEDUCE ME INTO falling for them, Poseidon's the only one who could have managed it. The man has no deception in him. It's refreshing, even if many of our conversations have been uncomfortably frank. With this man, I'll never have to wonder where I stand.

And where I stand?

He's watching me with something like wonder. It defies belief that he's managed to live this long when every thought is right there on his face. I don't think I'll ever get used to it, even as it warms me right through. It makes my skin go hot, and I have the uncomfortable suspicion that I'm blushing.

Instead of addressing *that*, I take his cock back into my mouth and resume tormenting him. He's wide and thick. My jaw already aches—I'm out of practice—but I'm not about to stop, not when his thighs are shaking and he's gripping the headboard so tightly it's a wonder he doesn't warp the metal. He's certainly strong enough to manage it.

"*Icarus.*"

The pleading desperation gets me. If we had more than a few hours, if we had days and weeks and months and years, I would keep him on this knife's edge until all the fight went out of his big body and he wasn't capable of doing anything but take what I give to him. Until I'd imprinted myself right into his soul.

We don't have that kind of time.

I hold his gaze as I loosen my grip. He's so attuned to me, I don't need to give the verbal command to orgasm. Poseidon's amber eyes go wide and panicked. "Wait—"

It's too late. He's coming, shooting down my throat in great spurts. I give him one last long suck and ease off his cock. I'm so hard I can barely think, but I've spent most of my life in some sort of misery. At least this is in pursuit of pleasure. Of making someone I care about feel good. Of washing away Poseidon's fears about tonight. I can't help more than I already have—assuming Deo doesn't try some kind of double-cross—but I can give him peace. At least for a little while.

I move up his body to straddle his hips. I'm still wearing my pants, mostly to remind myself to remain in control. "You did well. You've pleased me greatly." He looks so dazed I can't help leaning down and kissing him gently. "Can you take more?"

"Yes." No hesitation.

Fuck, but I might love this man. How godsdamned tragic.

I sit back so I can grab the candle. It was so fucking tempting to find a needle or knife and scar him so he'll remember me always, but apparently my lifetime selfish streak doesn't apply to Poseidon. This thing between us will be over far too soon, no matter what words we've exchanged in the moments before we sail off into battle. Promises made when neither party thinks they'll survive the night are as substantial as wishing on stars.

He'll survive to have a nice long life, and I'm selfish enough to want to be a fond memory instead of a literal scar. One will fade with time, becoming something to reminisce about when he's in some rocking chair on his front porch, the golden afternoon sunlight warming his skin. The other could turn bitter, could be a point of contention between him and whatever partner he finally settles on. Someone worthy of the good man he is.

No matter what he says, it won't be me.

The candle has melted enough for my purposes. I use my free hand to cup Poseidon's face. "There are proper waxes to use for this sort of thing that won't burn. This candle isn't one of them. It won't harm you in any long-term way, but you will have a light burn for a few days."

He blinks a few times, obviously trying to focus through the post-orgasm bliss. "You went over this earlier."

"Yes." I don't move. "But it's worth repeating. Do you want me to go an alternate route?"

"No." He shakes his head sharply. "No, Icarus. I want this from you. Please."

I don't ask him again. As he said, he agreed before, when pleasure wasn't weighing him down and lifting him up in equal measure. But, for the first time in my life, I'm not looking to take advantage. I don't want him to have any regrets about our time together.

His chest isn't particularly hairy, so it's only the burn we have to worry about. I hold his gaze and tilt the candle. The wax wells and drips onto his skin. Poseidon flinches, surprise making his eyes go wide, and then *whimpers*.

I trace around the edges of the hardening wax, careful not to touch it. "How we doing, big guy?"

"Good," he whispers. "Don't stop. Please."

I don't stop. I trail wax over his chest, mapping his freckles in hectic lines that are somehow more beautiful for their imperfections—because they're on him. This beautiful, rough man who shakes and whimpers at every drop, who arches into it all the same, whose cock is already hardening again in response to this pain.

And through it all, he looks up at me with wonder, as if I'm a god who's wandered down to earth. As if I'm someone of value. Someone *he* values.

By the time I'm done, his chest and stomach are covered in a hectic pattern of wax. I could keep going, but the knowledge that our time is limited is never far from my mind, no matter how much I'm enjoying myself.

I set the candle aside and stroke him gently. "You've done so well. Are you ready for your reward?"

He blinks. "Reward?"

"Mmm, yes." I skate my fingers over his cock. "Tell me what you want and I'll give it to you."

Poseidon doesn't hesitate. He draws in a shaking breath. "I want you."

I want you.

The proclamation rings between us like a bell, drawing forth an answering call from within me. *I want you, too.* More than

I've wanted anything in my life. I don't speak the words, though. I can't. Poseidon isn't a child and he isn't a fool, but he's not thinking clearly. When this conflict with Circe is over and peace is restored, he'll realize we have no future. If he's forced to choose between me and his city—his people—it won't be a contest.

I grab the lube and a condom. This might all be over tonight. Circe's conquest. My romance with Poseidon. I want to give him something to remember me by.

I push his legs wide and spread a generous amount of lube over his ass. "You've been so wonderful at keeping your hands on the headboard. Keep them there a bit longer, big guy."

"Icarus."

If I live another seventy years, I'll never forget the desperate, loving way he says my name. "What do you need?"

"Let me touch you. Please."

It's dangerous, but I've already thrown myself fully into the reality of walking away from this with a broken heart. If I walk away at all. There's every possibility that my body will join my father's in some unmarked grave outside the city proper. What will it hurt to allow this moment of total intimacy? I drag in a rough breath. "Okay."

He doesn't hesitate. He wraps his arms around me even as I sink into him, one slow inch at a time. It's like being held by a mountain, like in his embrace, nothing would dare touch me. In this moment, I can't help but believe it. My heart lurches and a horrible burning starts behind my eyes. "This city doesn't deserve you." I withdraw almost completely and shove back into him. "I don't deserve you."

"You have me," he moans. He strokes those work-roughened hands down my back as I keep fucking him.

Except it doesn't feel like fucking.

It feels like love.

It doesn't matter how hard I thrust, how intense the pleasure. There's no denying the current of caring between us. It's there in the way he arches up, in the way I catch his mouth, in the press of his fingertips against my skin.

He breaks the kiss. "Icarus! I'm going to—"

"Come for me, big guy." I nip his bottom lip. "Please."

That single word is his undoing. I angle back so I can fuck him more thoroughly. It takes a single stroke and he cries out, coming in great jerks all over his stomach as I take him. A fucking masterpiece, his freckles, his seed, my wax. It's too much. I follow him over the precipice. Too good. Everything with him is too damn good.

It's like my bones dissolve. I slump onto his chest, mess and all, and he immediately wraps his arms around me and hugs me to him. Words blossom in my chest, words I can't allow myself to speak. If I tell Poseidon that I love him, he'll never let me go. Even if it hurts him in the end. Even if it *kills* him.

I don't tell him I love him. I don't tell him that he's given me a gift beyond measure. He's cared for me, seen value in me that no one else in my life recognized—not even my beloved sister. For Poseidon, I can put away my selfish ways. For him, I can be brave enough to do the right thing.

To leave him.

POSEIDON

WE MANAGE A SHOWER BEFORE FALLING BACK INTO BED. I have the presence of mind to set an alarm and then I pass out, Icarus tucked against my body. At least until my phone wakes me up sometime later. I roll over, relishing the sting of the tiny burns Icarus made, the languidness of my body, and fumble the phone up to my ear. "What?"

"What did you do?" Hera is so coldly furious that I'm half-surprised she doesn't manage to ice the entire room with her displeasure alone.

I check the alarm next to the bed but can't quite manage to breathe a sigh of relief when I realize I have two hours before I need to meet Zeus and Hades. Except there's no relief to be had because Hera is on the phone. She said something... "What?"

"What. Did. You. Do?"

"I don't know what you're talking about." I don't sound the least bit convincing. I'm a shit liar even when I have time to prepare. Icarus shifts next to me and makes a small sound. I don't hesitate to cover his mouth with my free hand and give him a little shake to wake him up. I don't think Hera is waiting outside the door to murder us, but I'd be a fool to underestimate her.

"Don't insult me by trying to lie. You're terrible at it," she snaps. "Why is my husband missing, Poseidon? Did you warn him of my plans?"

"Zeus is…missing." Belatedly, understanding rolls over me. Of course Zeus isn't where his wife expects him to be. He's staging a coup and planning a midnight attack.

She pauses for a beat. "That time, I almost believed you have no idea where he is."

"I don't." That, at least, is the truth. I know where he'll be, and I could take a guess or two to figure out where he is now—coordinating with Ares and Athena tops the list—but it's not as if he provided me with an itinerary.

"Fuck," Hera breathes. "This is a problem."

She has no idea. "It might be a good idea if you go to the countryside with Psyche and your mother. Eurydice is safe enough with Persephone behind the lower city barrier." For now. "If you're worried about what Zeus is planning—"

"I'm not going to flee on the possibility that he's finally got his shit together." Sharp footsteps echo down the line. She's pacing.

I knew that suggestion was a long shot, but I had to try. Hera's the one person who can blow this plan right off the tracks, and while I'd like to think that she values her family more than she hates her husband and the city, I can't be sure. "Well, I don't know where he is. Is that all you needed?"

"Don't get bitchy with me now." She inhales and exhales slowly.

When she speaks again, she sounds more like herself. Controlled. "I'm concerned about Hermes."

"Everyone is concerned about Hermes." And they should be. She was pretty clear with her endgame when she broke into my kitchen. I don't necessarily disagree with her goals, but there's a reason I refused to work with her. Her methods are just as suspect as the rest of the Thirteen. Which I suppose proves her point. "And no one can find her, so there's not much to be done about it."

I glance at Icarus. He's fully awake now, watching me with large dark eyes. What little relaxation we claimed through the... claiming...of each other is gone. He lies there, tense and silent. I don't stop to think. I set my phone down on the bed between us and put it on speaker.

She continues to pace, the sound echoing through the phone. "I think she's working with Circe."

"I don't." That, at least, I know to be true. If she was working with Circe, then we would likely all be dead and scattered among the ashes of the city. "It doesn't make sense. She wouldn't do that."

"Well, you're fucking Icarus right now, so I don't think we can stand on *your* character judgment."

I sigh. "Is there an actionable step you're requesting, Hera? Or did you just call to yell at me over things neither of us can control?"

"You are *such* an asshole." She hangs up.

Icarus props his head on one hand. "She's going to be a problem."

"Zeus's problem. Not ours." I wish I believed it. I never should have allowed her to convince me to join in that ill-fated coup attempt. It's been nothing but trouble, pulling me deeper and deeper

into the messy politics and backstabbing—literal and otherwise—
that I've spent most of my time as Poseidon avoiding.

"If you really believe that, big guy, I have an ocean-front property in Arkansas to sell you." He leans over and brushes a kiss to my
lips. "You'll handle it. I have no doubt about that."

I huff out a laugh. "You have more faith in me than I deserve."

"I have exactly as much faith as you deserve." He kisses me
again, longer this time. It's surprisingly sweet and sincere enough
to worry me.

I pull back and search his face. He's still a better liar than I'll ever
be, but I'm starting to be able to read the real emotions beneath the
careless mask. He...means it. He really has that much faith in me.
It scares the shit out of me. "I don't deserve you."

Icarus chuckles awkwardly and sits up. "I think you'll find that
the situation is reversed. Hera is right, you know. As soon as the
Thirteen and the rest of Olympus find out you're fucking me, any
credibility you've gained over your tenure as Poseidon will be gone.
They'll call you a traitor and worse."

"Fuck them." The words burst out of me, far stronger than I
intended. I didn't *intend* to say them at all. "I never signed up for
any of this, and I've still done my duty to them for most of my life.
You're the only person who's actually seen what I need and tried to
give it to me. You're the only person who's seen *me*."

"Poseidon." I hate the way he says my name, like I'm a silly
teenager experiencing puppy love instead of a man who's seen the
backside of forty. Icarus turns away, his shoulders hunching a little.
"I know the sex is good, but it's just sex—and good kink. You're
experiencing emotions that are the result of that, not because of me."

"Shut the fuck up."

He flinches and spins to face me. "Excuse me?"

I stand and cross to him in two steps. He backs up and I shadow him, stalking him across the room until his back hits the wall. Icarus stares up at me with wide eyes, nothing like the sweetly sadistic Dominant he is when we engage in a scene. Both are him, but the other is at peace with how much I want him. This version needs more assurance. Is it any wonder? He's experienced so much trauma in the last few weeks—watched his abusive father die and his beloved sister sail off without him. Of course he doesn't believe that I might have actual feelings for him.

I plant my hands on either side of his head and lean down until our faces are even. "I need you to listen to me. Are you listening?"

"Kind of hard not to," he murmurs. He's not panicking, though. He's certainly not afraid. Good. I don't want him scared. I just want his attention.

"I'm not one of your marks who only sees the fantasy and not the man beneath." I'm not the kind of person who always knows the right thing to say. I'm pretty sure I've *never* known the right thing to say. It's a damn shame, because I need the words to chase the lost look from his eyes and I don't fucking have them. "I see you. What I feel for you is the result of you seeing me, too. I'm not distracted by the sex and kink. It's simply part of the whole picture."

He blinks at me, looking wounded and confused, and I don't know how to fucking fix it. Especially when he licks his lips. "It will never work. Olympus will never accept me. If you appear to choose me over the city, even your own people will hate you. It will ruin everything good you've spent decades creating. You'll start to resent me, and eventually that resentment will turn to hate."

We might both die tonight, so I don't see the point in worrying about a future that might never come. I know better than to say as much, though. It will come across as dismissive and will hurt him, which is the last thing I want.

"I never wanted to be Poseidon. I've held the title this long because there was no one else." Technically, Triton could have held it if something happened to me, but he would have been an unmitigated disaster as Poseidon. "I can train Triton's eldest daughter to take the title and step down. It will take some time, but once I'm no longer Poseidon, it won't matter what the city thinks. We could..." I take a deep breath and a leap of faith. "We could meet your sister in Brazil for Carnaval. We could go anywhere, do anything. Whatever you want."

Icarus laughs in my face. It's a desperate sound. Wounded. "Stop it." He pushes at my chest, and I release him and step back so he can slip past me. He drags a hand through his wavy hair. "I know I can be an asshole, but you're being cruel. Even if the title and the city didn't stand between us, *we* stand between us. We're too different. I'll disappoint you. You'll drive me to distraction with your rigidity."

I flinch. *Rigidity.* That's one way to put it. It's almost kind, which somehow makes it worse. I'm a fool for thinking he might not find me lacking the way every one of my past lovers have. "If you don't want me, all you had to do was say so, Icarus. I have no desire to force you into anything."

"That's not what I meant!"

Frustration is thick on my tongue, a buzzing beneath my skin. I have to turn away, have to release the pressure by tapping my fingers against my thigh even though I know it's giving my agitation away by doing so. "Then what do you mean?" This isn't the time for this conversation. I should have known better than to start it. I'm a fool a thousand times over for thinking he felt the same way.

"Poseidon," he says softly. He waits for me to turn and face him to continue. Icarus looks as lost as I feel, and somehow instead of comforting me, it only makes me feel worse because I'm the one who's put that expression on his face. He takes a deep breath. "I'm fucking this up. Can we pause, please?"

"Of course." There's nothing else to say. I can't push forward and drag him along behind me when he obviously wants to be anywhere but here.

"Okay." He paces from one side of the room to the other. "Okay, give me a second."

There's nothing to do but sit on the chair and wait him out. His mind moves so fast, he doesn't make me wait long. He spins to face me, pointing an accusing finger at my face. "If I trust you to know your own mind, then you have to give me the same courtesy. Deal?"

I swallow down the instinctive agreement and examine his words from all angles. I don't know if I'm sensing a trap, or if I've simply been a member of the Thirteen for too long and have trust issues. It seems simple enough, though. I nod slowly. "That seems reasonable."

"Good. Great." His body shifts like he was about to start pacing again but he forcibly jerked himself to a stop. "I meant what I said about caring about you. That isn't just sex and that isn't manipulation because you're keeping me safe. I don't understand how we could possibly have a future together, but that doesn't mean I don't want the idea of it."

I have to grip the edge of the chair to keep from going to him, from hugging him until he loses that ragged edge of fear, because that's what you do when people are upset and you have a certain level of intimacy with them. But it's not the right move right here, right now, with him.

I force myself to pause and think and reason through this the way I promised I would. "I care about you, too," I say slowly. "I appreciate how similarly our tastes run sexually and that you've opened up a new world there for me, but I also appreciate how brave you were on the docks to defend your sister. I hate that you don't feel like you're good enough when you're clever and kind and have a great capacity for love."

"I'm not kind."

I narrow my eyes. "I thought we were agreeing to know our own minds."

Icarus lifts his hands but lets them fall back to his sides in defeat. "We are. You're just...you're seeing an idealized version of me."

"No, I'm not." I don't know how to get him to *understand*. "I don't see the idealized versions of people. I see what I have evidence to see. You may be capable of monstrous things, but that doesn't make you a monster. It doesn't mean you're not worthy of love."

"Love," he says faintly. He scoffs. "Love doesn't exist."

"You love your sister."

"That's different."

"Yes, but it's proof that love exists." I can't quite contain my agitation, so I push to my feet and cross my arms over my chest to keep from fidgeting. "I'm not saying what I feel for you is love, but it could be. It *will* be if we live long enough."

"Poseidon…"

"My *point* is that the future is one I'm willing to work for and reach a compromise about that makes both of us feel good. But I fully intend to be an active participant in that conversation—and expect you to be one as well. You don't get to make sweeping generalizations. I'll resist doing the same. Understand?"

"But—"

I swallow hard. "You've been forced into too many relationships throughout your life. I won't be another one to hurt you with my selfishness. If all you want is sex and your freedom, I understand."

"What? *No*." He crosses to me in a rush. "That's not what I'm saying at all."

"Icarus." I feel like I'm drowning. I don't want him to end this, but I don't know how to say that without it coming across the wrong way. "What *are* you saying?"

"Fuck, I don't know what I'm doing." He drags his fingers through his hair again. He looks actually tormented. "This wasn't supposed to happen. I never bargained on you, on feeling…"

That makes two of us. "If it helps, I don't know what I'm doing, either."

He sucks in a breath, pauses, and exhales slowly. "That does help, actually." Icarus smiles a little, though he's clearly still frazzled. "I just… I've never been in a real relationship where I didn't have a goal in mind. Which is really fucking sad, but there it is. I don't know how to do this."

"I don't, either. I've never been with anyone like you."

"There's no one else like me, big guy." His attempt at humor falls a little flat, but I think it's a good sign that he's trying.

I carefully take his hands. "We can figure it out. Together. If you want to try. With me."

Icarus searches my expression. I don't know what he sees. I've never been particularly good at hiding my thoughts; something I've never had cause to be grateful of before now. I want him to see how confident I am that we can make this work, how much I care about him...how I'll force myself to let him go if that's really what he needs.

"Together," he repeats slowly. "I guess that's a fair ask."

"Only if you want to."

This time, his smile is smaller, but significantly steadier. "I do want to try, Poseidon. With you. Even if it seems impossible right now."

I slowly pull him closer until he slides his hands up my chest to loop around my neck. It feels good. It feels *right*. "Then we'll try."

He hugs me tightly. "Promise me that you'll stay safe tonight," he whispers. "Promise that you'll come back to me."

"I can't promise that without lying." I brush a kiss to his forehead. "But I promise to try."

ICARUS

I DON'T KNOW WHAT TO SAY TO POSEIDON. IT FEELS LIKE I've been in this strange new territory for days on end, something new accosting me every time I turn around. Tender care. Open communication, even if it's uncomfortable. Sex unlike anything I've ever experienced before. No wonder he's talking about a potential future—he's falling just as hard and unexpectedly as I am.

That should comfort me. I'm not dancing past the point of no return alone; he's right there with me, every step of the way. But I don't quite believe we're moving toward some happy ending with rainbows and sunshine and *happy endings*. How can we when we have so many obstacles before us?

"Trust me."

I jolt and glance to where Poseidon sits behind the steering wheel of his SUV—truly, I don't think he even has a driver—tense and still. We've been sitting in this parking lot for thirty minutes, looking out over the water to where the ships linger, dark shadows against the increasingly darker water. Five, still.

It's not time yet. Deo will text when they're leaving so we can time our attack. I haven't failed.

"Icarus." He waits for me to drag my gaze back to him. "It will be okay. Trust me."

"It's not too late to lock me up and throw away the key. Better not risk having an enemy at your back for what comes next." I don't exactly *want* to be locked up, but for all that he's one of the legacy titles, cutting his teeth on politics and backstabbing, Poseidon isn't acting to type. He's too trusting. It's only been a couple days. I could be anyone. I could be *me*, belligerent playboy of an enemy country, sent to Olympus to bring it down.

He places his big hand on my jostling knee. "Breathe. Slowly. Through your nose."

"I'm not—" At his sharp look, I stop arguing and obey. Within a few breaths, I feel better, calmer. I hate that. I love it, too. "They're going to send me away. You might as well have done it first."

"No." Just that. No explanation, no doubt.

As the sun finishes setting and darkness takes root, Poseidon only becomes calmer, more in control. I don't understand it. Personally, I feel like I'm one mild inconvenience away from spinning out entirely. I flip wildly between believing the blackmail will work and being absolutely sure that Deo and the others are going to bet that they can kill me before I can release my blackmail to Circe and Aeaea. It's what my father would do.

My father. Who's dead.

"Did you toss my father's body in a dumpster like I told you to?" The words feel jagged in my throat.

"You know I didn't." He squeezes my knee. "There's a small

funeral home for my people and their families. He's been moved there and will remain until you're ready to face him."

Of course he will. Of course Poseidon has thought of everything—and brought a level of caring that I suspect has nothing to do with the fact we're sleeping together. It's just *Poseidon*. "Cremate him and toss him in the trash."

He's silent for several minutes that feel like a small eternity. "If that's truly what you want to do, then tell me again tomorrow and I'll see it done. Not the trash. I'll store his remains somewhere safe in case you ever change your mind." He pauses. "An alternate option is to have his body converted to soil and plant a tree. We have a designated space outside the city for people who want to utilize that option."

I have spent all of my adult life and no small amount of my childhood learning to lie and shield my emotions from those around me. There's absolutely no reason for Poseidon's kindness to have my throat closing and my eyes burning. I blink a few times, but it only makes the sensation worse. "He was a monster. Not just to everyone else, but to me and Ariadne, too. He hated every part of me, and the more I tried to please him, the more he loathed the weakness that drove me to seek his approval."

Poseidon shifts his hand to mine, linking our fingers together. "It's okay to mourn him. Or to mourn the father and person he should have been. It doesn't mean you excuse all the bad things he did."

A single tear slips free and I have to close my eyes to keep the rest in. "You're pretty smart, you know that?"

"I can't take credit for it." He chuckles a little. "I read a lot and try to learn from people smarter than me. That's from one of my books."

I don't have to ask why he was reading a book apparently about grief for a person who was terrible—his uncle. My laugh is watery. "Shit is complicated."

"Life usually is."

I breathe slowly, giving myself time to get under control. He waits me out with a patience I can't quantify. Finally, I manage, "If we live through this mess, I think I'd like to read that book." It's nowhere close to the promises of a potential future we made earlier today, but it feels monumental all the same.

"I'm happy to give it to you." He squeezes my hand. "And there's no *if*, Icarus. You're living through the night."

I wish I had his confidence. I wish I had a lot of things. I open my mouth to say as much, but two cars pull in on either side of us before I can. They're identical to the one we sit in, black SUVs with deeply tinted windows. I tense, expecting an ambush. When a door opens and Zeus steps into the cold night, I'm not exactly reassured. This is all part of the plan, but I can't help the worry nibbling at the back of my mind that I've missed something, that everything is about to go terribly wrong.

That *Poseidon* will be the one to pay the price.

Zeus walks right up to my window and stares so pointedly, there's nothing to do but roll it down. I'll never get used to how cold his blue eyes are. My father had a terrifying presence, but he covered it up with charm. Zeus doesn't try to cover up anything. He's like a piece of ice carved into a man's shape. It makes me shiver.

His gaze flicks over me and lands on Poseidon. "Clock's ticking."

Poseidon seems to struggle with something but finally clears his throat. "Hera called me this afternoon."

If I wasn't watching Zeus so closely, I wouldn't notice the way he clenches his jaw. His reaction is nowhere in evidence in his voice. "And?"

"And if this doesn't work—and even if it does—I would sleep with one eye open."

"Let me worry about my wife." Normal people would react to the late autumn wind surging past Zeus and into the car. He just stands as if he really is untouchable. I don't believe in that shit. I've seduced and betrayed people who thought they were untouchable—it's why we're here tonight—but he's on another level. It scares the shit out of me.

Poseidon must notice my shivers, because he says, "Let's go up to the warehouse while we wait for Hades and the rest. The coffee isn't good, but it's hot, and there's plenty of room for everyone."

"Lead the way."

Poseidon glances at me, his eyes filled with something I don't have a name for, and then he steps out of the SUV. I have to wait for Zeus to move before I can do the same.

He levels a cold look at me. "If you attempt to double-cross us, I'll cut you down, but I won't stop there. I'll find your sister and ensure she knows exactly who's to blame before she dies."

As threats go, it's a good one. Except for one notable detail. "That's like the twelfth time someone has issued that exact threat. It's getting old. You're not touching Ariadne. You'd have to get through the Minotaur, and he's the scariest motherfucker I've ever met—including you."

His lips quirk, and it should warm his expression, but somehow it just makes him look less kind, less *human*. "I suppose we'll see, won't we?" He finally moves back enough for me to get out of the vehicle.

I very much would like to keep the metal door between us, but I've dealt with enough predators in my time to know never to show fear. No matter how much it's chilled me to the bone. Especially when Zeus follows soundlessly on my heels around the back of the car to where Poseidon waits.

Poseidon steps between us immediately, slipping an arm around my shoulder and tucking me against his body. It serves to protect me from the wind, but I can't help how aware I am of Zeus watching us. Or of the woman who steps out of the second car and moves to join us. Athena.

A pair of people join her, and I glare at the Black woman with a scarred face and medium-brown skin at her right shoulder. Atalanta is built for combat, with a muscular body and her locs pulled back and fastened up to prevent anyone from using them as handholds. She made a name for herself in the Ares tournament, but after the ill-fated party in the countryside, she changed allegiance from Artemis to Athena.

She also hunted me and my sister through Olympus just days ago. She catches me watching her and winks. I just stare, but that doesn't dampen her grin any.

At her side is a tall Black person with warm brown skin, a head of thick curls, and an intense look on their handsome face. Bellerophon, Athena's second-in-command. They don't even look at me, choosing instead to focus on Poseidon. "We've tapped into the cameras in the area to supplement your people's watches, but I have no way of getting eyes on those ships. They seem to be on a closed network."

They are, but I don't bother to say as much. There's no point. They won't take my word for it, and even if they did, there's nothing we can do about it.

Bellerophon keeps talking. "Based on the ship models, we have blueprints, but we can't guarantee the interior will look like we expect."

That, I know nothing about. Blueprints of ships I never intended to set foot on weren't something that interested me. I follow Poseidon inside the warehouse. The huge space feels significantly smaller because of all the shit in here, pallets stacked nearly to the tall ceiling. I can't identify what any of them contain before we step through a door into a makeshift break room that's been built inside the warehouse.

Atalanta makes a beeline for the coffee. She sniffs the pot and laughs. "Not the worst I've ever had."

Bellerophon gives her a faintly put-upon look as Atalanta sips the coffee that looks too thick to be termed liquid. They turn back to Poseidon and hold up a tablet. "I have a map to go over our plan of attack."

Athena crosses her arms over her chest. For once, she's not wearing an impeccably tailored suit, choosing to forgo that in exchange for cargo pants and a formfitting long-sleeved shirt that shows off a lean body. She's also bristling with guns. I count four in various holsters, and I'm sure there are a few extra tucked away. She's held her title for quite a while and survived multiple assassination attempts in the last couple weeks; it's clear that she is just as capable of murder as the people who work under her. Of course she is; this is Olympus, after all.

She catches me watching her and raises a brow. "If you go for one of *my* guns, all you'll get for the effort is a new hole in your head."

"Enough, Athena."

She snorts and turns to Zeus. "Hades isn't coming. We shouldn't wait."

"He's coming." He sits down in a rickety chair, somehow transforming the impression of it into a throne. It's a neat trick. I don't understand how he can be so calm, but I suppose he's been raised to the role. Unlike me, this man wasn't a disappointment to *his* father.

We mill around in somewhat awkward silence. Poseidon hovers at my shoulder, all his earlier relaxation gone. It makes me want to stand between him and the rest of them, but that will only make things worse. Still, the impulse is a new one and I marvel at it. The big guy has me acting against type. I really have gone and fallen for him, haven't I?

I reach out tentatively and press my hand to the center of his back. I actually *feel* his exhale. He gives me a brief smile, but then his gaze lands over my head and he freezes.

There's nothing to do but turn around. I almost wish I didn't. A group of black-clad people walk into the room as if they own it, fanning out almost as if they intend to block off the exits.

Hades is here.

POSEIDON

IT DOESN'T MATTER THAT I HAD A CONVERSATION WITH Zeus and Hades just a short time ago. It feels different having them *here*, in my space, not bickering over a fancy boardroom table but actively planning an assault on our enemy. The coup is in action. We're gathered around the digital map Bellerophon projects onto the blank wall. It depicts the five ships and our coastline.

"We launch from here, here, and here." Athena points to each spot in turn. "Even if the jammers work on their radar like you say, we don't want to gather and present a pretty target for them to shoot at if someone happens to see us."

Hades stands with his arms crossed over his chest. Like Athena and the rest of their respective people, he's dressed for war, not for the boardroom. I don't know what Zeus was thinking, showing up in a suit.

Hades leans over to speak to the white woman with short blond hair at his side. Medusa. Normally, his ever-present shadow is Charon, who I fully expected to accompany him. When Charon ferried Hades across the river, I assumed rumors of his injuries in the recent attacks in the lower city were exaggerated. Apparently not. I do question the decision to bring Medusa, though. She's got a reputation for being dangerous—because she used to work for Athena. At least until that mess with Odysseus and Calypso. I would have expected her to avoid coming back to the upper city, *especially* since this meeting requires Athena's presence.

"Don't be shy, Hades," Athena says drily. "Share it with the class."

He gives her a long look, expression carefully blank. "Normally, I would recommend splitting our respective forces to be represented on each of the boats, but in this case, I think it would do more harm than good. We don't have time for the potential pissing contests or the slightest hesitation."

Athena's lips thin, probably at the insinuation that any of *her* people would let a silly thing like loyalty get in their way of obeying an order. She runs a tight ship, so to speak, but surely she realizes he's right. The Thirteen, myself included, have spent too much time ensuring our people are loyal to *us*, not the Thirteen as a whole. It's the only way to sleep soundly at night, even as a legacy title. For someone like Athena, that's doubly true; her title can be claimed through the assassination clause. Since that knowledge became public, she's fielded no less than three attacks...that we know about.

"He's right," Zeus cuts in. "We can't afford to waste energy ensuring we all play nice. We have to make this work the first time."

"Fine." She turns back to the projected map. "Zeus." She points to the spot in the middle. "Hades." The next one to the left, a little dock a quarter mile away that's rarely used by anyone but teenagers. "Me." Her arm sweeps back to the right to the farthest point. "Poseidon's people will have to be on each boat."

"Poseidon himself will be with me," Zeus says, still sitting in that damn chair as if it's his throne in Dodona Tower. He doesn't raise his voice, but he doesn't have to. "Icarus as well."

That stops me short. "No. Absolutely not." No one protested Icarus's presence for this meeting, but I figured that was because they didn't see him as a threat. It's not as if he can call Circe and tell her we're coming.

He managed to call his past lovers with the aim of blackmailing them.

I ignore that logical voice murmuring in the back of my head. It's true enough, but I can't believe Icarus will betray us. Betray *me*. He might be as good a liar as anyone else in Olympus, but beneath that, he's scared out of his mind and starting to care deeply for me. I don't doubt his feelings, not when I've seen and heard and felt the evidence. He's not going to betray us. I'm staking my life on it.

"No, he's right." Hades speaks softly, but it still draws every eye in the room. "We'll be out there for some time before we reach the ships. Plenty of opportunity for him to slip your guard and make a few calls. That won't happen if he's on a boat with one of us."

I'm already shaking my head. "It's too dangerous. He's not trained."

"He doesn't need to be." Zeus stands and stretches. "He just needs to sit there and not betray us. It's easy enough. Right, Icarus?"

I glance down at Icarus. He's gone waxy with fear, but his dark eyes are determined. That worries me. All of it worries me. I have a suspicion he thinks he has something to prove, and that means he's going to do something dangerous. "No. If that's the requirement, then this whole thing is off."

"Poseidon." Icarus takes my arm and tugs me a few steps away. I don't think we're actually out of earshot, but he doesn't seem to care one way or another. He steps close and lowers his voice. "You can't call the whole thing off. This might be your only chance to turn the tide."

"I don't care."

"Yes, you do."

"Fine, yes I do." Agitation is a live thing inside me. I want to roar at how unfair this is, at the fact that I already know I'm going to lose this argument. Normally, that would be enough for me to change gears or simply give in, but this is *Icarus*. I don't trust that he's not motivated by some fatalistic bullshit. "You're injured."

"Not injured enough to keep me from having pretty athletic sex." He smiles sadly. "I'm fine. I'll be okay."

I don't believe him. But even as I open my mouth to keep arguing, I remember what happened the last time I left him in someone else's care. My attention falls to his chest, a chest I am now intimately acquainted with. His bandages might have come off, but the healing wounds there will scar. All because I misjudged a situation and the depth of Polyphemus's grief and anger. Polyphemus will be piloting one of the boats, but there are others who have plenty of motivation to hate the Vitalis family, and Icarus is the only Vitalis left in Olympus. Theseus hardly counts, even before he fully switched sides after marrying Zeus's sister.

"Poseidon." Icarus presses a hand to my chest. "We don't have time for this. You are going to have to agree. Let's just find a way to do this right." His eyes go troubled. "And hope Deo and the rest actually leave."

"Even if they don't, we'll handle it."

He shakes his head. "It will be significantly more dangerous."

He's right, and I can't lie well enough to comfort him about it. "I don't like this."

"Look around, big guy. No one likes it. No one wants to be here. We're all just playing hero because we're the only ones who can." He smirks, looking a little more like the rakish spoiled prince I once believed him to be. "The Thirteen are finally pulling their weight. All it took was a coup to make it happen. Someone better call MuseWatch and alert the presses."

"Not until after we've succeeded and Zeus has abandoned the coup officially," Athena snaps, proving the entire room was party to this attempt at a private conversation. "If you're done, there are still several details to finalize."

Icarus is right. I'm not winning this argument. Not with him and the others firmly in the opposite camp. "Nothing is going to happen to you. I won't let it," I whisper.

He smiles, taps my chest a few times, and moves around me to walk back to the others. It's only as I turn to follow that I realize I recognize the pattern. It's the one I tap out when I'm concentrating. He's been paying attention.

With that bolstering me, I find the strength to turn to face the rest of the room. "Fine. Let's move on."

"Gladly." Athena continues to walk us through the plan.

It's simple enough. As soon as we're done here, we'll split off to our respective launch locations and wait for the agreed-upon time to slip into the dark water and head for the ships. She's planning on Icarus failing, which leaves us to deal with five ships. Each pair of boats will hit one, her and Hades's people scaling the sides and going to our best assumption of where the captain's quarters are—and where the rest of those in charge will be sleeping. After killing their targets and setting explosive charges, each team will make an announcement that the crew has fifteen minutes to abandon ship before it goes down—and that any attempt to make landing on Olympus's shores will result in a quick and fatal end. Then it's back to the boats and a quick retreat to shore, just in time for the charges to blow and sink the ships. Simple.

Except for the fact that there are half a dozen points off the top of my head where everything can go wrong. The captain's quarters are nowhere near where we need to set the charges, and even in the middle of the night, there will be people awake and moving about. Getting to the designated locations will likely mean killing anyone we come across.

I glance at Icarus, seeing the same knowledge reflected in his expression. He doesn't protest, though, likely for the same reason I don't. There's no other way. Making the announcement is a compromise Athena didn't want to make, but it still feels like it's not enough. There will be lifeboats to allow the crew to get to safety. Probably. The nearest non-Olympian coastline is only a few hours of rowing, which isn't ideal but it's still better than mass murder. I just hope they won't try to row to the nearest shore.

Athena stops and turns to face us. "Anything to add?"

Hades shrugs. "Seems simple enough." He glances at me. "The only risk is of one of her generals betraying *us* instead of Circe."

"The generals won't betray us," I say. My face heats when

everyone turns their attention on me, but I've dealt with the uncomfortable sensation of being the center of attention enough times in the last few decades that I'm able to keep speaking. "Circe has no reason to expect them to sail away, and she certainly has no evidence to support an attack. She knows Olympus's politics well enough to recognize that the Thirteen will never vote to go to war. Zeus's coup will catch her flat-footed."

"That's the plan," Athena murmurs. She cuts a look to Zeus, the threat clear in her tense stance. "Though the coup won't last past dawn."

As long as he keeps his word. I don't say that aloud, though. There's no reason to introduce doubt right now, when we need to trust each other the most. "When the other ships are gone, Hades's people can continue with the plan to plant the charges and remove Circe and the others, and the rest of the boats will assist with the evacuation efforts."

"Poseidon." Athena sighs. "We're under no obligation to ferry them to safety. To suggest that is absurd. They have their own boats. They'll be fine." *And if they're not, it's not our problem.* The unsaid words sit there in the space between us, the knowledge that most people in this room don't care about an enemy crew, recruited under duress or not.

"I insist." I look around, meeting each of their gazes in turn. "This all started because most of the people in this room stood by and did nothing to curtail the last Zeus's abuse of power. If we want to end the cycle, this is how we do it."

"They're the enemy," Medusa scoffs. "They wouldn't give us the same courtesy."

"All the more reason to extend it to them." I speak softly, all too aware that Medusa has history with the title Poseidon. It's my uncle's abuse of power that resulted in her ending up under Athena's command, indirectly responsible for her landing in the lower city. Knowing that makes me cautious with her.

Athena crosses her arms over her chest and glares. "Then you can play savior if you want. The rest of us will stick to *our* plan."

Zeus rises, effectively ending the discussion. "Let's get moving."

There's nothing left to say. It's only as we're walking out the door and breaking off to our respective destinations that I realize I should have pushed harder to keep Icarus behind. He keeps pace at my side, but it seems like every step he takes bows his shoulders more. I hate it. I want to protect him and I don't know where to begin. "Icarus."

He glances up. "Yeah?"

"It will be okay. I promise." I hate that it feels like a lie, like I'm making a promise I can't possibly uphold. But for him, it's worth it.

ICARUS

THERE'S A PAIR OF LOW BLACK BOATS WAITING AS OUR group files down to the docks. Even though I know better, I can't help searching the faces of the people gathered for Polyphemus's one-eyed gaze. A lot can go wrong on the waves in the middle of the night—in a fucking sneak attack—and it would be just my luck to get a knife between my ribs from him, instead of an Aeaean.

"He's with Athena's group," Poseidon says softly. "Orion is with Hades."

I glance at him, that warm and fuzzy feeling he brings about inside me gaining strength. Not only because he guessed the direction of my thoughts, but because he obviously took what steps he could to ensure my safety and comfort. A week ago, I would have laughed in his face and pointed out that there's nothing safe about our plans, that he wasted that time and effort. I don't. It would hurt him.

I want to gather up this evidence of his goodness in the palm of my hand, a light to hold the darkness at bay.

"Remember your promise," I finally say. To live through the night. To be okay.

He doesn't get a chance to respond. Zeus steps toward a boat. "Let's go." He pulls on a long coat he's been handed over his fucking suit. I wish I didn't get why he made that choice. We're the ones confronting Circe—killing Circe, if Zeus has anything to say about it—and appearances matter.

Finishing the job his father started.

We file into the two boats. I stick close to Poseidon's side, and despite Athena's insistence that Zeus take his own boat, he ends up on my other side. It's uncomfortable, to say the least.

My father was never much of a sailor, but I've spent a fair amount of time on sailboats and pleasure crafts since my teens. This boat is nothing like that. It's low and sleek and it charges through the waves with dizzying strength. It's also freakishly quiet. It feels like we're flying along above the surface of the waves instead of on them.

Nausea slaps me in the face almost immediately. I press my hand to my stomach and close my eyes, but it only makes the sensation worse.

"Here." Something presses against my lips and I open without hesitation because it's Poseidon offering.

Spicy flavor explodes on my tongue. Ginger. It's so strong, it almost burns me, but it does help the seasickness. "Thanks," I manage.

By the time I open my eyes, the relative light from Olympus's proximity feels distant. I cautiously look back to see the city twinkling in the distance. It didn't seem like the ships were that far offshore, but I guess distances are tricky on the water.

"The jamming devices are doing their job," Athena murmurs. I don't know how she can tell that. I can barely see anything at all.

I glance at Poseidon, close enough that I can pick out his familiar features in the near-perfect dark, and find him grinning. He catches me looking and shrugs. "I like being out on the water, even in these circumstances."

"You would love Aeaea." I say it without thinking, without considering the implications. "At least the sea surrounding it."

He seems like he might respond, but he doesn't get a chance. "Stop here." Zeus doesn't raise his voice. He doesn't have to; the motor is damn near silent even as the person at the helm obeys, easing our pace until we're only holding our location instead of moving forward.

Now, we wait.

Even with the clothing Poseidon provided, I'm so cold, I can't stop shivering. Zeus seems not to feel the weather. He stares at the ships as if he can sink them through sheer willpower. I'm not certain he can't.

"Fifteen minutes to midnight," he finally says. "We move in twenty, regardless of whether we get a signal or not."

"Understood," Poseidon says.

We all understand. Fifteen minutes has never seemed like a particularly long time, but as we sit in the bobbing waves, ginger practically burning my tongue, it might as well be years ticking by. Poseidon sits at my side, but he's a million miles away.

To distract myself, I stare into the darkness, trying to pick out any indication of the ships. It's an impossible task. They aren't plea- sure vessels with large windows to shine their light out across the water. Poseidon found it strange that Deo and the others were personal owners of what amounts to military ships, but on Aeaea, the military is privatized. It's just how things are. I never questioned it, but now, sitting here freezing my ass off while we try to break the siege on Olympus, I wonder if maybe I *should* have questioned it.

I should have questioned a lot of things.

Something vibrates against my leg and I flinch instinctively. He pats my thigh. "It's my phone."

"Right. Of course." It's everything I can do not to dig it out of his pocket myself to read whatever text just came through. It has to be from Deo. It *has* to be.

He shifts away just enough to pull his phone out—the screen already turned down so low that I can't read it—and sighs. "They're leaving."

"I'll believe it when I see it," Athena mutters. "Five minutes."

"Poseidon." The woman, I've already forgotten her name, leans forward with a tiny screen lit neon green. "They're moving." She points to one of the tiny dots among the lines.

We sit silently and watch four of the dots peel away from the fifth, taking varying angles and moving toward the open ocean. It's…happening. I did it. I haven't failed. This might not be what I originally planned to use the blackmail for, but it's actually serving a noble purpose instead of a selfish one. With only one ship to contend with, Poseidon has a better chance of living to see sunrise. He'll be okay, in part, because of *me*.

"It could be a trap," Zeus says.

"It could be. But it's not." I don't deserve the faith Poseidon puts in me. I've done nothing to earn it. It still feels good. Especially when the little dots don't turn back. They seem to be picking up speed, though it's hard to tell for sure. Poseidon touches my back, a light brushing of his palm between my shoulder blades. "Icarus came through for us."

"Apparently so." Zeus doesn't sound particularly pleased, but he never sounds like anything but ice. "Let's go. The others will see the same thing we are and will be shifting positions."

One ship. They still outnumber us, but even if I haven't spent much time among the normal people in Aeaea, the ones who existed outside the guarded gates at my father's property, I still know the reality they live in.

It's honestly not that different from Olympus's civilians—worse, in some ways. Ironic, that. Circe doesn't seem to care that she's allied with people who, if given half a chance, would have done exactly what the Thirteen did in Olympus.

But then, vengeance has a way of narrowing focus and allowing for all manner of compromises of one's ethics.

"When we reach the ship, stay in the boat with Ceto."

Zeus speaks before I can protest. "No, he's coming with us." There's no give in his voice, just a command he obviously expects to be obeyed without question.

He should know better. Poseidon shakes his head. "Absolutely not."

"It's entirely possible that this is all an elaborate maneuver to get the three legacy titles on their knees in front of Circe. I'm not taking any chances. He comes with us."

Poseidon opens his mouth to continue to argue, but I reach out and squeeze his big thigh. "It's fine. I'll go onto the ship." I turn my attention to Zeus. "If only to ensure you keep your word about the crew."

"If I wanted to kill the entire crew, there's little you could do to stop me."

"You're right. But if that's your plan, then I will stand witness to you breaking your word."

He nods almost imperceptibly. "Noted. Let's move." The last to the woman at the motor. Ceto, apparently.

She puts the radar thing away and guides us soundlessly through the waves. I expected them to be less choppy now that we're past the surf, but they only seem to be getting worse. As if hearing my thoughts, she clears her throat. "There's a storm coming in."

I instinctively look up, but there's nothing to be seen except darkness. Nothing on the horizon, either. The only indication that she's correct is the increasing ditch between swells. Every time we crest one and drop in, my stomach lodges itself into my throat. We're not that far from shore. An athletic person could probably swim it if they were smart and experienced. I'm none of those things. If I go over, I'll drown.

I laugh. I can't help it. This whole situation is so fucked. "I suppose now's not the time to mention that I'm not the strongest swimmer."

Poseidon gives me a look and, even in the darkness, I can tell he wants to throttle me. "You don't think that's something you should have mentioned before getting on this boat?"

"It doesn't matter." I jerk my chin at Zeus. He's ignoring us, leaning forward as if he can will the boat to move even faster.

For a moment, I actually think Poseidon will grab Zeus and toss him bodily into the water. It would be a mistake but entertaining enough that it might be worth it. Poseidon isn't a man ruled by his baser impulses, though, so he manages to muscle down his anger. Barely.

He grabs my arm and drags me close enough that we're pressed tightly together. "Listen to me, Icarus. I don't care what happens when we get on that ship—you stick by my side. Do you hear me?"

"Trust me, I'm not going anywhere." I fully intend to make a smart-ass remark in an attempt to break the growing tension, but between one blink and the next, a giant hull rears out of the darkness in front of us. I can barely pick up the white name printed against its black side. *Penelope.* Circe's ship.

We're here.

POSEIDON

CLIMBING UP THE SIDE OF THE SHIP IN INCREASINGLY unsteady conditions isn't something I'd choose to do on any given day. Doing it while worrying that Icarus's arms will give out and send him into the unforgiving sea is agonizing. I made him go before me, following Zeus, and I'm certain I can see the tremors in his body.

This was a mistake. Leaving him behind would have been hard, but Ceto is one of my best. She would have kept him safe…probably. But I can't guarantee that, can I? Polyphemus is also one of my best, and look how that turned out.

It doesn't matter. Zeus didn't give me a choice. Icarus is here, and I have to keep him safe. I reach the top and haul myself over the edge. My knees crack as I land in a crouch and Icarus gives a faint wheeze that might be a laugh if he had the air for it. "I should stop calling you 'big guy' and start calling you 'old man.'"

"No, thank you." My knees crack again as I straighten to join him next to Zeus, which makes my cheeks flame despite the circumstances. The rest of Athena and Zeus's people slip onto the deck and look around.

It's eerily quiet on deck. I know Deo said that this ship was run by a skeleton crew, but I didn't believe him any more than Icarus did. Now, though? It's hard not to wonder what Circe could possibly have been thinking. Yes, we have jammers and our boats are quiet and we were all dressed in dark clothing so nothing would give us away, but we shouldn't be able to climb aboard and mill around without *someone* noticing.

Zeus straightens his jacket as if he's about to step into a board meeting. "Let's go before they have a chance to rally."

Rally suggests they're in disarray, but best I can tell, no one even knows we're here. The Circe who met Hera and me out on the water was one of the most self-possessed people I've ever encountered. Even more so than she was as a young bride to the last Zeus. There's no way she could know Zeus would stage a one-night coup to come here to kill her, but... "Something's wrong."

Zeus looks at me and, for a moment, I swear I can see the intent to just shove me overboard so he doesn't have to deal with someone questioning him. He shuts down the thought immediately, but the slip showcases how on edge he is. "It's too late to do anything but move forward." He motions to Bellerophon. "Lead the way."

Icarus and I fall into step behind him. Athena's people create a wedge around us. Even now, when we're about to charge into combat, they're protecting the Thirteen. As if their lives matter any less than ours. As if I earned my title through any merit beyond the blood in my veins—same as Zeus. We're no better than any other citizen of our city.

"Unclench your jaw, big guy," Icarus murmurs at my shoulder. "That's a good way to give yourself a tension headache."

I match his low tone, barely more than a whisper. "This is wrong. Even with a skeleton crew, there should be more people here."

"Yeah." He nods down at the butt of the pistol my hand has instinctively found. "I hope you know how to use one of those."

"I wouldn't wear if it I didn't. That's grossly irresponsible. I go to the range once a week and am up to date on all safety material." I belatedly recognize that I'm earnestly responding to what was clearly a joke.

"Of course you do and you are." He laughs a little, but his eyes are shining strangely in the moonlight. "I expect nothing less."

"Quiet," Zeus says. "Hades is in position on the other side of the ship. We're going in."

I don't want to. Fuck, I don't want to do any of this. I'm not a soldier. I'm barely even a leader. I'm not sure I even believe in the same Olympus that Zeus and the others do. The one ruled by the Thirteen. But we're here and we're the only thing standing between Circe and a potentially catastrophic loss of civilian life.

I reluctantly draw my gun, pause to reach back and guide Icarus behind me, and then follow Zeus through the door. He, at least, shows no hesitation. He's focused in a way that makes the small hairs rise on the back of my neck.

This ship is strange. It's not quite military, but it's not a cargo carrier, either. We're on the starboard side nearest the stern, tucked back behind where the officer cabins should be. I would wager Circe's is at the top, but we have to get to her first.

"This all ends tonight," Zeus murmurs, almost too low to hear. He nods at Bellerophon. "Kick down the door."

Bellerophon obeys without hesitation, kicking open the door and moving gracefully to the side right as someone in the room fires. They didn't even wait to see who it was.

I shove Icarus back, putting him between me and the wall. I think he makes a sound of protest, but it's hard to hear over the ringing in my ears. Where I'm floundering in the first real combat of my life, Zeus isn't.

When the person comes through the door, a shotgun in their hands, he grabs the barrel and shoves it skyward as they fire. He punches them in the throat, rips the gun from their hands, and shoves them at Bellerophon. Two pulls of their trigger and the enemy is dead.

It took all of three heartbeats. Zeus's expression never changed. It still doesn't as he turns to me. "Clear the cabin. We're going to keep moving."

I manage to nod, and then they're gone, hustling down the hallway to the next door. The body is still on the floor at my feet. I've seen bodies before, but not like this. I never wanted to see them like this.

"Poseidon?" Icarus presses his hand to my back. "I don't like this, either, but we can't afford to freeze."

Because if we freeze, we might end up dead. *He* might end up dead.

That gets me moving. "They came here to kill us." Maybe if I say it enough times, this will feel right. Or maybe that's just a lie we tell ourselves so we can sleep at night. If we're getting the crew to safety outside of Olympus, there's no reason we couldn't do the same with the rest of the officers.

Not with Circe, but with the rest.

"Breathe, big guy." Icarus is so close, he's practically plastered to my back. I have no idea how he's not stepping on my heels. He rubs small circles between my shoulder blades. "The man is an officer, and he's the same guy who runs a fighting ring for street kids. Where do you think the Minotaur came from? Theseus? They didn't crop up in a vacuum. Aeaea has just as much rot as Olympus."

Knowing that doesn't make me feel better, but it *does* keep me moving. I step into the room to clear it. It takes only a single sweep to recognize that no one else is here. The cabin is familiar enough—it seems all maritime vessels have similar ones. Bed bolted to the floor in the event of tumultuous seas, a narrow door leading to a small bathroom barely big enough for someone to hide in. But when I open the door to the shower, there's a person cowering there.

I jolt. "Shit."

Icarus steps forward before I can stop him. Gone is the flirty playboy, gone are the lies. The compassion on his handsome face is so honest, it makes my chest ache. "It's okay," he says softly. He makes no move to close the distance further. "You're safe."

The only response is for the person to curl even more in on themselves, their arms around their knees and their long hair covering their face. Icarus glances at me, but I don't have the right words for this situation. I don't know if there *are* right words.

He eases down into a crouch. "They're only after the officers. No one will hurt you."

They lift their head a little, recognition shining in their dark eyes. "You're Icarus Vitalis."

He flinches. "I, uh, yes, I am." On his next breath, he seems to gather himself. "You're safe. No one is going to hurt you. I promise."

"Okay," they whisper.

He hesitates. "Do you know where Circe is?"

"No." They shake their head. "He...kept me here. Away from the others." I catch sight of bruises, both new and old, marking the light-brown skin of their arms.

"I'm sorry." He reaches out, but hesitates before making contact. When they don't flinch away, he carefully grips their shoulder. "It won't happen again."

It's like the strength goes out of their body. They slump down against the wall. "It always happens again. It's how things are."

"Not anymore. Stay here. This will be over soon." He gently shuts the shower door and turns to me. "Do you understand now?"

Yeah, I guess I do. This person is obviously part of the crew, and is just as obviously being abused by the officer now dead on the floor outside. It's just one person, but it certainly supports Icarus's insistence that the crew wouldn't choose to be here if they had a choice.

"Let's keep moving," I finally say. I almost tell him to stay here and barricade himself in, but I don't want to let him out of my sight.

Out in the hallway, we find more dead bodies. I edge around them and follow the sound of fighting, Icarus close on my heels. "We just need to find Circe," I huff. "Then this ends."

"I hope so."

We catch up with the team at the bottom of a set of stairs.

Bellerophon glances at their tablet. "This should be the main suite. She'll be there."

"Let's go." Zeus doesn't hesitate. He rushes up the stairs and slams the door open, the stolen shotgun still in his hands. He doesn't spare us a look before disappearing into the room.

Fuck. I drag in a breath and follow him in, steeling myself to pull the trigger if necessary. Circe has been the cause of so much pain and suffering. She may have been victim to it herself, but even as I empathize with the pain she's experienced, I cannot condone the harm she's committed. She's too clever, too driven. As long as she lives, Olympus won't be safe.

Except the room is empty.

I slowly lower my gun, following Icarus's touch to shift away from the door and put our backs to the wall. The room isn't anything particularly fancy. There's a desk bolted to the floor, and a short divider that has a single bunk on the other side, sheets tucked in with military precision.

Zeus charges into the only other door, one leading to a tiny bathroom. It's pristine in a way that suggests no one has been here in some time. There are no toiletries on the sink or in the shower. I look back at the room again. No computer, no personal effects, no *clothes.* "She's not here. She might never have been here at all."

Zeus spins around, blue eyes showing emotion for the first time all night. They're wide and wild. "Where is she? *Where the fuck is she?*"

"We'll find her."

"She was here. You met her out on the water with my wife." He clenches his fists. "She went back to her ship after that meeting."

"I thought she did." I catch sight of a stack of papers on the desk and move toward it. "She went in that direction, but we didn't follow her. It's possible she changed course once she was out of sight. She didn't land where my sentries could see but…"

"But without the barrier, there's more land than there are sentries," Icarus murmurs, finishing my thought.

Zeus veers around me and plucks the piece of paper I noticed from the desk. He reads it and curses. "That fucking *bitch*."

It takes my eyes a moment to adjust to the darkness enough to read the words written in thick marker, their meaning almost obscene in their cute bubble letters. Circe even drew hearts over the tops of the *i*'s.

> It's so cute that you thought you could get the best of me. Darling Zeus, you should know by now that I'm always three steps ahead. Tell Icarus that Deo sends his regards. Better luck next time.
>
> —C

"What—?" I can't even get the sentence out before Zeus shoves everything off the desk and roars in rage. "Zeus, stop." I start to step forward but Icarus grabs the back of my shirt, pulling me up short. Or, more accurately, as soon as I feel the resistance, I stop. "There might be evidence we need in the room."

"There isn't." He kicks down the divider between the bed and the rest of the room. It's also bolted to the floor, so it only bends drunkenly until he kicks it again and again.

Shock roots my feet to the floor, but Icarus has the presence of mind to shut and lock the door before any of Athena's people see. I've never witnessed Zeus as anything other than cold and composed, even when he was still Perseus, heir to the title his father held.

He continues to rampage. Icarus and I stand as silent witnesses. I'm aware of the tension in Icarus's frame, but there's not a damn thing I can say that won't make things worse. I'm not letting Zeus turn his ire on the man I care for, but I'm also not going to say as much and give Zeus any ideas.

He finally slumps against the desk. "Damn it. This is so fucked. It was supposed to end tonight."

This is my cue. We aren't friends—he hasn't earned the effort it takes me to manage his emotions—but there's no one else. I step forward carefully. "This is still a victory."

"How do you figure?" He doesn't look up, fisting the fabric of his expensive slacks.

"It's pretty fucking clear. Circe lost her squadron. Four of her generals sailed off without her."

He snorts. "So they can circle the coast and come back. She said Deo sends his regards." He narrows his eyes at Icarus. "He played you. He played *us*."

"*Think*, Zeus." I want to shake him but manage to resist the urge. "She has no reason to deceive us. With five ships, she could bomb the city to oblivion with little risk to herself. The only reason she didn't get around to it yet was because she was sure the Thirteen wouldn't vote—something she was correct about. She didn't see the coup coming. We stopped her."

He finally drags a hand through his blond hair and curses. "We didn't stop anything, but at least the blockade is no longer an issue." As he speaks, I can actually see the walls coming back, his control once again reasserting itself. "Take this ship."

"Excuse me?"

"Take this ship," he repeats slowly. "You and your little boyfriend wanted to free the crew? Do it. Then bring the ship back to port and we'll take it apart with a fine-tooth comb." Zeus jerks open the door and stalks out of the room.

I blink, still trying to process this unexpected turn of events. I glance at Icarus, who surveys the room with a strange look on his face. "Is it a trap?" I ask. "It's what she did with Hades in the lower city."

"Circe isn't the type to try the same trick twice." He drifts to the mess of papers on the floor and picks up the note. "And no matter what kind of monster she is, I don't think she'd blow this ship and its crew up—not even to get you and Zeus."

"And Hades."

He opens his mouth, seems to reconsider what he was about to say, and shrugs. "My father would make that play. The last Zeus would make that play. Circe is terrifying, but she's terrifying in her intent. It's more likely…"

I follow his thought, even though I desperately don't want to. I clear my throat. "It's more likely that this blockade was a distraction." A clever one at that. She knew we'd vote and vote and vote again, trying to get the Thirteen to unite enough to stand against the ships. Just like she knew it wouldn't work. While we were fighting each other, she was already moving onto the next step in her plan. "Are there even large-scale weapons on the *Penelope?*"

Icarus laughs bitterly. "I have no idea, but now that you've asked the question, I think we know the answer, don't we?"

I feel sick. This has all gone so wrong. It's been going wrong from the beginning, but I had no reference for the sheer gauge. "If Circe isn't here, if these ships were never meant to attack Olympus, then where is she?"

"I have a feeling we're going to find out, sooner rather than later."

ICARUS

IT TAKES OVER AN HOUR TO ROOT OUT EVERY CREW member and arrange them on the deck, sitting cross-legged with their hands laced behind their heads. As I suspected, not a single one of them put up a fight once the officers were dealt with. They all surrendered the moment they realized there was an attack.

They all...recognize me. Just like the person in the shower— who we've now recovered and brought to the deck. As I walk in Poseidon's shadow, I hear the whispers.

"Icarus..."

"That's Icarus Vitalis..."

Zeus stalks in front of them, his movements still too jerky to fully pull off his customary ice-king routine. He's been questioning them for twenty minutes with little success.

They don't know where Circe is. None of them even saw her at all, which confirms what we suspected about her not being on the ship for any length of time. They were recruited with the promise of steady wages and a nice bonus when they returned to Aeaea—one that would be paid out even in the event of their death, as long as it happened in the pursuit of Olympus. It's an offer designed to pull in those with poverty's boot on their necks, and the great irony is that the leaders of Aeaea could have fixed the poverty levels if they'd been less greedy. Instead, they recruited people who couldn't afford to say no to being cannon fodder.

It pisses me off.

I rub my arms, disliking this new sensation. I've spent so long only caring for myself—and Ariadne—that I don't know how to deal with this feeling. I can hardly go back to Aeaea and expect to have the power to change things.

Except you're technically your father's heir, no matter how little he wanted you. You've likely inherited everything.

I stop short. In all this frantic scrambling and free-falling of the last couple days, *that* never sank in. My father is dead. Gone forever. That means his extensive holdings and properties are all mine and Ariadne's. Without him hanging over my head as a threat, I *can* go back to Aeaea. My father held significant influence among the wealthy. I might not have his charm, but I know all their dirty secrets.

I could...make a difference. I think I even *want* to.

"We're done here." Zeus spins on his heel and stalks to where Bellerophon and the others wait by the railing. He stops halfway and looks back at us. "If they give you any trouble, kill them."

"Absolutely not." I'm speaking before I can fully process that I've stepped forward—stepped between Zeus and the Aeaeans. "No one is touching them."

Zeus turns to me. The survivor in me, the one who will do

anything to save his own skin, screams that I need to do something to draw his attention away from me. But that survivor isn't the only voice inside me. *These are my people.* I don't recognize the feeling of those words, but they resonate in a way that snaps my spine straight.

"I will not risk Olympus because of your misguided heroism," he snarls.

I laugh. I can't help it. "I'm no hero. But I *will* hold you to your word. Or is that as changeable as your father's was?"

The calculated words hit their mark. He doesn't react, other than to turn away. "Get them out of my sight and bring the ship round by morning."

"We'll see it done," Poseidon says quietly. He places his hand in the middle of my back as we watch Zeus stalk away. As soon as the blond man vanishes from sight, Poseidon turns to me. "You should talk to them."

"What?"

"The crew." He watches me carefully. "They recognize you, the same way the person down in the cabin did."

"I have a recognizable face." The words are right, a perfect side step, but I can't help turning to the crew. It's easy enough to pick out the leaders among them. They're the people the others crowd around, the ones who move with a little more steadiness, trying to bolster everyone's courage. It's false bravado, but I respect it.

One of them holds my gaze, a man with light-brown skin weathered from the sun and years, his short hair long since gone gray. "What happens now?"

"We are going to get you home."

He laughs bitterly. "For all the good it will do. We don't get our wages until the end of this disaster. What home do we have to go back to?"

He's right, and yet it doesn't sit well with me. I look around at the people gathered. There are easily fifty of them. "I'll pay you for your lost wages when we return to Aeaea."

Instead of looking comforted, the man crosses his arms over his chest. "And what of the others?"

"The others?"

"The other crews," he supplies. "They sailed off without accomplishing their goals. No doubt Deo Artino and the others will use that as an excuse not to pay them for the work they did."

I glance at Poseidon, but he's simply watching me, letting me take the lead. I could use some of his deep well of confidence now. There's none to be had inside of me, but I've always known how to fake it. "That sounds like something Deo would do. He's a bastard like that." I shrug. "Then I'll pay their wages, too." My father was the kind of rich that borders on absurdity. It's an easy enough promise to make.

"Why?"

I blink. "Why?"

"Yeah. What's in it for you?"

It's a fair question, and one I don't have an answer to. "It's the right thing to do."

The man laughs again, even harsher this time. "Since when has an Aeaean noble cared about the *right thing* to do when it comes to people like us?"

I have to fight down the tremble that threatens. He's right. My father and his ilk are selfish creatures who hoard their money and are only concerned with getting more. I'm just like them...but that doesn't mean I *have* to be. I could...choose to be different? "Since now." My voice is even steady as I say it.

"We need to get moving," Poseidon says softly. "We don't have long to get them to safety."

"Right." I meet this stranger's eyes. "Stay here. We're going to travel outside of Olympus's waters and then the crew will be freed, but if you cause trouble, I can't save you."

"I understand." He sinks back down to speak in a low voice with the others gathered around him.

A couple of Athena's people stand over the crew with guns held easily in their hands, but they look significantly more inscrutable than Zeus was, so I'm not worried about them panicking and shooting someone—or killing them out of anger. They're true professionals, because of course they are; they work for Athena, after all.

Poseidon leads me up to the bridge. We're alone for the first time since we left his apartment, and the relative silence feels so fucking loud. He scrubs his hands over his face. "Okay. Okay, next steps."

Next steps. "We need a way to get my people back to Aeaea." I already meant for it to happen, but after seeing the crew on this ship, having it driven home exactly how fucked over they've been by every single person in power.

Poseidon turns and looks at me, really *looks* at me. "Your people."

"It's the truth," I whisper. I have lied, cheated, and stole and never felt a fraction of the guilt blooming inside me as I realize what I have to do. "You were right about the corruption in Aeaea. Hermes was too, in her way. I couldn't do anything about it before, not with my father in the mix, but the blackmail I used against Circe's generals was only one piece of my arsenal. If I go back, if I step into the position my father left with his death, I could actually change things for the people who need it the most. People like this crew."

It hurts to say it. It hurts to even contemplate it. I've been selfish my entire damn life, and it's fucked beyond measure that I'm going to develop a selfless streak right now, in the moment when I find an honorable man who loves me. An honorable man that I love, too.

Poseidon doesn't yell. He doesn't accuse me of using him. He just studies me for so long, it feels like he's seeing me right down to my tarnished soul. "You have to do this."

It's not a question, but I answer it all the same. "I have to do this." I drag in a harsh breath. "I won't ask you to leave Olympus and your people. Not with the threat of Circe hanging over your head. But…" Fuck, this hurts. I want to stay. I want to spend whatever stolen moments we can find in his bed.

I want everything.

But I wouldn't be worthy of his love if I ignored the deep wound in Aeaea that I have the potential to help heal. It's what he would do in my position. I swallow past my increasingly tight throat. "Fuck it, I will ask you. Come with me. You never wanted to be Poseidon. You never wanted any of this. Fuck this city. Stay with me. Love *me*."

He pulls me into his arms and kisses me with a desperation that conveys his answer even before he speaks. I cling to him, trying to communicate a feeling I don't know how to put into words. I don't know if I succeed.

When he finally breaks the kiss, he presses his forehead to mine. "I can't."

Even expecting his answer, it strikes right through all the bull-shit. "I know," I whisper.

"I love you." He says it with a quiet certainty that shakes me right down to my core. "But I can't leave my people with this threat hanging over them."

"I know," I repeat. And I do. He wouldn't be the man I fell for if he was willing to shirk his responsibilities. If he was as selfish as I've been my entire life.

Poseidon holds me so tightly, I can barely breathe. "After." He kisses my forehead, his whole body shaking. "After this is over, I'll come for you."

Hope flares, so strong that it almost takes me to my knees. I dare to lift my head, to meet his amber eyes. "What?"

"I *love* you." He stares intently at me. "I can't abandon the city and my people now, but this will be over one way or another soon. When it is, I'll leave Olympus and come to you. I promise."

It's not something he can really promise, not beyond a shadow of a doubt. There are so many things that could get between where we are now and the future I want so desperately that I can almost feel it in my hands. Circe could win. Zeus could win and demand Poseidon's presence for reconstruction efforts. Poseidon could *die*.

Or none of that could happen and time will unravel the spell we've cast on ourselves. He'll come to his senses and realize what he feels for me is a confused mix of hormones and proximity.

But even as I think that, it can't kill the hope inside me. This *isn't* circumstantial. It's real. I know it is. I just have to have faith. "When you come, I'll be waiting. No matter how long it takes."

"I won't hold you to that."

It's such a Poseidon thing to say that I go onto my toes and kiss him. "You don't have to. I'm holding myself to it. I love you, too, big guy. No one else compares."

We stand like that for several long beats before he sighs and steps back. "I have to make a call."

I wander around the bridge as he pulls out his phone. After the efficiency of the attack, it feels strange to be out of danger, at least temporarily. I'll have to watch for knives in my back after I get back to Aeaea.

Fuck, I can't believe I'm doing this. That deep selfish part of me that I don't think I'll ever fully shed wants to walk back on my plans. I could stay here…and be a burden Poseidon has to constantly worry about protecting. Zeus probably still wants me dead, my helping them or no. He doesn't seem like the type to allow loose ends to become a problem. There are other people under Poseidon's command like Polyphemus who were hurt by my father's plans and actions. Poseidon won't be able to focus fully if he's worried about me.

My staying here could get Poseidon killed.

Even without that? I can't help thinking of the crew member hiding in that officer's shower, the rest of them kneeling on the deck and waiting to hear if they'll live or die, all dependent on the whims of the rich and powerful. All because they wanted to provide for their families. How many people like them have been hurt by those in power in Aeaea? I'll probably never know the number, but for every one of them who is hurt because I was selfish when I could have done something to change their lives for the better…

I have to go home. I have to do the right thing. Not to benefit me, but *because* it's the right thing to do.

Poseidon hangs up and turns to me. "Let's get going."

Watching him move about the bridge, getting the ship ready to head out, is a lesson in delicious agony. He's so capable and focused and beautiful, and I can't believe I'm planning on walking away, even if it's not forever. It certainly feels like forever.

The ship starts moving slowly, but quickly picks up speed, angling away from Olympus and taking the most direct route to leave the bay. It seems like something that should take hours— days—but all too soon we're leaving Olympus's waters.

It's almost anticlimactic. I watched my sister fight for her life in the waves created by the barrier coming down, and now I'm just... sailing to freedom.

Again, that selfish part of me, the one that's kept me alive all this time, whispers that I should embrace that freedom fully, should hand off leadership to one of the crewmates on the deck and take off for wherever Ariadne has landed. There's no one to stop me, no one to check up on if I'm going where I said I would.

But it would be the wrong thing to do.

I sigh. "It's really frustrating prioritizing the well-being of many over myself."

At the helm, Poseidon huffs out a sound that's almost a laugh. "Tell me about it."

"You could come with me." I guess I still am that selfish, because I don't hesitate to throw the offer at him again. "Fuck Olympus. They've never deserved you. I don't, either, but at least I'm aware of that fact."

His smile is sad and weighs me down from across the room. "You know better."

Yeah, I guess I do. I cross to him and hug him from behind, letting the steady beat of his heart soothe me as much as I can be soothed in our current circumstances. "Can you sail?"

He tenses slightly. "Yes. I haven't in a long time, but it used to be something I did often."

"I'm going to leave you a sailboat in the port closest to Aeaea." He tenses further, but I keep going. "It's an open invitation, big guy. I'll wait, however long it takes. When you're done with what you have to do here, come for me."

He's silent for what feels like forever. "I will. I promise."

There are so many other things I want to say, but what's the point? He knows. We both know. We can circle this until we're blue in the face and the results will be the same. I'm leaving. He's staying. So I just hold him. He covers one of my hands with his and uses his other to guide the ship to our destination.

It takes far less time that I'd like. All too soon, Poseidon says, "We're here."

I lift my head and shift to look past him out the windows. Dawn is just a hint on the horizon, the first fingers of light diffusing the night. I can barely see the shore in the distance. We're much farther out to sea than I realized. I frown. "I sincerely hope you're not going to make us walk the plank and swim for shore."

"Icarus, no one walks the plank anymore." The fond exasperation in his deep tone makes my heart ache.

"Then..."

"How will you get home without a ship?" He turns in my arms and pulls away just enough to be able to see my face. "You were right to spare the crew, and you're right to help those who need it. I'll

be damned before I strand you out here for doing the right thing."
He blushes. "And I'll worry about you."

That horrible, amazing feeling in my chest only gets stronger.
"What did you do?"

"Ceto will be here shortly with a ship large enough to carry you
all to safety. After you've reached Aeaea, she'll return to Olympus."

So *that's* the call he was making. My throat tries to close, but
I swallow rapidly past it. "Thank you." I won't let her go back to
Olympus without loading her up on supplies to haul in. With all
the civilians in the countryside, it's bound to affect Olympus's food
stores. "Poseidon, *thank you.*"

He takes my hand and leads me back down to the deck. There
are moments that are too full for words, and this is one of them. We
stand together and watch the Olympian ship get larger and larger,
until it comes even with us and the crew hurry to toss ropes to temporarily bind us together. A heavy metal plank is lowered and the
shivering crew are ushered over.

I'll have to spend some time reassuring them that we're going
home, but I'm having a hard time focusing on that right now.
"Poseidon—"

"I need an additional three months."

I twist to face him fully. "What?"

"This thing with Circe will be over soon, but no matter what
the outcome, there will need to be a transition period." His voice
hitches. "Three months, Icarus. Three months after Circe falls and
I'm coming for you. I promise."

Another promise. I don't tell him that it has the flavor of a
hope-saturated lie. I want to believe the lie too much to poke holes

in it. "I'll be waiting. No matter how long it takes." How can I do anything else?

For him, I'll wait forever.

POSEIDON

A THOUSAND TIMES, I ALMOST TELL ICARUS I'VE CHANGED my mind. A thousand times, I almost go against everything I am and sail away from Olympus and all the trouble that awaits my return. A thousand times, I stay silent instead.

"Poseidon, I have to go."

I look askance at Icarus, only to realize I'm still gripping his hand too tightly for him to slip free. He's not trying, but he's right. The entire Aeaean crew is milling about on the deck of the other ship, unsure what to do. They need him, need his direction and his comforting words. I just…need it, too.

"Three months," I repeat. I've never believed in mantras before, but I have a feeling I'm about to. Two words, a promise I am determined to uphold.

"Three months," he confirms. He kisses me hard enough to buckle my knees, and then he's gone, slipping through my fingers as if he was never truly mine to hold.

No. Damn it, *no*.

I can't afford to lose faith the moment he stops touching me. I don't make promises I don't intend to keep, that I'm not sure I *can* keep, and I'll do everything in my power to reunite with him. I've never felt a connection like this before, and I suspect I never will. I just have to survive long enough to realize it.

He walks away, easily crossing the plank, and steps down onto the deck of the other ship. Several of my people who came with Ceto cross to me and help unhook the plank and ropes keeping the ships near each other.

"Where do you want us?"

"Nowhere yet." I glance at Ida. Zir is Orion's next in command, a solid, reliable person with pale skin and a nearly shaved head. Tattoos crawl up zir neck to frame zir pointed chin, all nautical themed.

Even that glance is too long looking away from Icarus, growing small in the distance as Ceto guides the ship away from the coast, from Olympus, from *me*.

Am I making a mistake?

I don't know. I don't fucking *know*. If there was someone else to step into Poseidon's shoes without completely undermining any attempts to fight Circe, if we weren't actively under attack, if, if, if. But there's no one else. Triton's eldest daughter can be trained, at least enough to take over, and Orion and Polyphemus and the rest can help her settle in and find her feet once I'm gone.

All that takes time, though. I'll be hard pressed to keep my promise to find Icarus in three months, but the thought of it taking longer is untenable. I have given Olympus everything, have done my best for a city and people who were never supposed to be under my command. For the first time in my life, I want something for *me* and me alone.

I want Icarus. I want a life at his side, whatever that ends up looking like. I have no preconceived notions. The idea of years stretching out without having every detail in place is a little scary, but it means leaving behind the memory of my uncle for good. It means...I get to choose.

In the distance, I can no longer make out Icarus on the deck. I swallow past the sudden tightness in my throat. "Let's go."

Ida doesn't make me say it twice. Ze strides away from me, issuing orders with the ease of someone who's used to being obeyed. Ze has held zir position for years now and has several ships under zir direct command. It shows.

All too soon, we're sailing back into Olympian waters. The city looks much like it did when we left, and yet it feels dramatically different. As if this morning is the first in a new era. That's the kind of superstitious thought process I rarely indulge in, but I can't shake the feeling that everything has changed.

That sensation solidifies as we reach the docks and the group of Athena's and Hades's people waiting for us. Zeus is nowhere to be found, but Athena and Hades stand a careful distance apart as their people file onto the ship and separate into groups, obviously following orders given out while they waited for me to arrive.

I walk down the metal plank to the dock and head to Athena first. "The Aeaeans have been taken care of."

She nods, her gaze on the ship. "I think it was a mistake to let them go. There's little enough reason for the other four ships to keep going instead of turning around and picking up where they left off."

"They won't." They'll have their hands full with Icarus making moves on Aeaea. Even if they were inclined to continue the assault on Olympus, they'll have to choose a course of action to prioritize and it will certainly be their home.

"We'll see." She crosses her arms over her chest. "We have no idea where Circe is. It's a problem."

"More than a problem." I twist and look toward the city center, even though I can't see Dodona Tower from this position. "Zeus?"

She smiles tightly. "He's going to call a meeting officially relinquishing control of his coup."

"I'm sure the rest of the Thirteen will love that."

"Undoubtedly."

Especially Hera. But she's not my problem any longer. Our alliance is at its end. I want to believe she wouldn't have gone behind my back and opened the gates for Circe, but I can't say it with any amount of surety. She's ruthless to a fault, and if she thinks she can save her family, there's no depths she won't descend to.

Hades shifts closer, his expression unreadable. "I'll leave some of my people here to assist with things—and continue reporting to me—but I'm returning to the lower city." To his people and his pregnant wife.

I extend my hand. "Thank you for your help tonight." I have no doubt Zeus would want to press the importance of continuing with a legacy-title alliance, even without a coup in the works, but I don't bother saying it. Hades knows everything I do; it's why he's here. He'll show up when we need him next time, too.

"Keep me updated."

"I will." I watch him leave and then glance at Athena. "Do you need me here for this?"

"Go." She waves me away. "I know how to reach you if I need you."

I go. After a brief internal debate, I call Orion and Polyphemus and tell them to meet me at the main house. After a longer internal debate, I call Pallas.

It's early but she answers on the third ring. "Hello?"

"It's Poseidon."

"Yes, I know. What can I do for you?"

This is the moment of no return. If I hand over the title, I'll lose the control it gives me. I won't be able to protect the people under my command any longer. I'll have to trust that my read on Pallas is correct and that she'll step up with enough support. I had intended to hold this title until my dying day, but...Gods, I'm tired. I didn't even realize how tired until I shared the burden with another person for a few days. No, not just another person. With *Icarus*.

"I would like you to come to the house for a meeting. Now, if you're available."

She's quiet for a moment, and then says, "Okay. I'll be there in fifteen."

There's no going back now. No time to second-guess myself. "I'll see you shortly." I hang up and head for my SUV.

Twenty minutes later, the four of us are closed in my rarely used study as I outline my plan. Orion and Polyphemus are shocked, but it's Pallas who speaks first. "But...are you sure? You're *Poseidon* and I'm just—"

"You're not *just* anything," I cut in gently. "But I understand better than anyone the burden I'm asking you to take up, especially considering our current circumstances. I won't abandon you in the midst of this conflict—have no fear of that—but after…"

Pallas favors her late mother more than her father. She's a slight woman with light-brown skin and long, straight black hair. She's been spared the blue eyes that plague our line as well. She sits perfectly still, her spine straight and her gaze a little too direct to be perfectly comfortable. "My father never would have agreed to this."

There's no point in arguing that. She's right. "I know. But it's not his decision. It's yours."

She swallows visibly. "I…" Pallas pauses and shakes her head sharply. "I want it. Not just because you've served for so long and deserve your own happiness. I want the chance to prove myself. To…well, to do it all."

I focus on Orion and Polyphemus. "You have thoughts. Let's hear them."

Polyphemus speaks first, his words practically tripping over each other as they leave his mouth. "You're going to throw it all away for *him*? You've known him a couple of days, and he's the enemy!"

"I'm not throwing anything away." It's so strange that the longer I sit with this plan, the calmer I feel. "I'm passing on a burden I've been carrying most of my life. One I never would have chosen for myself. I think I've earned that, don't you?"

Polyphemus sputters, but Orion nods. "He's right, Po." They turn to Pallas. "Treat us fairly and we'll support you unquestionably."

She blushes prettily. "I don't expect unquestionable support. There's plenty I won't know, even after Poseidon, uh, vacates the title." Her voice firms the longer she speaks. "I will value any and all of your input for as long as you're willing to give it."

She's going to be fine.

The realization washes over me, bringing a tide of exhaustion in its wake. We've done so much, and yet there's still so much left to do. The threat of Circe has never been greater, and we don't even know where she is. Zeus and Hera's war might be even more dangerous to Olympus as a whole. There's mess wherever I look, and it's a tangled knot of one disaster after another.

And yet...

Hope has taken up residence in my chest, and there's no dimming it. As Pallas keeps talking with my people, I shift to look out the window to the east. The ocean is hidden from view, but the promise remains, beating in time with my heart.

Three months. Wait for me, Icarus. I'm coming to you. I promise.

ICARUS

FOUR AND A HALF MONTHS LATER

EVERY MORNING FOR THE LAST SIX WEEKS, I'VE GONE through the same ritual. I make myself a cup of coffee and walk down to the beach on the west side of the property. It's a spot where Ariadne and I used to play when we were young, pretending to be literal royalty and believing that all we needed to be happy was to wish hard enough.

These past months have proved that wishes aren't worth the breath required to voice them. If I want something to change, I have to *work*. It's all I've done for four and a half months. The battle for Aeaea won't be over anytime soon, but I've made good progress from my new seat among the council.

The older members aren't happy, but I have more than enough information about their less-than-pure habits to keep them on the straight and narrow.

I don't know why I'm surprised that I'm good at politics. Maybe I shouldn't be surprised, considering how I was raised.

When I got back to the island with the saved crew in tow, one of the first things I did was get a new phone. I've listened to my sister's voicemail dozens of times in the intervening months, but aside from texting her to say that I'm safe and I'll be in contact soon, I haven't talked to her.

If I answered her calls, I'd have to tell her what happened after she sailed away. Maybe she'd understand what I feel for Poseidon, maybe she'd even support me in my foolish belief that he'll really come for me, but…maybe she won't.

That *maybe* is one too many. I'm already teetering on the edge of a sorrow so deep, I don't know how I'll survive it. And the promise of it only gets more harrowing with every day that passes without seeing black sails on the horizon.

That doesn't stop me from showing up every morning and evening like clockwork. I refuse to admit that the steady whoosh of the waves reaching the shore soothes me. Or that the crisp sea air makes me alert. Or that, possibly, I would enjoy this ritual if it didn't always end in disappointment.

I haven't had any contact from Poseidon, but how would I? It's not as if we exchanged phone numbers. I've followed the news coming out of Olympus closely, and to the best of my knowledge he survived everything that followed my leaving…but he still hasn't come.

He could have changed his mind. No matter what promises we exchanged, I should know better than most that emotion blossoming in traumatic times isn't trustworthy. And yet I continue to wait. To *hope*, the sensation so fierce that some days it feels more like agony.

So fiercely that, when I notice irregular black in the distance, I almost convince myself that it's some fisherman bringing in the morning's catch. Even though this ship is far outside the prime fishing waters and obviously coming from the mainland.

That doesn't mean it's him.

It might not be. It likely isn't. It couldn't possibly be...

Even as doubt yells at me to go back to the house to avoid disappointment for a little longer, to not let hope take the reins, I stand there rooted long after my coffee has gone cold and the sun is high in the sky. Long enough for my brain to finally admit that I *know* this ship, that it's one I haven't seen since I left it in a slip at a dock on the mainland. That I specifically left for one man.

I still try to deny it when the man himself appears and tosses the anchor into the shallow water. He lifts a hand to his brow and goes still. I barely have time to process that he's seen me when he dives into the water and starts swimming to shore.

There's no room for thought. Not when I drop my coffee mug and start running. Not when the waves hit my knees, ruining my shoes. Not when Poseidon rises out of the water like some kind of siren and I launch myself into his arms and wrap my legs around his waist.

He loses his footing and we go under, but only for a moment. I don't care. I'm too busy clinging to him, kissing every part of his sunburned face I can reach. As he haphazardly carries me to shallower water, I finally manage the breath to speak between gasps. Only two words, over and over. "You came, you came, you came."

We finally reach the shore and he holds me to him tighter. "I'm sorry it took so long," he gasps. "I wanted to be here sooner."

"I don't care. *You came.*" I kiss him properly, putting four months' worth of fear and hope and need and love into it.

His knees buckle. We hit the sand and then I'm on my back, his big body pressing me down in a way I never want to stop. I never *have* to stop because he's here. *He came.*

Poseidon eases up just enough to look down at me. "You waited."

"I would have waited forever." I can't quite catch my breath. "I love you."

"Still?"

"Always."

His grin is like the sun coming out from behind a cloud. It warms me right through. "I have a present for you."

"Your being here is present enough."

He laughs, sounding more at ease than I've ever heard him, and moves to the side, pulling me up into his lap. "No, this is a real present. It's back on the sailboat, but I have plane tickets."

I blink. "Plane tickets?"

"Yeah." He keeps touching me like he can't quite believe I'm here. "To Rio. I'm cutting it a little close but..."

Carnaval.

Where Ariadne will be waiting for me. I hadn't forgotten, exactly, but I'd been putting off buying my own ticket, the thought of so many days away from Aeaea and this beach almost more than I could bear. "You didn't have to."

"I wanted to." He kisses my forehead. "I love you, too. So much."

"Poseidon—"

"Proteus."

I frown. "What?"

"I'm not Poseidon anymore. I never will be again." He takes a slow breath and despite the fact that he looks tired, he seems… unburdened. He smiles. "My name is Proteus. Or it was before I took the title, and now it is again."

We have so much to talk about, and yet there's only one question that matters. "Are you staying?"

"Yes." He nods seriously. "As long as you'll have me."

I find myself laughing, the sound of hope winning over despair. "Be careful what you say, big guy. If I have my way, you'll be mine forever."

"Then I'll be yours forever, and happily." He makes a face. "As much as I want to sit here until we're caught up, I'm wet and covered in sand and I'm not going to be able to focus on a single thing until that's fixed."

"Of course." I scramble to my feet and take his hand after he does the same. "Let's go home."

"Home." He says the word as if weighing it. "I like that. I want to have a home with you, Icarus. Not just somewhere we rest our heads. A true home."

I'm already tugging him toward the winding path leading up to the house. We'll have to deal with the ship at some point, but it will be safe enough for now. "I've made some changes to the house since I got back." I'm blushing and smiling like a fool and I can't seem to stop. "You're welcome to change anything that doesn't work, but I had you in mind when I redecorated."

"I'm sure it's perfect." Poseidon—Proteus—keeps pace with me easily. He's smiling, too. "I can't wait to see your—our—home."

Our home. His. Mine. *Ours.* A place where we can play out a future. *Together.*

And not even Olympus can get in our way.

ACKNOWLEDGMENTS

Acknowledgments always come at the part of the process where I'm ready to toss the book out of my window and into traffic. As a result, while I've done my best to list out everyone who helped a project come into being, they were a bit...dry. So let's try something new for this one. Shoutout to Stephen Graham Jones for so charming me with his acknowledgments that he inspired me to do better with mine.

Thank you, Dear Reader. It's hard to quantify all the amazing ways my life has changed in the last few years, but it really comes down to *you*. You've picked up my books again and again. You've shared them with your friends and talked about them on social media and in book clubs. You've hand-sold them in your bookstores and recommended them to your library patrons. Every single one of you is a blessing, and I truly hope you know that. I joke that I'm trying to arm-wrestle traditional publishing into acknowledging that queer stories—*inclusive* stories—can find an audience just as easily as their cishet counterparts, but I wouldn't have the power to even consider this fight without your buying and recommending habits proving the truth of it. So thank you! You've allowed me reach a space where I can lower the ladder to so many people.

Special thanks to the folks on social media and in my newsletter who share my reading taste and trust my recommendations for authors who aren't me. Your trust means so much!

This book has been a long time coming. It's the first gay romance I've written, something like a hundred books into my career. I'll admit that part of the resistance I've had to writing a romance with only two guys is just pure spite for how undervalued sapphic romance tends to be. If not for a stray comment about how Icarus falls into the sea, Poseidon may have had a different love interest. But I'm glad these two were my first. This book is incredibly vulnerable in a number of ways, and I've worked hard to take care with Icarus and Poseidon, both on their own and as a pair.

I'm sorry it's taken eight books to mention this, but a deep thank you to my fourth grade teacher for allowing me to do a book report on *The Odyssey*. In hindsight, I'm sure that presentation raised some eyebrows, but it was the first time I sank my teeth into Greek myths, and I haven't stopped chewing on them since.

While the framework for Circe as villain (No spoilers, I promise!) has existed in my mind for a very long time, several key components fell into place while writing this book. This was due in no small part to Jorge Rivera-Herrans's *Epic*, particularly the Circe Saga (of course!) and even more particularly *Done For*.

I have the utmost gratitude to Mary Altman for being one hell of a partner on this epic journey. Every step of the way, you've pushed me to go harder and do better, and we wouldn't be in this place without your input and support. Thank you for trusting me to take big swings, and thank you for helping me ensure those big swings aren't misses.

That saying about a tree falling in a forest is equally true for a book being published without promotion and marketing support. We're all overworked and drowning, but my deepest appreciation to Pam Jaffee, whose constant energy and innovation has ensured the Dark Olympus series continues to gain new readers and end up with excellent placement. This series wouldn't have such an extended reach without your efforts, and I am endlessly grateful.

Shoutout to the team at Sourcebooks who have tirelessly worked to make these books successful, from cover to all the little details that would make my brain melt if I tried to handle myself. Thanks to Jackie Cummings, Diane Dannenfeldt, Stephanie Gafron, and India Hunter.

Thank you to Jenny Nordbak for always being there to brainstorm, as a voice of support, and honestly just the best friend a person could ask for. I'm feeling a bit sappy as I write this. We're days away from our third Kickstarter together, and no doubt by the time you read this, it will have been a massive success. I couldn't do this shit without you, but even if we didn't work together, I value your friendship on a level I have a hard time putting into words. Even though putting shit into words is kind of my job.

Thank you to Hilary Brady for all the support! You're right, as always. Why be a sad bitch when we can be a bad bitch?! The laughs we have playing Fortnite have been the perfect ending to so many stressful days. Thank you to Nisha Sharma for being a safe space to talk about touchy subjects and always calling me to tell me about what you're studying for your PhD. You're the smartest person I know, and I deeply appreciate you sharing your thoughts with me. You make me a better person and a better writer for giving me so much to consider. Thank you to Asa Maria Bradley and Dani Romero for our monthly dinners. You're my safe space and you're both so damn smart, and I appreciate your perspectives and your friendship!

To B and C. I know having me as a parent isn't always the easiest, but you put up with my shenanigans admirably. Thank you for being so damn cool, even when you're being little shits. I'm so damn proud of the people you're becoming, and while I'd love to take credit for all of it, the truth is that you're just good kids and you're going to be amazing adults.

To M. My dude, you aren't allowed to read this anytime soon, but I hope someday you'll go back through some of these acknowledgments and get a kick out of how cringy you'll no doubt find them. Thank you for keeping me young even when I'm feeling particularly old and crotchety.

And Tim, the love of my life. When people say romance authors set too high of a standard for real men to achieve, you're the reason I laugh in their face. We're living a true insta-love second chance romance, and I wouldn't be able to accomplish half the shit I do without you behind me, pushing me to be fearless and taking care of me when I stumble. You're the fucking best, and I love you.

ABOUT THE AUTHOR

Katee Robert (she/they) is a *New York Times* and *USA Today* bestselling author of spicy romance. *Entertainment Weekly* calls their writing "unspeakably hot." Their books have sold over two million copies. They live in the Pacific Northwest with their husband, children, a cat who thinks he's a dog, and two Great Danes who think they're lap dogs.

Website: kateerobert.com
Facebook: AuthorKateeRobert
Instagram: @katee_robert
TikTok: @authorkateerobert